DOWN DON'T BOTHER ME

ALSO BY JASON MILLER

REDBALL 6, with Ian Miller

PHILOSOPHER REX, with Ian Miller

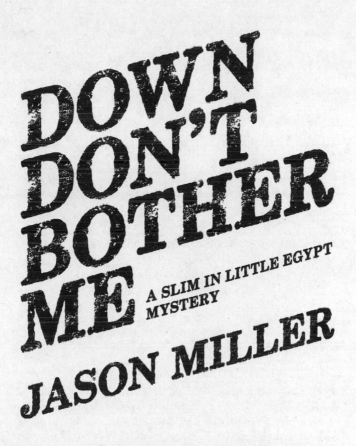

DOWN DON'T BOTHER ME

A SLIM IN LITTLE EGYPT MYSTERY

JASON MILLER

BOURBON STREET BOOKS

An Imprint of HarperCollinsPublishers

HarperCollins books may be purchased for educational, business, or sales promotional use. For information, please e-mail the Special Markets Department at SPsales@harpercollins.com.

Designed by William Ruoto

Library of Congress Cataloging-in-Publication Data has been applied for.

ISBN 978-0-06-236219-3

15 16 17 18 19 OV/RRD 10 9 8 7 6 5 4 3 2 1

For LMC

SOUTHERN ILLINOIS and its surrounding environs have a specific geography, of course, but you won't necessarily find an honest depiction of it in this book. Any apparent errors in the placement or relationships of its many towns should be chalked up to the whim of the author.

Envy's a coal comes hissing hot from hell.

— Philip James Bailey

PART ONE

IN
DEEP

ONE

I'd been demoted and was shoveling slide-back and minding my own business when they found Dwayne Mays's body in a pile of gob. This was up in Coulterville at a coal mine called Knight Hawk, last of the great old Randolph County mines and one of the few remaining great collieries in the Illinois downstate. A young guy called Ham Body—you guess why—tripped over Mays in the dark and went down, headfirst and hard, into a Sandvik dual-boom roof bolter and a half an hour or so worth of what I'm sure were uneasy dreams. When Ham Body finally came to, he raised the alarm and soon a great and calamitous ruckus was spreading its way through the work area: Ham Body to Plodder, Plodder to Bunny, Bunny to a guy called Neil (despite that his name wasn't Neil), and from there outward until Insane Wayne called it up to the surface with his characteristic restraint. Miners are dramatic sorts, you see, and sometimes the difference between a coal mine and an opera house seems not very much. Adding to it, this was shortly after that bad union business in Wolf Creek, where in the heat of a picket somebody (Neil, maybe) got his asshole in a knot and threatened to strangle a local reporter. When they discovered that Dwayne Mays had a mini-recorder wrapped round his neck and a notepad stuffed in his mouth, someone said, "Well, they got one." And then the cops came.

It'll sound heartless, maybe, but I didn't dwell on it overmuch or stay to catch the show. Like with most days, I had plenty on my mind. I was raising a daughter basically on my own and there were mountains of bills to pay and trouble to stay out of. The bills never ebbed, and trouble was everywhere and mostly the same, but the daughter was always changing and keeping me on my toes. Mostly, though, I never wanted to hang around the mine longer than necessary. The Knight Hawk paid okay, I guess, but the work bit the big one and I hated it like poison. Coal mining is terrible work generally, but the Knight Hawk had driven the union out twenty years earlier and the mine had gone from a reasonably decent place to make a living to like something out of a nightmare. The leash was off, and as long as everyone met their load requirements, they were free to do all kinds of malevolent and stupid shit down there. There wasn't anybody left to spank their behinds or say boo. The result was a kind of industrial slapstick. Hands were lopped off wrists, bodies fried by electrical currents. Heads were crushed like melons under falling rock. A couple years back, I had the misfortune of seeing a miner killed by his own trench digger. The rig's cable got hung up in a trolley-wire gap, and this guy—we called him Putzy—climbed down to move his nip across the gap and restart the digger. And restart it he did, but he was standing in front of it now, and the machine lurched forward suddenly and ran him over and cut off his leg. That's coal mine work these days.

Shoveling slide-back is maybe the worst job in the mine, but I'd mouthed off once or twice too often to one of the less-forgiving shift bosses and lost my roof bolter. Slide-back is what they give you when they want you to quit. It's a punishment.

The Knight Hawk was what's called a longwall mine,

and in a longwall mine what you have is basically a giant shearing machine that bites apart the coal seam and sends the pieces up a conveyor belt into daylight. Problem is, as the coal is traveling up, water is rushing down from the surface—water is almost always rushing into a coal mine from some place—and it washes the coal off the belt and into the empty space beneath the system. Your job, when you're shoveling slide-back, is to scoop out that wet muck and throw it back on the belt. At which point, it comes down again. It's a little like being one of those characters in Hades from Greek myth, but without the fun or glamour.

I shoveled out my shift until the cops and bosses came through and hustled us from the work area. The cop in charge was a big guy with graying hair and . . . soft eyes, I guess you'd say. I don't know how else to describe them. The rest of him didn't look so soft, but he was a rural cop and that was to be expected. He took my name and asked what I'd seen, which was nothing, really, and then he let me go. I went out and rode the thousand feet to the surface and hurried across the colliery to the shower house. You had to hurry or you ended up waiting in a line that stretched to China and back. I hung my pit clothes on the meat hook above the stall and turned on the stream. I'd made it just in time, and in another moment there was a line out the door of miners waiting with their towels and pumice soaps and shakers of Comet. Once coal mine grit gets in you, it doesn't come out easy. You have to fight it, but eventually the grit wins.

Nobody that day was too interested in grit. There was a corpse in the coal mine, so they wanted to talk about that, and so they did. They were buzzing. It was almost like

Christmas, but with murder. Mays, someone said his name was. Dwayne Mays, a journalist. I'd never heard of him. I finished my shower and got out of the way for the next guy. I dressed and went out to my bike and rode south to meet my daughter and Peggy.

I was working the day shift then, but my trip home through rural southern Illinois was across country distances, and by the time I roared down Shake-a-Rag Road the sun was smearing its lazy self across the line of foothills to the west. The sky darkened and the first stars bit through the sky like broken silver teeth. The air turned cool and the restless late-autumn stir calmed to a distant rustle. It's a poetic kind of country, Little Egypt, and it makes you think like that.

I lived way out in a place called Indian Vale. Probably no Indians ever lived there, so who exactly it was named after was a mystery and subject of frequent speculation between my daughter, Anci, and me. Influenced by some recent movies, Anci said it was probably pirates.

"Pirates?" I said. "But there's no ocean."

"So?"

"So pirates need an ocean. Otherwise, what's it all for?"

"Lost pirates then."

I said more likely it was backwoods gangsters or shine smugglers. Anci said I lacked imagination. She added that I'd have made a terrible pirate, which as an insult felt like overkill to me. Whatever the case, the only anyone living there now was Anci and me and a couple of house cats, Morris and Anthony. The house was my father's, or had been once upon a time—a raised-ranch dwelling roughly the size of a large hatbox, situated off a lonely county road where our only neighbors were a den of foxes in a patch of mockernut hickories and Johnson grass and, farther distant, a big truck farm up the hill west of the valley.

As I pulled in the drive, I could just make out the *inmigrante* working beneath the lights to bring in the last of the spinach harvest before the promise of an early snow turned into more than just promise. As I climbed off the bike and walked up the lane, the phone buzzed in my pocket. I thought maybe it was Anci or Peggy calling to check in on me, as they sometimes did, but the little screen said *Matthew Luster*, a name I didn't recognize. I don't know technology, really, so how it knew his name was something of a mystery, but not an interesting one, to me anyway. I was tired from work, and that evening in a particular hurry, so I just turned off the cell and put it away. Probably it was a wrong number. Or a creditor. Still, something worryingly familiar tickled at the back of my brain.

Just then a voice ahead of me said, "Hey there, Slim."

I looked up and forgot all about it, tickles and brains and whoever on earth Matthew Luster might be. Peggy was leaning in the doorway, grinning. She was gorgeous—what the old folks would have called a looker, forty-one and fit, with a figure that would have made Jesus punch a mule. She had bourbon-colored eyes and a mane of silver hair that settled around a pretty face. On her chin was the specter of a scar, a childhood accident from her first and only roughstock riding competition. She'd slipped off ineptly girthed tack into the Z-brace of a bull gate and nearly bitten off the tip of her tongue, leaving her forever after with a slight lisp. Even then, she climbed on again and won the day. So the story went, anyway. And I believed it. She was tough like that, with tough left over.

She said, "You're running late. We were starting to worry."

"There was a bit of a dustup."

"There usually is," she said, "Anyway, you just made it, darlin'. Anci's been eyeing that ice cream cake like a wolf eyes the wild turkey."

"She's a little wolf, all right. What about you?"

"I've been eyeing it, too, but I've got to keep one eye on the little wolf, so I'm pulling double duty."

"I'll see there's a little something extra in your next paycheck maybe."

"Thanks. What was the dustup about?"

I told her what I knew, about the body in the gob pile. Her face blanched and she took a step backward, into the shadow of the doorway.

I said, "Whoa there, you okay?"

"Sure, sure," she said, but she didn't look it. "It's just shocking, is all."

"It is that."

"Killing like that. A murder. It's shocking. What do you think it's all about?"

"No idea," I said. "Someone stepped on someone else's dick, probably. That's usually it. Right now, though, better let me inside before all that's left in this cake box is two quarts of cream and a cold memory."

The cake was more or less intact, but it was a close thing. The big "12" in the middle was conspicuously missing part of its "1," but I pretended not to notice, and Anci let me get away with it. She tossed down whatever book she was reading, and we kicked off her birthday party. I braved the slight chill to grill burgers and some corn on the cob I'd put away earlier in the season. The food must have been good. We scraped holes in our plates. Now and then Peggy lapsed into an uncharacteristic silence, but I guessed I knew what that was about: I'd recently asked her a pretty big question, and I figured she was mulling it over. Anyway, I hoped she was.

"Hey, guess what?" Anci said.

"Chicken butt?"

"Be serious."

"Okay, what?"

"One more year and I'll be a teenager."

"So you've reminded me."

"Might remind you again once or twice," she said.

I said, "Okay. One more year. But remember, getting older's not always what it's cracked up to be."

"That's what you say. From where I sit, it looks okay."

"I remember feeling the same way," I said. "But there's always a downside. For one thing, about the time you're ready to start paying bills, they take away your allowance."

"Who's *they*?"

I panned my hands in the air. "Unjust forces in the world."

"That'd be your daddy," Peggy put in.

"Not helpful," I said.

"Sorry."

Anci said, "You can try." And I knew the challenge was genuine. Fathers without daughters will never understand the fearful influence they wield over you. But let me tell you, it is real. I've had fights with Anci where I woke up later wondering how I managed to get hit by more than one train.

Peggy said, "Anci, I think your daddy is asking you not to be in such a hurry to grow up."

"I don't get it."

"We big people don't always get it either, darlin'. It's just something we worry about."

Anci shrugged at this, the mysteries of the big people. If we didn't understand it, why should she try? She didn't try. She cleared our dishes, then kissed Peggy on the cheek, scowled a threat at me, and went inside. Every time she walked out the door, any door, my heart ached for her to come back, even if she was occasionally a royal pain in my behind. Probably sooner than later, she'd go away to college or meet someone and fall in love or want to live somewhere else on account of a job that didn't involve shoveling anything, and my ache would move in for good, and live with me for the rest of my lonesome days.

I stopped thinking about it. Thinking about the dead body in the Knight Hawk was more pleasant, so I gave my brain to that. I wondered who this Dwayne Mays really was, whether he'd left behind any precocious tweens of his own. I wondered whether anyone was missing him tonight or was lonely because of his loss. Mostly, though, I wondered what he'd done to make someone hate him so bad they dragged him all the way down into the mine just to kill him and stuff his notepad in his mouth. It was hard to guess a reason, little as I knew, but then nothing on earth was more inventive and surprising than the wickedness of people.

Besides being dangerous, coal mines could be violent places, especially since the methamphetamine trade had moved in and put out its shingle. And this was one of those double-edged sword situations, too, because with the meth business you got it from both angles. Dealers inside the mine moved their evil product and did battle with their competitors. Meth gangs outside the mine laid siege to the colliery itself. Just recently, in fact, the Knight Hawk had undergone a rash of break-ins targeting its supply of anhydrous ammonia.

Let me tell you a thing or two about that. This can get a bit technical, but to start simple: a coal mine is just a giant hole in the ground. It's a complicated hole, but a hole just the same, and, as with any hole, water will find its way in. But when water gets in *this* hole, it comes into contact with rocks the miners have cut, and through a chemical process it turns itself into acid. If it stayed down there, maybe that'd be okay, but just as water inevitably finds its way into the hole, it inevitably finds it way back out into the world, where it tends to make its way into rivers and streams and lakes. All the places you don't want it to be. Once there, it poisons the water and kills the fish and birds and raises all kinds of hell with local ecosystems. Acid mine drainage, we call it. That's a bad deal for everyone, so the state and federal regulatory agencies force coal mine operations to clean it up. It's an ongoing and expensive treatment process, and the mine owners hate it like hot death and grumble about environmental extremists and the crushing weight of government regulation and all the other grievances they nurse while they're blowing the tops off our mountains and raking in the cash. Anyway, a lot of coal mines use anhydrous ammonia to neutralize the acid drainage.

So far, so good, but somewhere along the line some evil genius discovered that anhydrous ammonia could also be used to produce methamphetamine. And since mining operations bought the stuff in bulk, there was always plenty of it around. We need it to eliminate poison; meth dealers want it to make poison. It's a match made in hell.

A while back, after local gangs destroyed three new chain-link fences to get at the Knight Hawk's storage tanks, the mine bosses hired armed guards to patrol the area. As yet no one had been shot, but that was only a matter of hours, probably.

"I tell you," Peggy said, interrupting my happy thoughts with a glance in Anci's direction. "That little one's more like an adult every day. It's impressive."

"I call it unnerving."

"That too. She was talking earlier about her career. That's the word she used, too. 'Career.' Said she might want to be a lawyer."

"Oh, hell's bells."

Peggy put her hand on my shoulder. "Environmental law, at least."

"Small consolation."

"I think we're at the point where small consolations are all we can hope for, Slim. Still, she's something else."

"She is," I said, "but she's had to grow up fast. Too fast, probably. And she's had a lot put on her, and a lot of questions I can't answer."

"It's a tough age," Peggy said. She frowned a little at her thoughts. "And like to get tougher. I have some vague memories of those years, and let me tell you, it can be a hard time for a young woman who wants to turn herself into something."

"I do what I can."

"Darlin', no offense, but that's a little like turning a bull loose in the hatchery."

"So you've settled on honesty for tonight."

"I try to be honest every night, Slim. Or at least good."

"Or very bad."

"Depends on the night, sugar," she said. She lost herself again in her thoughts, then looked back up at me. "I don't suppose I can get you to be serious for a moment?"

"Well, since you went out of your way to put some icing on it."

"I mean it. I got something to tell you."

"Okay, I'll be serious, too. Try to, anyway. What's the story?"

Before she could tell me, though, the door opened and Anci reappeared.

She said, "My memory is we had a date."

"Reality TV and YouTube videos," I explained to Peggy.

"Looks like it's time to get back inside," she said, collecting the cats who'd trailed outside after Anci and leaving it lie.

I'll be honest, leaving it lie wasn't really my thing. Never has been. When I die, they'll probably chisel it on my headstone: *Slim: Wouldn't Leave It Lie.*

Long time ago, I'd married a hippie woman for love. And love her I did, and she loved me. Or so I believed. For a long time it was good, and I thought we'd beat the weary world and its cynical ways. I worked my kip at the Knight Hawk or wherever would have me. She practiced Reiki or sold magical stones or whatever was hitting the new age markets that year. In the end, she gave me both good and bad. The good was Anci. The bad was heartache. We'd been going along okay as a family until, one morning, just like that, she announced that she'd dissolved our marriage in a dream. She was done and ready to move on. More to the point, she'd taken up with another guy, one who spoke her language or understood more fully the language of runes or the whispers of the earth or whatever it was. At first, I figured he was some kind of Svengali, maybe, that he'd put her under some kind of a spell, but you always want to let the ones you love off the hook or create an excuse for their badness. In the end, I had to face it: she was gone, and gone of her own will. She packed up our only car, and she and her new fella struck for the golden West and whatever spiritual quest awaited them.

Situation like that, you want to spend some time—five or six years, maybe—staring at a wall and hoping an airplane lands on your bed. But when you've got a kid, you can't do that. All of a sudden, there's slack to pick up. Miles of slack. You've got to do all the cooking and cleaning and helping with homework. You've got to hold her hand and tell her everything's going to be all right, that her mother didn't leave because of her, and you have to keep telling her until she believes it. You wish there was someone around to tell you the same things, but there almost never is. I guess that's just the way of things.

Orders received, we went inside with Anci. The YouTubes weren't bad, but the reality shows were a terror. Some of them were basically singing and dancing contests, and those were okay, I guess, but the worst seemed to pit people of bad character against one another for no other reason than to raise serious doubts about the value of the human race. I hate to be like that—I hated when my parents yelled at me about the Rolling Stones—but some things just get to you. Every one of these shows was the same: Young folks spinning webs of deceit and treachery that Dante himself would pass over as unrealistically mean-spirited. Anci asked me if I liked them and—it being her birthday—I said I did, but secretly I wanted to find the responsible parties and show them images of earthly suffering until they devoted their lives to something less heinous.

After basically a million years of these terrible things, Anci stood up and yawned and stretched and said, "I think I'm calling that a birthday."

"You're giving out already?" I said. "I thought we'd be watching until midnight at least."

"I've decided to give you a break," she said. "I know that look you get."

"What look?"

"The look you're wearing right now. One like you want to kick a hole in the baby Moses."

"I thought I was hiding it better than that."

"Well, you're not," she said. "Besides, my guess is you'll want to get on to complaining about your taxes or how bad your back aches or whatever it is old folks talk about when the young people aren't around."

"I have this whole thing planned about my arthritis," I said. "There are pictures and everything."

She looked at Peggy.

"You're good to put up with him."

"Don't I know it."

"I hate it when you two team up," I said. "I can barely keep up with one of you. A team-up just isn't fair."

"You mean like state fair?"

"Go to bed."

She hefted her book—it was as big as a cinder block—and thanked us for her presents and cake and hugged Peggy around the neck one last time and went up to her room, singing.

When we were alone, we sat there quietly a moment or two with our thoughts. I switched off the TV, and the terrible people went away. At last, I said to Peggy, "Well, that was a party now."

"It was. Shame they only come once a year."

"Strongly agree. I'll tell you, I got the post-party blues."

"Me, too."

"Do you want to hear my presentation on arthritis now?"

"No. No, I do not."

"Well, what do you want to do then?" I asked.

"Darling, I want to fuck."

"Bless you."

And that's what we did. It was nice, playful and playfully rough and fun. Mostly fun. Afterward, we lay in bed, laughing and licking our wounds and feeling content. Peggy had some grass. I rolled a joint, and we shared it back and forth.

I said, "Well, that wasn't half bad."

"Honey, I'm only *getting* old." She hit me gently with her pillow. "I figure I got another fifteen years or so of screwing the gray out of your beard."

"Possibly I should get a dye job, give you a run for your money. What do you think?"

"I think middle-aged men who color their hair look like serial killers, TV ministers, or porno producers, but whatever keeps you motivated, love."

"It's a deal then," I said. "Speaking of which . . ."

"Yeah?"

"Have you thought any more about my offer?"

"About moving in here with the two of you?"

"No, about my come-to-Jesus pitch. Of course about moving in here."

"I'm thinking about it, Slim. I really am."

"Been a while now."

"I'm a slow thinker."

"You hate your place in Zeigler."

"Only because it's drafty, creaky, and possibly haunted. It has its good points, though. One thing, the ghosts appear to have frightened off the snakes."

"And Anci would love it."

"I know," she said, turning serious.

"I wouldn't dislike it so much my own self. We could make a nice life together, maybe."

"More than nice, even."

"That's what I think. How long have we been seeing each other?"

"A year and a half, two weeks ago Thursday," she said. "Not that I'm counting."

"Wednesday, actually. Not that I'm counting," I said. "I think by the time my parents had known one another that long, they had three kids and my daddy had been to war and back."

"Your math might be just a little off, love, to say nothing of your biology. Anyway, in case you haven't noticed, times have changed a little since the olden days."

"Olden days? I'm talking about the *sixties*."

"Uh-huh. Slim, 1961 was a half century or so ago, believe it or not. Meantime, I've been married. I've been married and a half. Married a damn meth dealer."

"I know."

"And I've made other mistakes."

"That's just another way of saying you're an adult."

"True enough. And this adult needs more time. To think things through. To be sure about us."

"And me."

"And you," she agreed. "And where we're headed."

"Fair enough."

She kissed me on the lips.

"Good. You're a good man, Slim. I appreciate your patience."

"I like to think it's more than just something like patience."

"I like to think so, too. Do me a favor? Ask me again soon."

"Deal," I said. "And speaking of asking, you had something to ask *me* earlier."

"I did?"

"Or something to tell me."

She was quiet a moment then said, "Ah, that. Let's save that for another time, okay? It's a rule. I don't do serious conversations in the buff, and I'm sure as hell not about to start tonight."

"Darling, I hate to tell you, I think you've broken your rule. I think we both have."

"Broke it and danced on the pieces, sug, but I tell you what, I'm done."

"Well, what do you do in the buff, then?" I asked. I reached for the roach cradled in the V of a punch-metal ashtray.

"Let me show you."

She showed me. Following another earthquake, we again lay in the dark. The house was still with that nighttime country quiet. Peggy breathed softly beside me, snoring a little, her body tingling with the warmth of sleep. The cool autumn air sighed against the windowpanes. I lay there awake and wondering how I could have gotten old enough to have a twelve-year-old. It seemed impossible, but I guess the passage of time always does. Then I lay there hoping that Peggy would eventually take me up on my offer, and I got mad at myself for hoping things. I hoped I really was a good man, like Peggy had said. I wished I could right the mistakes of the past or at least straighten them out some so that it all made sense, but you could never do that. It was what it was and always would be, just like I was always going to be a coal miner whose wife had run away, and that's all there was to it. Things were what they were, and I tried to be resolved about it, but trying only made me more blue. I'm not usually a depressive sort, but the nighttime brings it out in you sometimes. You know how it is. After what felt like a long time, I grew drowsy with my thoughts.

Before I drifted off to sleep, I rolled over and glanced at my phone to check the hour. Whoever this Matthew Luster was, he'd called five more times.

TWO

A report on the Mays killing led off the local radio news that morning, but there didn't seem to be any new information. No suspects were named and no arrests had been made. The section of the mine where they'd found Mays's body was still closed and like to be for some time. There was the usual business from the cops about it being an ongoing investigation, then someone from the Knight Hawk issued the kind of statement that's carefully constructed to convey no meaning whatsoever, and that was the end of it.

I got out of bed quietly so as not to wake Peggy. I slipped into a robe and came downstairs, where I found Anci staring mournfully at the remains of the ice cream cake. Somehow in all the fun the night before we'd neglected to put it away and the cats had been at it. There were sticky white paw prints everywhere. I half expected to see them on the ceiling.

Anci said, "Well, that's kind of a kick in the teeth. That was going to be my breakfast."

"I was hoping you'd try something a little more healthy."

"French toast with lots of syrup?"

"Little powdered sugar makes it nice, too."

"Sure does."

"Right on."

We dapped and blew it up.

I got started on the toast. Anci turned on some music—"Ready for the Time to Get Better" by Crystal Gayle, I think it was—and we sang along together with that. After a while, Peggy heard us carrying on and came staggering in. She was a beautiful woman, but morning was not her time. She looked like she'd slept through a cyclone. Her hair was a tangled mess and she'd put on a pajamas shirt but missed a buttonhole, and the whole thing was cockeyed. She was wearing one sock. The other had gone AWOL.

I said, "The reports of your demise . . ."

"Fewer jokes," she said, "more coffee."

While Anci ate and Peggy mainlined caffeine, I excused myself and had a quick workout: pushups and some stomach crunches. I worked the heavy bag for a while and then tied on my sneakers and went for a run up to Shake-a-Rag and back. It was a gray morning. The clouds pushed in and blanketed the sky, and though the air was touched cool, by the time I got back to the house I was a sweaty mess. Meantime, Peggy and Anci had showered and dressed and were heading out to school, Anci for learning and Peggy for teaching.

"Stay out of trouble today, Slim," Peggy said.

"I always do," I said.

"That'll be the day," Anci said.

I kissed them both and saw them off. I went back inside and sipped another cup of coffee. The house was always too quiet when they were gone, and I soon found myself singing along to some more old-school country songs, Willie and Emmylou and Dolly. "Gulf Coast Highway" came on with its tale of patient love and I started getting teary. I didn't know what was wrong with me lately. Probably I was getting sentimental in my old age. I switched off the radio and checked my cell for more calls and found none. I contemplated calling this Luster back to find out what he was on about, but I was already running late, so I mopped up some of the ice cream mess I'd missed, then hopped on the bike and cruised up IL–13 north and west to Coulterville. Along the way, it started to rain.

I arrived at the Hawk just as it really started turning loose. I flashed my ID, rode through the gates, and headed up to the shaft to wait for the elevator. Some of the men in line wanted to talk about the body in the gob pile, but coal miners basically have the attention span of small children and pretty soon they were on to other things, including the rack on the new shift nurse. The gist of it was that she put them in a romantic mood. Mercifully, the elevator soon arrived and took us below.

My section was at the far end of the active work area, north and east a ways and beneath the edge of the lake. I climbed off the man-trip—the vehicle that transports miners to the face, I mean—and then walked a half mile or so to where a pile of slide-back roughly the size of Angkor Wat was waiting. Just looking at it made my back ache. I was searching around for my shovel when my least favorite shift boss came over. He had a head like a bearded ham and an ass it would take two ordinary men to pull. Everybody called him Big Sexy. He always looked at me like something he wanted to wipe up with a hanky.

He said, "Hold up on that boodle there, Slim. You're wanted up top."

"Up top? You're shitting me. I just got down here."

"I know. Saw you come in."

"Goddamn it, Big Sexy, why didn't you save me the trip?"

He shrugged. "'Cause I don't like you."

If my shovel had been there, I would have shoved it up his giant ass. It wasn't, so I'd have to get my vengeance bare-handed, and I was about to when another of the bosses took my arm and led me away.

"C'mon, Slim," he said quietly. "Boss is waiting."

So I went out again, back on the man-trip, and to the cage, and up into daytime. It was raining harder now, cold slashes of rain, and from somewhere west came the bark of thunder. I walked across the tipple to the fiberglass shed they called the main office, and went inside to the reception desk.

A blond woman with a hair bun the size of a small dog looked up at me.

"Help you there, Slam?"

"It's Slim."

"Oh." She made a face. "Why'd I think Slam then?"

"I don't know."

She thought about it a moment. I just stood there, letting her think. The phone didn't ring. The computer on the desk didn't catch fire. No one threw a folding chair through the office window.

"I think maybe there was a Slam who worked one of them Asheville mines. You know the ones."

"I guess I do."

"You don't have to worry about your name being close to his, though," she went on. My mind briefly entertained the idea of hitting her with her keyboard. "He's dead."

"Billy Bear sent for me," I put in.

She thought about a dead guy named Slam for another moment or two, frowning, then came back to the present and shook her head.

"He didn't."

"I was told he did."

"Well, if he did, he didn't do it from here. He's up to Rock Island this week. Got a daughter getting hitched."

"That's a hell of a thing."

She blinked at me.

"The wedding or Billy Bear not being here?"

"The second one," I said. "I don't know about a wedding."

She shrugged and said, "I've met him. She could do worse. Your thing, though? Maybe someone's pulling your chain."

"I'm starting to think so. Fact, I'm starting to think this whole day is a big joke on me. What's the penalty these days for running your shift captain through the crusher house?"

"I don't know, but they'll probably dock you both."

I thanked her and went out with murder in my heart. He was coming in at the same time, and we nearly collided. He was short—five foot five or thereabouts—with a head like an artillery shell and a pile of white hair. He was maybe seventy and with the hair looked a little like a mad scientist from one of the old movies. He was wearing a light brown suit and a display handkerchief and, somewhat preciously, rough work boots.

"You're Slim?" he said.

That's me. I'm Slim.

The man nodded and scowled and reached out to take my hand. His clasp was firm and felt like money in the bank.

I was right on that count, at least. "I'm the one sent for you, son," he said. "My name's Matthew Luster. And this is my coal mine."

Like most folks with his kind of money and power, Luster looked the part. His suit was neatly tailored and his red display handkerchief was fine like raw silk. His wristwatch was one of those fancy Omega numbers that does everything but man the phones and spank the babies. Even his mad-science hairstyle looked better than my ten-dollar Walmart trim.

We went back inside and into Billy Bear's office. There was a desk with Billy Bear's name on it and some framed pictures of kids playing ball and such. The little girl in some of them was the one who'd grown up to get married, I guess. A good-looking young man in a dark suit hurried to join us. Luster sat in the big leather chair behind the desk. The young man leaned casually against it. They owned the place and acted like they did. There wasn't a chair for me so I just stood there like a dope, dripping from the rain and wondering why I'd been summoned to an audience with the owner.

Luster said, "I was starting to worry something had happened to you, boy. You always ignore your phone calls?"

"Sorry. I didn't recognize your name on my cell. I don't even know how you managed to *get* your name on my cell. Usually it's just a number, unless I know you."

"Oh, that. You can pay extra for that," he said. "It's a service."

"Well, service or no, I didn't recognize your name out of context. Thought you might be a salesman."

Luster sniffed. "*Context?* What the hell kind of a thing is that? Let me ask you, you have some college, Slim?"

"I've driven past a couple," I said. "You could have left a voicemail, you know? That's a service, too."

"Okay. Fair enough. But this ain't the kind of thing you leave phone messages lying around about." He waved a hand. He wanted to get down to it. "Let's turkey shoot. What job you working down there these days?"

I told him, and he sucked it around for a moment. He looked at the young guy and nodded, and the young guy slid off the desk and out of the room without a word.

"You're off that as of now," Luster said. "You want your bolter back, you can have that. You want to be shift captain or dust boss, or you want to get up here in the daylight for a while, maybe, you can have that, too. Jonathan is off taking care of it for you now."

"He got all that from you with just a look?"

"We been together since he was a pup. We got to where words aren't always needed." He crawled forward some on the top of the desk. Words were needed between us, I guess. "Listen, Slim, I do this for you because I want you to *see* what I can do for you."

"Okay."

"I can do more," he said. "Don't think I can't. I'm what you call a person of means."

"I'd say that's putting it mildly. I'm guessing you own most of the county. Underside of it, anyway, which is just as well, because that's where the money is."

Luster shrugged. His lips pressed together and for an instant his eyes showed memory and a spark of something like regret. He said, "One time, maybe. Not so much these days. Business ain't what it used to be. I've sold out some to Roy Galligan, too. You know Roy Galligan?"

"We've never been introduced."

"Know of him, I mean. Anyway, I've sold out some to him. Couple of them smaller outfits, and that surface mine over there to Holly. Headaches for cash. Still, what I've got left pays the bills."

"I bet," I said. "Maybe a little left over. Only question is what any of it has to do with me."

"You know a guy name of Sam Dooley?"

"Dooley-Bug? Yeah, him I know," I said.

"You worked with him once."

"More than once. Dooley-Bug's been in the mines a long time."

"True that. So long he owes Underground Jesus a nickel. But what I mean is, last year you found his kid for him."

I hesitated. This was suddenly getting into some pretty confidential territory. I wondered how Luster knew about it. Surely not from Dooley, who was a close-lipped sort, but others were involved, too, not least Dooley's daughter. Some of them weren't so close-lipped. Not least Dooley's daughter. Others, too, probably.

I decided to play noncommittal. "Something like that might have happened, one time or another."

Luster waved his hand.

"Don't lawyer me, boy. Word is, the kid started running with a pretty dubious crowd. Something to do with this meth shit we got running wild these days. Maybe the kid was just using or maybe she was selling, too. Whichever it was, she was being used by her gang. Bag whoring, they call it. Pussy for drugs. You know anything about that?"

"Nope."

"Nasty business. Anyway, story is that Dooley went to retrieve her. I hear he didn't want her back so much. The kid had been trouble for a long time, a bad seed. But his wife was brokenhearted over the whole deal and talked him into it. So off he goes to confront these black-toothed bastards, and for his trouble he gets the holy dog shit beat out of him. Word then has it that he set you loose on them, and you tore through 'em like a tornado through a trailer park. They say you left a lot of hats on the ground."

"I can't say."

"Hell, Slim, I don't expect you to tell," he said, and smiled and winked at me because we were men sharing things. "Secrets are secrets. It's a rare man these days who understands that and can keep his hole shut. I just wanted you to know that I know. They say you've got a bloodhound's nose, and you're either too brave or too stupid to be afraid."

"Thanks."

He didn't care for that. He had a wealthy man's touchiness, and he showed it to me.

"I just mean you got tangled up in a rough situation with bad actors and came out of it on top. Jesus, Slim, sit down."

His words were barely audible over the sound of rain tapping the window glass, but as soon as he said it, Jonathan came back in through the door pushing a roller chair. It was like a magic act. I sat down.

Luster pressed on. "And I hear you helped out a few more fellas here at the mine. Finding folks for them, I mean. Bringing 'em home. They say you have a knack for that kind of thing. Bloodhounding. That true?"

I didn't like saying so, at least not until I had better idea of where all this was headed. Facts were facts, though, and the fact was that after the aforementioned business with Dooley I'd been approached by a handful of folks eager to locate this missing person or that. Sometimes I found them and brought them home—runaway kids, mostly—and sometimes I found them and left them alone, if leaving them alone felt like the right thing to do. But I always found them.

Luster waited. I waited. Jonathan waited. Somewhere, a turkey buzzard fell out of the sky. Finally, the old man said, "Okay, let's assume it's true, then. And let's assume also that this talent of yours is something I'm currently in the market for. You know about this business in the Knight Hawk? The body they found down there?"

"It was in my section, so I knew right away. I even got a look at him."

"Name was Dwayne Mays. Local press, dead-tree division. Someone screwed a pistol in his ear and separated him from his brains, so this won't be one of those things that burns off with the morning dew. The cops are plenty interested in how and why Mays's body ended up down in my Knight Hawk."

"It makes sense they would be," I said. "It's their job, isn't it?"

"Backcountry parts, their job is usually stroking their chickens and soaking the local yokels, boy, but this county sheriff might be different. Name of Wince. You know him?"

I said I didn't.

Luster said, "Well, keep clear. He's the worst kind of cop there is."

"Corrupt?"

"Committed." He leaned back in his seat and looked at me, about the way a gator eyes the bird on its nose. He tapped a finger on the desk and said, "Lot of bad press for coal mines these days. You follow the Upper Big Branch story?"

"Everybody did."

"Lot of bad press," he said again.

"Lot of dead miners."

Luster considered that. He did a powerful job of considering. For a moment, I was afraid his hair would catch fire. He said, "You got politics, Slim?"

"Some. Some politics, some college."

"Liberal?"

"Because I don't like a company killing its miners through sheer stupidity? Sure. Liberal as hell."

Luster looked at Jonathan. Jonathan looked back, his face handsome but empty. Probably he'd been to some fancy school somewhere and they'd taught him the trick of emptying expression from his face. Probably charged him a pretty penny for it, too. He shrugged. Luster looked at me again. I felt my asshole tighten. It was coming, whatever it was.

"I'd like to see about having you do a little work for me. You be interested in something like that?"

I already worked for him, so I didn't say anything. He didn't want me to anyway. I just sat there.

He seemed okay with that. "What we got here is an industry under watch. Handful of things go wrong. Bullshit or bad fortune. Fire breaks out. Meteor strikes. Miners die. Lawsuits happen. You're right: Massey Energy stepped in it good with that UBB thing down in West Virginia. Worse was the way they handled it after. Exposed their shareholders to risk. And now we got a situation where reporters all over the country are looking to make a name for themselves, trying to catch any big mining outfit they can in a slipup."

"You think that's what Dwayne Mays was doing?"

"I don't know. Maybe. He was up to something, though. Chances are he didn't end up down there by accident."

"Chances are."

"Problem for him is, we're not up to anything."

"That, plus the problem that he's murdered and half buried in a gob pile."

"That, too. But what I said stands. We're entirely and completely aboveboard, Slim."

I just sat there.

"You believe me?" he asked.

"You need me to?"

"I do not," he said. "Meantime, the cops are all over us, stink on a monkey's ass. They've already shut down part of our operation, and it's likely they'll shut down more of it, this thing drags out any kind of time. That's bad for business. These are lean days as it is, and we just can't take them getting any leaner. Plus, a shutdown will attract attention—all kinds of attention, some of it the wrong kind. Before you know it, we're completely under the microscope. All that's not bad enough, we got us another complication here."

"Which is?"

Jonathan sat there like a stump, except for one hand, which came to life and slid a photograph across the desk: a balding Average, early fifties or so, striking a pose in the Herrin city park. They've got this memorial statue out there of a World War I doughboy, and the Average was standing beneath it and staring off into space like he'd worked out a plan to beat the kaiser.

Luster pointed at the picture. "Name's Beckett. Guy Allan Beckett. He's Dwayne Mays's photographer. Or they paired up on quite a few jobs, anyway. Beckett went missing the same time Dwayne Mays showed up in pieces, and ain't nobody seen or heard from him since. He can't be raised by any means, and his bank card hasn't been used. His wife thinks he's come to evil. The cops are probably thinking the same thing, though they're not talking just yet."

I set down the picture and breathed out heavily and said, "Mr. Luster, I appreciate your moving me upstairs. More to the point, my back appreciates it. You probably saved me from an early wheelchair. But I'm not a policeman. I'm not a private eye, and I don't know a thing about professional mystery-solving. Top of that, near as I can tell, cops like folks poking around in their business about as much as they like the criminals themselves. And that's just what I get from books and TV. I can't even imagine what they do to you in real life. It's true, I once helped some friends who were having family woes, but I've got a soft spot for that kind of thing—family stuff—and I let them talk me into it. It wasn't maybe the prettiest thing I've ever done, but in the end it was small fuss and the law was never involved in any way. I don't know what I can do for you."

For the first time, Jonathan spoke. I didn't know he could, frankly, and the sound of his voice shocked me like a clap of thunder.

"What you can do for us, Slim," he said, "is attempt to locate Mr. Beckett. At least look for him. Use that nose of yours to track him until you find him, then bring him to us."

"Not the cops?"

"Us first. Remember who got you off slide-back."

I guess Luster liked that one okay. He nodded. Jonathan nodded. I didn't nod. The whole thing was ridiculous. But these were the type of people you couldn't easily say no to, so instead I decided to go for the stall. I glanced at the picture again. He went maybe five ten or so, Beckett, though it was hard to tell from just a photo. He sported the regulation middle-age gut but otherwise appeared reasonably fit. Nothing interesting about him—no missing limbs or scars or anything like that. From a seek-and-find standpoint, that would probably make things tougher.

I said, "You don't think you ought to give the police investigation some time? This only happened yesterday. They probably haven't even finished brewing the coffee yet."

"Not my style, Slim," Luster said. "I've made my whole life by jumping into the game early and with both feet. You know who stands around waiting for other people to solve their problems?"

"I got a sense of it, yeah. Why me, though? I got to tell you, I can't figure out your angle here. Why not hire a real detective?"

"Hell, son, hire one from *where*? Case you haven't noticed, Slim, this ain't exactly what you'd call a major metropolitan area. Southern Illinois has all of three private investigators, all of them graduates of a community college summer program and not a one of them worth using to scrape shit off your shoe."

Jonathan said, "We checked into them." He made a purse with his mouth and shut his eyes and shook his head slowly at me.

Luster said, "Besides, I use some outsider, I have to dick around bringing 'em up to speed on the local terrain. Whereas you already know the territory. And the people. Oh, and then there's your daddy. That's the other reason we called on you."

"My daddy?"

"Not my favorite person, I admit," Luster said. "But there's no denying what he was and what he did down here. A lot of folks think he's a damn hero."

I said, "He'd probably agree with them."

Luster just shrugged. He said, "I got to think there's not a door in the downstate his name won't kick down. Do more than a badge or a private investigator's ID from godforsaken

Chicago, that's for sure. Slim, I feel pretty sure you can get to places a pro couldn't, and I know you've got contacts it would take someone else months to cultivate. That's time I don't have, son."

"I wouldn't know where to start."

"Just start anywhere. Hell, it's what the police do. Pull on some thread, see where it leads. You think they've got a team of Sherlock Holmeses stashed away in the Randolph County sheriff's station? Goddamn, boy, it used to be a Pizza Hut."

"Pizza Palace." Jonathan.

"Pizza Palace. Just jump in anywhere. Ask a few questions. See what you turn up. You might get lucky. If not, well, we can at least say we tried." He fixed me with his frosted eyes. "Like I said, we can do things for you."

"You already got me off the worst shift-duty of them all," I said. "That's probably enough."

"Oh, hell, Slim, that was just for openers. I'm talking about something more substantial. And permanent."

Jonathan said, "Your job, one. As long as Mr. Luster owns this mine, it's guaranteed."

"Your pension, too."

The bit about the job was nice, but that last thing knocked me asshole-over-teakettle. Jonathan produced a glass of water. I drank it. The glass went away. He really was a magician. I waited for him to fart out a platinum coin.

Luster said, "Times are tough, Slim. You know how it is. Lot of pensions guaranteed at one point are disappearing today. And that's health coverage, too. Security for you and your family. You got a family?"

"A daughter."

Luster nodded. "Security for your daughter. I sell this

place eventually, it gets bought up, and suddenly those pensions aren't worth the promises they're printed on. You've seen it happen before. But yours goes into a special account. Starting today. This afternoon."

Jonathan said, "It's a generous offer, Slim."

"This is southern Illinois, son," Luster said. "Coal country. The best friends to have around here are friends in low places."

This was the case and I said so to Luster, but I wasn't really listening to me. I was thinking about that pension and all that it meant. For a coal miner—or any working person, really—a pension means just about everything. Luster was right: a pension was health insurance into your dotage and financial security after you retired. It was a monthly paycheck and food in your tummy and a roof to keep the sun off your bald spot. But more than that, it was a promise kept. That pension was the reason a lot of miners went into the mines in the first place, and it was the reason a lot of them stayed longer than they should. It was, in a very real sense, the light at the end of a very long, very dark night.

Luster picked up my thoughts and carried them forward. "So do it for that. Do it for your daughter," Luster said. "Hell, Slim, do it for Beckett's wife."

"Beckett's wife?"

Luster cleared his throat. "You told me you have a soft spot for family, Slim," he said. "Well, this woman, her name's Temple."

Jonathan said, "Temple Luster Beckett."

Luster said, "She's my daughter. This Beckett who's gone missing is my son-in-law."

THREE

It was a Saturday afternoon in the springtime, and my mother was crying in the kitchen with a gun in her hand. My sisters were huddled on the floor away from the windows with their backs to the stove and they were crying, too. I was crying. I was six years old. The door opened. My sisters screamed and my mother screamed with them and discharged the gun into the floor, and then my father walked in.

Like I'd be one day, my father was a coal man, but unlike me he was an important one. Maybe the most important in the downstate. He was a union leader and strike organizer and an inspiration to every other coal miner in the area. His name opened doors, or closed them, sometimes slammed them. He was an organizer or a bureaucrat or a thug, depending on whom you asked, and I hated him and was afraid of him. He was tall and skinny like I was becoming and had slightly stooped shoulders and a hawkish nose on an angular face. His eyes were gray and his hair graying prematurely. He looked at us now without expression and stepped smartly to my mother and took the gun from her.

He said, "You'll hurt somebody," but he might have been chiding her for being careless with a potato peeler.

My mother said, "There was a person here."

"A person?"

"A man. A big man. He had red hair and a mark on his cheek. Like a birthmark."

My father said, "His name is Deaton. He's a company goon. What did he want?"

"Just to say hello," she said. "And that he knew us. He wanted us to know that he knew us. He said the girls' names."

My father nodded slowly and then turned and walked further into the house with the gun, and that was the last that was said of any of it, at least in front of us. We were in the midst of a strike that year, a monster that had stretched on since early in the winter, and my father was leading the local UMWA. His friends had been beaten. His truck had been set on fire. But no one had ever come to the house before. No one had ever said my sisters' names. In another few weeks, the strike had ended—quietly, the way those things always seemed to end—but it wasn't until late summer that I happened to hear a news report on the radio, the discovery of a body in the waters of the Hog Thief, shot full of bullets. The man had been missing since sometime in the spring, and his name was Deaton.

Until further notice, I had been reassigned to my current task: finder of missing photographers. I'll be honest: as career changes go, it was jarring. I left the Knight Hawk around twelve-thirty and headed south and east along the IL-13/127 corridor. The thinking was, I should at least talk to Luster's daughter and get some sense of this Guy Beckett and what he might have been working on and where he might have gone. Way I saw it, the most likely explanation for Mays's murder and Beckett's sudden disappearance was that Beckett's committing the former—for whatever motive—had necessitated the latter. I had a feeling that the cops were probably thinking the same thing. I had a second feeling that Luster and Jonathan were maybe thinking the same thing, too, but neither had said so. We can get as advanced as we want as a species, but something in us will never let go of the idea that giving voice to an unpleasant possibility will somehow make it real.

I rolled the bike past Grubbs, Vergennes, and Grange Hall. Like a lot of rural places, southern Illinois is basically a bunch of small towns knit together, a Babel's Tower mix of rednecks, rubes, freaks, tweakers, gun nuts, and aging hippies––real hippies, not the newfangled crunchy kids they're turning out these days––who'd fled into the dark-licked hills sometime during the bloodiest days of a war that wouldn't stop shaping their lives and had never come out. The land they occupy is low farmland, or river basin, or rock-clotted hill country, evidence of the Illinois glacial advance of some two hundred thousand years ago.

It's a pretty place, too, at least it is when it's not turning itself into a mudhole. By the time I reached Spillway Road, the clouds had rolled over to show their dark bellies, and the rain was coming down in sideways sheets, sucking little plumes of white smoke from the asphalt. The wind picked up and snakes of gray water slithered across the paved ribbon of highway. I tell you, at this point, I started seriously regretting my decision to ride to work. I soaked down to the skivvies in seconds, and the rain buffeted the bike across the lane and nearly off into the woodsy roadside. Somehow I held on, but there were moments in there when I felt like a spider clinging to her web during a typhoon.

The address Jonathan gave me was inside something called the Crab Orchard Estates. I wasn't sure what that was—it sounded like some kind of nineties real estate agent's wet dream—but I had a sense of where it must be. I aimed the bike toward the Crab Orchard wildlife preserve and took the shoreline road until I spied a gated community spreading its way west and north along the edge of the water. There was a check-in box with a black man sitting inside. When I pulled up, he leaned closer to the window and slid back the glass.

He said, "Little damp today."

"I don't know, I'm thinking of building an ark."

"Probably more practical than, say, a motorcycle."

"Probably," I said. Everybody was a comedian. "Let me ask you, you know where I can find Temple Beckett's place?"

"She know you're coming?"

"What I'm told."

This was getting down to business. He produced a clipboard and looked holes in it. He flipped some pages and put the clipboard back on its hook. He picked up a phone and dialed, but I guess no one answered because after a moment he set it down again, too.

"She ain't called down about anyone, and I can't raise the house. What'd you say your name is?"

"She'd probably have called me Slim."

"That a coal mine thing?"

"How'd you guess?"

"You got a bucket tied to your scooter there," he said. He sighed. "I let you go up and something happens—something ain't supposed to happen, I mean—I'm the one's gotta answer for it."

"Well, maybe I could leave something here with you. You know, some kind of collateral."

He lifted an eyebrow.

"Leave something? Like what?"

"My union card, maybe."

"You even got a union card?"

"Nope."

"Didn't think so. These days, I don't know anyone's got one. They're like unicorns."

"Getting to be."

He waved his hand at me.

"Go on up. Just don't do anything come back on me," he said, and gave me some sense of the direction I should go. Then he said, "You know, I used to be in the mines my own self. Worked a scratchback mine up at Olney years ago. My father worked it, and his brother, and some cousins of mine, and I swore I never would but damned if I didn't. I'll tell you, that was something like a hell on earth."

"Five-foot seam?"

He leaned forward in the window a little. The rain beaded on his short, silver hair and eyebrows.

"Lemme tell you, we'd have strangled our mothers for five-foot coal. You ever heard of Kelvin's Scratch-Ass Mine?"

"Can't say."

"Well, that was us. The Scratch-Ass Boys. Four feet in most places. Couple three-and-a-half foot spots. Like that old song, 'Thirty Inch Coal.' You know that one?"

"I heard it once or twice."

"*Ridin' on a lizard in thirty-inch coal,*" he sang. His voice was soft but deep, and it sounded like history. "It was like that. You raised your eyebrows, you'd hit the ceiling. You got so you had scabs all up and down your back and spine and on your knees and hands. My wife ain't like those scabs on my hands. Calluses, neither. Bought me this cream to use. Smelled like some kind of flower, lilacs, and wouldn't you know that's what those other Scratch-Ass sonsofbitches ended up nicknaming me. Lilac. I couldn't wait to get out of there, and after twenty years I finally did, and it's nice not being Lilac anymore, but look where I ended up. Sitting in a damn box all day."

"Least it's got a high ceiling," I said.

"Yeah, but it's dull. Go on up, Slim. But behave."

I promised to behave. I thanked him and started to roar away. He started to push shut his window. I stopped and said, "Hey, one more thing. I grew up around here, but I've never been to this development before. You happen to remember what used to be here?"

"Sure. Once upon a time, this was the old Grendel Mine company town."

"I thought I knew it. That was a Roy Galligan mine, memory serves."

He nodded.

"Still is, technically. The mine's up the hill there apiece, across from that King Coal outfit. You can kinda make out what's left of the tipple. It's dead, but Galligan still owns the land lease."

"Galligan and Luster. I guess they own most of them around here these days."

"Don't know," he said. "Don't know Luster. Heard his name, of course, but that's the extent of it. Roy Galligan, though, him I know."

"I can tell from your tone you don't like him," I said.

He chuckled. "He ain't on my holiday shopping list, no. You might think you've met a sonofabitch in your time, but let me tell you, you ain't. That old man is so bad, they'll have to come up with a new definition of the term just so ordinary bad men won't get all full of false piety."

"That's pretty good," I said.

"Thanks. You sit in this box all day, you have time to think about stuff like that and how to say it. Good old Roy," he said, but he didn't mean it. Nobody who said "Good old Roy" ever meant it.

I thanked him again and waved and puttered through the gate, which opened for me on its mechanical arm. Even with his directions in mind, it took a bit of getting lost on the shiny loops of paved road before I found my bearings. Sure enough, this was the old Grendel Mine company town. Way back when, it'd been the largest and most modern of its kind in the area, basically a self-sufficient community. There'd been company housing and a company store and company script stamped with the name of the company president and streets named after the important coal men of the time. The town had a mayor—who reported directly to the mine owner—and its own police force. The only thing it didn't have was a bill of rights for the residents. That's what the union was for, and the rifles. Anyway, it was gone now. The streets were renamed things like Candy Cane Lane and Golf Club Way, and the old lake shanties and company shacks had been torn down and replaced with starter mansions. South was the Duck Neck, and the marina with white boats resting uneasily in their slips, and more of the preserve. Up the piney slopes to the southeast was another mine, the old Grendel colliery, closed now these twenty years or more.

After a while, I managed to find Temple's address. It was at the far end of the development, abutting a wall of shingle oaks and, closer to the lake, bald cypress and tupelo and piles of duckweed. The house was an imposing gray foursquare with a lot of big, rectangular windows and a triangular projection like a silver toque near the back of the house. A mahogany-hulled Chris-Craft runabout bobbed near the quay, and a little red sports car with an eggshell ragtop and beaming chrome side pipes crouched in the bricked driveway. There didn't seem to be any airplanes or rocket ships around, but maybe they were in the back. I went up and knocked. After a moment, the door opened and a woman appeared.

She didn't look happy. That was the first thing that struck you. She was a small woman with white hair and wrinkled eyes, though she didn't look old enough for either, and her mouth was clenched like a fist. She was dressed in jeans and a blouse with a light pattern, and there was a wooden disk on a twine cord around her neck. She put a hand on her hip and frowned and said, "You the man from the mine?"

I told her I was the man from the mine. I said, "You're Temple Beckett?"

"Don't be an idiot." She closed the door, leaving me in the downpour. Bad guess, then. I stood there, getting as wet as a fish's teeth. A long time later, the hard-bitten woman opened the door again.

"All right, come in."

I came in. The hallway was dark wood and blue tile painted with little flowers, and it was what you'd call a good-size space. I've been on smaller runways. A life-size painting of a redheaded woman on horseback took up one wall. The other was partially covered by some kind of woven wall hanging, African or maybe Honduran. On either side of the doorway, widemouthed vases coughed dried

ornamental grass, and the ceiling was fitted with a seg-
mented skylight that ran the length of the space and let in
the day's stormy light.

"I didn't know any of this was back here," I said to the
woman.

She handed me a towel and said, "That's what the gate
is for."

The sitting room was pretty big, too. You could have parked
a bus in it and not missed the space. The ceilings couldn't have
been higher than twenty feet. The furniture was farmhouse,
but expensive-looking farmhouse, and tasteful, as were the
knickknacks and framed pictures. There were photos of an
older woman—Temple Beckett's mother, maybe—but none
of the old man. At least none that I could see. The floors were
polished walnut, stained very dark, and the walls were lined
with bookshelves so tall you'd need a man from the circus to
bring down the high volumes. Like in the hallway, the ceiling
was pitted with skylights, these as deep as wells, and the floors
were draped with worn Oriental rugs. As I often was, I was
again struck by the sheer amount of money in the world and
how much trouble the world went through to make sure none
of it ended up in my pockets.

I stood there, dripping on a rug. The wrinkle-eyed woman
frowned at me, then told me to wait and went out again. I
missed her immediately and consoled myself drying my hair
with the towel. There was a picture of Guy Beckett on the
coffee table, and I picked it up for a better look. He looked
the same. The doughboy was nowhere to be seen. Maybe it
was missing, too. I was still thinking about it when the door
opened again and a second woman came into the room.

"Put that picture down, please."

She was about my age, early forties, though I had to look at her hands to tell it. She was good-looking, too. Good-looking is putting it mildly, maybe. I looked around vaguely for a priest to strangle. She was tall and lean, with the kind of green eyes a lazy novelist would describe as "piercing." Her copper hair was pulled back from her face with a strip of brown cloth. I imagined that its more honest self was touched here and there with gray, but that was just a guess. The rest of her was dressed like a pioneer fashion model in a deerskin jacket with turquoise beads sewn on the pockets, a powder blue roll-neck sweater, faded jeans, and buskins made of the same stuff as the jacket.

I put down the picture. She looked at me and it and frowned the kind of desperate, exhausted frown that turns the room upside down and shakes the sympathy from its pockets.

"You're Slim?"

It was Luster's daughter, all right. You could see him in her, the way she moved and spoke. She held herself like the native she was—rock-shouldered, fighting shyness, full of Midwestern grit—but she held herself like a native who'd spent time and sweat and money to unlearn it all. Mostly money, probably. She didn't want to shake hands.

"You found us," she said. She didn't sound any too thrilled about it. "I guess I should offer you a drink. You people like to drink, don't you?"

"Ma'am?"

"Coal miners."

I'm a big boy who knows when he's being picked on, so I didn't take offense. I said, "I'll take coffee if you have it and it's not too much trouble."

She frowned some more in that beautiful way of hers, but nodded. She summoned someone named Susan, and the wrinkle-eyed woman came back. Temple asked her to put on a pot. Susan looked at me like something she wanted to sweep into the street and walked quickly out.

I said, "I'm just going to say it. I don't think she likes me."

"She doesn't. But don't take it personally. She doesn't like anyone."

"Even you?"

"Sometimes. Sometimes I'm not sure. Frankly, she's had a hard life. In some ways, terrible. But she's been a great help to me, and I'm willing to put up with her moods, even when she goes a little sour on me."

"So she takes care of you, you take care of her?"

Temple sat down on the sofa. It was one of these things swallows you like a biblical whale. She crossed her legs at the knee and pointed one of the buskins into space. She gestured for me to sit, and I spread my towel on a leather chair across from her and settled into it. The white leather on the armrests smelled like wealth and comfort.

Temple said, "A bit crude, but that's basically it. Isn't there anyone you take care of?"

"Oh, yeah."

"A kid?"

"Daughter. She just turned twelve yesterday. Or thirty. It's hard to tell sometimes."

I glanced around the big room. Rather subtly, I thought.

She shook her head and grinned meanly at me and flipped her hair. She had a sexy, toothy look about her that reminded me a little of Gene Tierney. I wanted to put on my finest JCPenney's suit and comb my hair and solve her mystery for her.

She said, "You can just ask me, you know?"

I felt myself blushing. I looked at her and smiled and shrugged.

"No young ones of your own, I guess?"

"No."

"Sorry. This really isn't my thing. Private-detecting, I mean."

"I guess not."

"I tried to convince your dad."

Temple said, "That's not always so easy. Believe me, I know. My father tends to get what he wants."

"Well, I think what he wanted was a detective of some kind. Instead, he got me."

She waved her hand at me. She wore a ring fixed with a chunk of black stone big enough to choke an elephant. "I think what he probably wanted was you," she said. "And here you sit. Big as life and wet as the lake. At least he seems to like you."

"More than he likes your husband?"

"Why do you ask that?"

"I don't know. The way you said it, I guess. Your voice. It didn't sound like you were talking about yourself. Top of that, your husband's a reporter, and I have a sense that Mr. Luster has a fairly low opinion of the fourth estate. I think maybe he thinks Guy is out to get him."

"He said that to you?"

"Not in so many words, but yeah. This story he and Dwayne Mays were working on, for example."

"I don't think . . ."

The coffee must have already been on because just then Susan came back in with a tray of it. In front of Temple she set a cup made of paper-thin bone china. Me, she gave a thick porcelain mug that might have lived in a garage for a few years, or maybe the crawlspace under the house. Susan dipped her head facetiously at Temple and went out again.

Temple watched her go. She looked at the door for a while after it shut, then turned back to me with hard eyes and said slowly, "I want be honest with you."

"Okay."

"It's no offense, okay, but I don't need you here. I don't need you and I don't want you. Let's be up front about that."

"Seems reasonable, really."

She ignored that. "You're my father's idiotic idea. Not mine. I tried talking him out of this, but he wouldn't listen. He never listens. And here you are, without the faintest idea what you're doing or where you're going or what to do, and none of the experience even to know that you don't know it. You don't, do you?"

"Not really."

"I'm worried that you're a danger to my husband, Slim. I'm worried that you're going to get in the way of the police investigation. If that happens, you could get Guy killed."

They were good points, all of them. I sipped some of my coffee and set the mug on the table. The coffee was hot and strong but didn't taste like poison. Maybe Susan liked me after all. Maybe we were dating now.

I said, "Fair enough. Truth is, I don't want to be here. Just between you, me, and Susan—who I assume has her ear pressed to the door right now—I don't think much of your old man's scheme, either. Your appraisal of my skills is sound, and I won't argue with it. On the other hand, I don't plan on getting in anyone's way, especially the police. I've got no reason to think they're doing anything but a bang-up job, and as far as I'm concerned they can keep doing it. Frankly, I just want to be able to report something to Mr. Luster and get my pension."

She gave me a look.

"Your . . . pension?"

"Yup."

"That's what he promised you?"

"All wrapped up like a newborn baby and stashed away somewhere warm and safe."

"Well, isn't that a little . . ."

"What?"

She blew out a breath and said, "I don't know. Desperate?"

"Ouch."

For the first time, she smiled a little. She seemed embarrassed.

"I'm sorry," she said. "I really don't know how to act right now."

"No harm," I said. "As for desperation, I guess it depends what your aspirations are. Mine's college for my daughter and an occasional haircut for myself."

Temple sighed quietly, then stood and paced behind the sofa. "Fine," she said finally. "Let's get it over with then. Ask your questions."

"Thanks," I said sincerely. "Let's start with what you think might have happened."

"I think Dwayne was murdered. I think my husband's disappeared. More than that . . ."

"I'll need to know about your marriage. What it's been like. Whether you've been happy with Guy."

She laughed at that. Kind of bitterly, too. But even her bitterness was like art. Her head went back and her ponytail poured over her shoulder like a vein of molten copper and curled up at the full swell of her breast. She was good-looking, all right. Peggy would turn me inside out with a butter knife to hear me say it, but there was something otherworldly about Temple Beckett, something that had to do with more than money.

I said, "Mrs. Beckett . . ."

"Temple," she said, interrupting. "I want to be called Temple. And none of this is about my husband and our marriage or our happiness."

"Well, wait a minute now. Why aren't you happy with Guy?"

"I didn't say I wasn't."

"You didn't, but your face did."

"My face?"

"Your expression. Your mouth, mostly. The way the corners flex when you talk about him. Not a happy look, Mrs. Beckett."

"*Temple.*"

"There's that, too."

She gave me a Susan look. Not gladsome. She came back around the couch and flopped down, as though exhausted.

"You're married?"

"Not anymore."

"But you were."

"A long time ago."

She said, "Then you know that no marriage is perfect."

But I got the sense that hers was less perfect even than that. "And I'm telling you, you're on the wrong path. You're thinking I was unhappy with Guy, for one reason or another. Deeply unhappy. Maybe you think he was having affairs. Maybe you think I was. Or both of us. Maybe he drank or knocked me around or just called me a cunt once too often or whatever. Anyway, you're thinking that maybe I had an affair with Dwayne and that Guy found out about it and killed him."

I said, "I admit the possibility crossed my mind. But my guess is that's usually how these things turn out. The simplest solution is usually the right one."

"I honestly don't know," she said. "I'm not interested in murder."

"I'm not, either. Tell me about Dwayne Mays."

She nodded her head. "I wondered when you'd get to that, but frankly there's not much to say. He and Guy came up together and went to school together. State school, nothing fancy. Neither of them could ever afford fancy. Dwayne's parents had a farm out near Union City, I think, and Guy's family never had two nickels to rub together. I went away to better schools but came back in time to be a kid with them. They were thick as thieves, but rivals, too, in that way men have. I learned to dislike Dwayne over time, the way he was always getting Guy into trouble, but Guy never saw it. Or wouldn't. Later, they worked together. Dwayne was rambunctious, egotistical, eternally horny, fanatically dedicated to his work, and principled to a fault."

"You've had time to think about this."

"I've thought about it," she said.

"Let's talk some more about the eternally horny thing."

"For . . . for men. Dwayne was gay."

"And your husband . . ."

"Wasn't," she said. "Not even half." She breathed out a sigh and looked at the watch on her perfect wrist. You could take a picture of that wrist and hang it in a museum and folks would come from all around to see it. "Now, if you don't mind, I think I've been more than fair with my time. I've got a hard afternoon ahead. I've got to talk to my father . . ."

"About me."

"About you. And then I'm meeting with the detectives in an hour. The *real* detectives."

"Sheriff Wince."

"You've met him?"

"No, but I've met some who have. My understanding is he's chewing on a theory that your husband and Mays ran into danger working their latest story."

She nodded. She said, "The meth story."

Well, that took me aback. Before I could stop myself, I said, "Meth story? Not the Knight Hawk's safety practices?"

It took her an instant. Then she glared, but there was fear behind it. The piercing eyes pierced deeper. "You sonofabitch. You have no idea how dangerous what you're saying is. To me. To my husband."

"Mrs. Beckett, do you have any idea who they might have been looking at? Chances are, if they're at the Knight Hawk, I know them."

"Get out. Now."

"Temple . . ."

"I said *now*."

She raised her voice enough that the door swung open immediately and Susan reappeared. I was right; she'd been there the whole time. I guess you couldn't fault her loyalty. I sighed and stood up to go, folding my towel.

"I hope everything works out," I said.

She didn't answer. Either it would or it wouldn't. She turned her back to me and faced the bank of windows along the western wall, down toward the waters of Crab Orchard Lake.

I followed Susan back through the house and the runway-hallway beneath the skylight. I had hoped the weather would be slowing some, but it was raining even harder now, and the glass was dark and loud with it. I'd have to find an over-pass to park beneath until it let off.

Susan opened the door. She indicated the folded towel. I was still holding it.

"I don't guess you were planning to walk off with that," she said.

I handed it to her. "It is awfully fluffy," I said. "The ones we have at home are like sandpaper."

"Everybody's got a problem."

"Just one? That sounds so nice. Hey, one thing . . ."

"Don't bother."

I ignored her. "Dwayne Mays. I ran out of questions before I could get his address."

"I don't care," she said. "Besides, you can get the address anywhere."

She was right about that. But I waited, looking at her. Truth was, I was starting to like her. I know that sounds weird, but it was true. She was the kind of person, when you met them, all you wanted to do was drown them in the nearest body of water, but then six weeks later you were BFFs. She wasn't bad looking, either, in a hard-bitten kind of way. She reminded me a bit of a dispatcher I'd had a fling with once, a tough bird who could drink just about any man under the table and who was so good with a knife she could shave the hairs off a flea's nuts without waking the dog.

At last, Susan sighed. Her wrinkled eyes flooded with the day's dark light. She said, "Crainville. North of town. He rented a place there." She gave me the address. "But if you go, beware."

"Too much curb appeal?"

"You're not funny."

"I'm not paid to be."

"There's no other way to say it: The place is a rat trap. Actually, I'm not even sure I can imagine rats living there," she said.

"So you've seen it?"

She sneered. "Clean your thoughts. I went there with Beckett sometimes, or dropped off negatives when Beckett couldn't get free."

"You mean photo negatives? I thought they did all that with computers these days."

She said, "Beckett couldn't stand them. He thought that digital cameras were ruining the art. Or"—she waved a contemptuous hand and changed her voice to what I guessed was an imitation of Beckett—"*diluting* it. Something like that. He insisted on using film. Dwayne transferred everything to a computer."

"This Mr. Beckett sounds like an interesting fella."

"If by *interesting* you mean *patronizing misogynist*, then yeah. He was interesting."

"You've got quite a vocabulary for someone who opens doors for a living," I said.

"And what do you do for dollars? You work in a hole, right?"

"Touché," I said. "So, if I'm hearing you correctly, the name Guy Beckett doesn't lift your heart."

"No, it does not. My gorge maybe."

I raised my chin back toward the house. "He didn't hit her," I said. "Her father would have him cut into pieces and melted the bones in a coking furnace. Drinking? Or drugs?"

"No more than the usual."

"I'm thinking it's women, then."

"It's women," she said. "Beckett has a weakness."

"A lot of men do."

"Not like him," she said. "He'd stack 'em five high at a time."

"He ever make a grab at you?"

"If he did, he didn't do it more than once. But everyone else was fair game. And this was a guy with some hustle. Book clubs, church groups. Name it. He'd join anything if there were women there. Even our local environmental club. Crab Orchard Friends, something like that."

"Saving the earth is not his thing, I guess?"

"Not his thing. Guy Beckett cares about Guy Beckett and his needs, period, full stop."

"And what do you care about?"

"More or less the same thing. But at least I'm honest about it."

"And here your mistress thinks you're loyal to her."

She glared at me. If she could, she would have unhinged her jaw and swallowed me whole.

"This *is* loyalty. This is what loyalty does. It raises its voice, and it tells a fool that she's running headlong down a dark tunnel toward an oncoming train."

"Beckett?"

She nodded. "Ruin on two feet. Believe me, she's better off without him."

"Well, someone must miss him. Family?"

She shook her head.

"Okay, friends, then. There's got to be someone."

"I don't know, really. Except for Dwayne, I rarely saw any friends. The ones I did see were mostly work people, but they never seemed to like him much, either."

"Sounds kind of lonely."

"I don't know that he ever noticed."

"Okay," I said. I stepped out onto the front porch. "One last thing."

"My God, what?"

"You said 'was' before."

She was confused. And as stern-looking as a chainsaw sculpture. "What?"

"A minute ago. I said Beckett sounds like an interesting character, and you said, yes, he was."

She said, "You can always hope."

She closed the door.

I drove back through the Estates. I stopped at the check-in box and thanked the old guy once more and got his name—besides Lilac, I mean—something I forgot to do the first time. I tried to imagine what I could do next. I'd asked my questions and learned something about Guy Beckett and his sad story of domestic disquietude. I guessed that, in the best case, he'd just run away from home. That seemed unlikely, but at least it was a possibility.

I'll tell you, though, the more likely angle, the meth-trade angle, wasn't something I was going to touch with a fifty-foot barbed pole. Hell, a pole of any kind. This isn't some nice, clean drug business with imported suits and orderly accounts like they show on TV. These people were animals; you come between them and their fix or their dollars, they'll kill you dead and lick your bones clean.

I didn't want my bones licked clean. I wanted more coffee. I found a place a few miles up the road and drank a hot cup and made idle chat with a former longwall operator who wanted the government to keep out of his Medicare. I made a couple of polite attempts to explain the situation, but he was impenetrable. After a while, I gave it up and paid for his coffee. I told him I hoped the government kept out of it, but he just sighed and shook his head. Like Susan said, everybody's got a problem.

A half hour later, the rain finally slowed down, till it was nothing more than a light mist, and I got on the bike and rolled east on IL-13 toward 148. Crainville was along the way, but Dwayne Mays's house would still be sealed off, most likely, so I decided to leave that for another day. Or never. Honestly, my real plan was to stall for time and hope the cops worked the whole thing out. Either Beckett would show up dead, or he'd turn himself in for the Mays murder, or he'd get caught. Less likely, he'd stumble home with a hangover and a crotch full of rot and a paternity suit. However it happened, I'd collect what had been promised me and that would be the end of it.

I thought it over for the next mile or so. I rehearsed it a couple times in my mind, the way you do when you're satisfied with yourself for outwitting the world. I passed the lake and its troubled waters. Some fool was out in a fishing boat, and the boat had gotten swamped and filled nearly to the gunnel, and another boat was on its way out to save the day. Probably he'd get swamped, too, and then they'd have to send another one. Life was like that sometimes. The only thing worse than the accident was the rescue. I didn't want that to be true of this thing I'd gotten involved in. I wanted what was best for my daughter and the family I was trying to build, sure, but there was a line I wouldn't cross—and places even my father's name wouldn't get me out of. I was still philosophizing about that, and life, and Guy Beckett, when my rearview mirrors winked red and blue at me, and I glanced back to find myself being pursued by a sheriff's department prowler.

Well, I wasn't speeding. It was too wet for that, and I'm always cautious on my bike. Illinois is one of these states that honors your right to severe brain damage in the name of personal liberty. But despite the lack of a helmet law, I always wear one, and I'm never one of these dummies you see riding in shorts and sandals or whatever other nonsense they dream up on their way to third-degree burns. A motorcycle is lethal in all kinds of ways, but weather and other motorists are the real risk. So I wasn't speeding. Maybe my brake light was out. I'm usually good at my pre-ride checks, but you never knew when something was going to go wrong and fuck you over. I pulled off 13 and onto the wide neck of Greenbriar Road where there's nothing but a dark cut of forestland and some empty fields. I switched off the bike, put down the stand, pulled off my helmet, and sat there.

Cops usually make you wait while they call in the stop, but this one kicked open his door and marched directly over. He was a tiny thing, five foot six at most, with a round face and a gut that would swallow punches like jellybeans. He was wearing the tan-and-brown and widescreen shades, despite the lack of sunshine, but everything was too small on him. His uniform hugged him like a second skin and revealed far too much of his manly side for my liking, like it'd been cut down to size to fit him but cut down too far. His pale wrists hung out of his sleeves a good two inches, and the temples of his sunglasses spread almost flat across the expanse of his face.

"Taillight?" I said.

For a moment he looked confused, or startled, that I'd spoken. Then he gathered himself again and shook his head and said, "You Slim?"

I said that I was Slim just as it dawned on me that he shouldn't know that yet.

It was too late. He said, "Okay. Good. This is for you, you sonofabitch."

"Wait," I said, but he wasn't paid to wait, I guess. His hand swept up and hit me upside the head with something hard. A baton, maybe, or a bank safe. I dropped sideways off the bike and hit the street and rolled down the hill and right into a ditch, where I belonged.

FOUR

The ditch water was filthy and reeked of rotting vegetation and road muck washed over by the rain. Good stuff. Worse, someone had dumped a deer carcass there. That was pretty common: They'd bag a buck or doe and field butcher it and dump the rest in some lonely place, the way you'd throw away an apple core. This one was skinned and dressed, and its exposed insides were as pink and bloody as a newborn. My mouth sucked up some of the swirling, greasy blood.

I spat it out. I tried to spit out my tongue, too, but it was still tied on. Behind me, I could hear the little bastard sliding down the grade on grass that had bowed over with the weight of the rain. Soon, though, he lost his footing and fell on his ass and shouted out in anger. I took that moment to attempt to pry myself from the mud pie, but it wasn't any good. Nothing was working. Arms, legs, brain. Nothing. The bank safe had done its work. The little dude clambered to his feet. He swore again and swatted in irritation at the mud on his clothes. Maybe he was worried about losing his deposit at the costume shop. I don't know. He came the rest of the way down the hill, and he was fuming. He'd suffered a professional setback, and he wasn't the least happy about it. The sunglasses were cockeyed on his face. He seized me by the scruff and spun me over and punched me in the mouth.

He said, "I'm guessing I don't have to tell you what this is about."

I gurgled out some blood and muddy water, and he

dropped me back in, faceup this time. He sneered down at me. He had the kind of face kids have nightmares about: dog turd eyes and a small, round mouth like a lamprey's. His nose had been broken at least once, maybe half a dozen times. His hands were thick and soft but as strong as steel clamps, and I might as well have been fighting drop-forged steel when he picked me up again and tossed me onto the road.

He squatted down next to me and said, "I've been told not to hurt you too bad yet, Slim, and that's a shame. I want to hurt you. I want to hurt you and keep on hurting you. Then I'd hurt everyone you know and love, too."

"Lot of hurting," I said. Something like that. My tongue wasn't exactly in top working order, and my voice sounded like Latin in a blender.

He shrugged. "That's what you wandered into with this. World of pain. And one more thing." He stood and stepped back a half step and wound one up and kicked me in the head. If it was a field goal attempt, he would have hit from eighty yards out. The world snapped to black, and I found myself dreaming of headache pills and angry redheads. Peggy appeared before me, holding a butter knife and calling me dirty names. Anci shook her head and went back to reading about dystopian futures and young girls with bows and arrows. Susan had me arrested for stealing a towel. When I woke up again at last, the women were gone. The bad man, too. I was lying in the rain, and some pecker behind the wheel of a yellow pickup was blaring his horn at me like I was a turtle crossing the road.

I called Jeep Mabry and asked him to meet me at my doctor's office. Some reason, I decided against ordering up an ambulance. Probably I was embarrassed about getting bush-whacked like that. It's a stupid man-thing. I pried myself up and climbed on the bike and rode slowly into Herrin. A couple of times, the traffic blurred out around me, or the road did, but eventually I arrived at my destination. I parked in the lot and went inside the little building on Lincoln Drive. It was a slow morning, and the staff looked at me and the blood on my swollen head and swallowed their tongues and sprang into action. After a while, I found myself in the examining room. A nurse was cleaning the cut on my lip with a cotton swab and some alcohol when Dr. Cooper came rumbling in. He was a fat man with thinning hair and sharply intelligent eyes. He had this little pinch on his top lip that twisted his mouth slightly upward and made him look like a smart-ass, which was just as well, because the rest of his mouth did that, too.

He said, "Fun times on that hog of yours?"

I said, "Not exactly."

"Listen to me, it'll happen sooner or later. What's it got in it?"

"Engine?"

"Yeah."

"Thirteen-hundred."

He said, "Not enough to outrun statistics. I tell you what, if I could get rid of one thing in my professional life, it'd be those wicked contraptions. Worst man-killers I ever saw."

"Women, too."

"True. They get everyone eventually. Equal opportunity carnage. I got a pamphlet around here somewhere I could let you see. You want to see it? Got some real pretty pictures. One guy ran off the road into barbed wire, came out look-ing like a sliced weenie."

"I'll be honest, I'm not too interested in that."

"You guys never are," he said. He thought for a moment. "I'll try again. This ain't something domestic, is it? Get hit with a frying pan?"

"That seems kinda sexist to me."

"And yet it happens," he said. "Besides, I always assumed they grabbed a frying pan because it was the object most likely to knock the sonofabitch's head clean off."

"There is that," I said.

"Gets the job done. Speaking of which, I had a situation up at the hospital a year or so back I'll tell you about."

"Isn't that violating some kind of doctor-patient thing?"

"Usually, but this thing was in all the papers later anyway. I was pulling a shift at the ER. Woman comes in with her arm all cut up. Ugly stuff. Torn to strings. Looked like she'd run it through a thresher."

"Did she?"

"Did she what?"

"Run it through a thresher? Because that's a common thing around here."

He said, "I know. No. Shut up. Anyway, I take her back and start looking at the arm, and it's cut up good by these little fragments embedded in the skin. Oddly shaped fragments. Like bits of china, but rough, not smooth. I start tweezing them out. Know what they were?"

"How much can I give you not to tell me?"

"Bone. Skull bone, to be precise. Few bits of scalp, too. Some with these little hairs still attached."

"I'm maybe not liking this story so much," I said. "Anyway, my stomach isn't."

"Uh-huh. Anyway, this woman, she'd been scheming

with her sister to kill her husband. He was an abuser. Wife-beater, I mean. Was beating her like a men's group drum for twenty years or so. Finally, she has enough. One night he comes through the door, three sheets to the wind as usual, ready to treat his wife like a speed bag, only this time her sister's there, too, with a shotgun. Crouched behind the dining room table, waiting to do the deed. You understand? She got her sister to pull the trigger. Couldn't do it herself."

"I get it."

"Thing is, though, it's a twenty-eight gauge."

"Oh, shit."

He shrugged and said, "Yeah. You know how it is, though. You inflate terrible things in your brain, make them out to be more than they are. Stronger, I mean. Twenty years of hitting and kicking and biting and worse, this sonofabitch must have seemed like a Godzilla to these two. So they choose too much weapon, thinking they'd need it to put him down. Damn thing is practically a cannon. Bastard's head explodes like a piñata, only there wasn't any candy inside."

"Doc . . ."

"So these bone fragments hit the wife in the arm and tear her up like she'd gone a round or two with a woodchipper."

"That's a pretty story."

"Thought you'd like that."

"It's not a domestic," I said. "I had a run-in with someone, but not with Peggy. Or any other woman, for that matter. And there weren't any shotguns involved."

He shook his head and grunted. The nurse finished what he was doing and hustled out without looking at either of us.

Dr. Cooper said, "Reckon we shouldn't be talking like

this in front of him. He's young and unwise as yet in the ways of the world. Something like this, a fight or an assault, I'm supposed to call the law."

"I was kinda hoping I could talk you out of that."

"I was kinda thinking that's what you were kinda hoping. I'll try one more time. This something happened at the mine?"

"Why do you ask?"

He hefted his shoulders and said, " 'Count of I get about as many of you guys in here for fighting as I do for work-related injuries. I tell you, Slim, think I've about seen it all. Had a guy in here couple weeks back had part of a rock-bolt stabilizer stuck in him."

"Ouch."

"That's what he said. Repeatedly. And that's just the violence cases. You guys are always doing stupid stuff down there, too. You happen to remember a guy went by the name of Bug Nuts?"

"Sure. Crazy little asshole, works that Gateway mine up near Red Bud."

"Not anymore. He's gone."

"Dead?"

"No, dummy. He went on vacation to hooker Disneyland. Yes, he's dead."

"Hooker Disneyland?"

Cooper ignored me. "Kid was, what, twenty-eight, twenty-nine? It ain't right, is it?"

"I don't know," I said. Your name gets to be Bug Nuts—and this is *underground coal miners* calling you this—a bad end is more or less in the cards. "What happened?"

"Well, you know, that little guy was loony as a Turkish

hermaphrodite. He pissed on the man-trip rail, set himself on fire through a stream of his own piss."

"Why in God's name did he do that?"

"On a dare," Cooper said.

That rang true. Ignorant idiots at coal mines were always daring one another to do lethally dangerous shit. And not just the inby men, either. I once saw a mine owner "prove" that filter masks were unnecessary by shoving his face into the longwall pan and sucking in heaping lungfuls of coal fine. When he died—and he would—he was going to die hard.

Cooper said, "That's the guess, anyway. Ain't no one took responsibility yet, and probably no one will. Hell, it's practically murder."

He picked up the cotton and alcohol and finished cleaning me up. He plucked a piece of gravel out of my ear the nurse had overlooked. He shined his light in my eyes and put his thumbs on either side of my nose. "This here don't look so bad. Eyes are working okay, and your face ain't broke. Maybe we'll just chalk this one up to household clumsiness."

"Thanks, Doc."

He accepted my gratitude with another grunt and gave me a shot. I don't know that there was any medicinal value in it. I sort of got the feeling he liked giving shots to assholes who dragged him into the office on his free time. He gave me another little lecture about motorcycles and forced me to take the pamphlet he'd mentioned with the guy cut up like a weenie. Then he shook my hand and let me go.

I hopped down from the table and went out into the waiting room, where they were waiting on me like a pack of hyenas. As soon as I was in sight, they jumped on me with armloads of paperwork and insurance forms. I was still working my way through it when, something like three or four years later, the office door opened and Jeep Mabry appeared.

Lemme tell you a thing or two about Jeep. This was a friend of mine from way back. Friend's maybe not the word, exactly. More like the brother I never had, the kind of brother who'd kill for you, or die. We came up together, dated the same girls, flunked the same classes, haunted the same haunts. Mostly, though, we raised all manner of hell together for so long that a lot of folks got to thinking of us as brothers. Which, like I said, in a way we were.

Jeep went six-eight or nine, four inches taller than me, and weighed in at 275 at least, not a bit of it fat. His head was as big and hard as one of those cast-iron tourist binocular stands, but his face was movie-star handsome and his eyes flashed with something might have been backcountry meanness, or cunning. We went back so far neither of could remember a time when we weren't attached at the hip, and we had a long-running agreement to ruin the funeral of whichever of us went first. We were pals, fellow coal miners, comrades in arms, and best buds.

"Jesus, Slick, you look like shit," he said.

"Thanks."

He said, "Correction: You look like shit took a shit."

"What?"

"I'm trying out some new lines."

"Keep trying."

"Motorcycle?"

"I've already done this routine with Cooper," I said. "You don't have a pamphlet, do you?"

"No. What?"

"Never mind."

"Coffee?"

"Buckets."

I rode into town and met him at the little restaurant on the corner of North Park and Poplar. Little place called Hardee's. I checked in by phone with Peggy at school—neglecting to mention my trip to the doctor's office—and then Jeep and I sat in a booth and ate a late breakfast of biscuits and those hash browns they serve in a paper sleeve and black coffee strong enough to kick your ass on Friday night and laugh in your face about it till Saturday morning. We barely spoke over our food. I had trouble chewing, but was hungry from my beating. Jeep was just hungry. Jeep was always hungry, like a locomotive furnace. We finished our meal and cleared our table. We chatted with a couple of the old-timers who seemed to gather there every morning and afternoon to mull over the state of the world. No shots or angry words were exchanged. It felt good, but temporary.

When we were settled again and ready to get down to it, Jeep said, "Maybe you should start at the top."

Which is what I did. I started at the beginning and told him all of it—the crazy, confusing all of it—and when I was finished he settled back and sighed and said, "So you've got yourself tangled up with Matt Luster, have you?"

"Looks that way."

"And his daughter."

"Yup. Well, by extension anyway."

"I'm going to be straight with you, Slick. This was maybe not your brightest idea."

"Hell, I know," I said, "but they dangled that pension in front of me and I snapped at it. Making it worse, there's at least a chance I've gotten myself involved in something has to do with those meth dealers."

"You're right. That would make things worse. Did you at least catch the department name on your friend's uniform?"

I shook my head. It hurt and I winced with it. I got the feeling I'd be wincing with it for weeks to come. That was an impressive kick.

I said, "No. Now that I think about it, though, the uni was too clean, like maybe he'd just unwrapped it, and I'm starting to think the badge was some kind of kid's toy. It all happened kind of fast."

"And you've never seen him before?"

"I think I'd remember. He had a face even Mother Mary would love to hit."

"I know I will, I ever catch up to him." He paused a moment to think. "This thing, you think you can just walk away from it now?"

"That's the idea. Run away from it, actually," I said. "Just as soon as I make a final report and get what's been promised to me."

"Noted. Maybe some good will come out of it."

"I'm hoping."

"Be nice for you and Anci."

"It would."

"How is she anyway?"

"Changing topics."

"Changing topics."

"As wonderful and terrifying as always," I said.

"Nice to know."

"You know," I mused, warming to the topic, "I was thinking the other day about her getting older and maybe moving away one day soon."

"No offense, Slick, but you always were too sentimental for your own good."

"Well, there's gotta be a right time for sentimentality sometimes, right?" I said. "Anyway, I was thinking about that, and how I might be looking at some time alone soon . . ."

Jeep said, "And you started to wonder whether asking whatshername to move in with you might have something to do with fear of being by yourself in that old house of yours."

I looked at him, slightly amazed. "How'd you guess?"

"Mostly because I've known you all my life, and I know you better than I know pretty much anyone," he said. "You're a worrier and an overthinker. Like that business with Dooley-Bug last year."

"That keeps coming up these days."

"Well, you fretted about it, didn't you?"

"I think something like that's worth fretting over. There was like to be trouble."

"Bad men, drugs, money, and guns, hoss. That always equals trouble. And what'd I tell you at the time?"

"You told me I'd end up doing it. I told you you were nuts."

"And?"

"And I ended up doing it."

Jeep nodded. "Because it was the right thing to do, whether Sam knew it or not."

"Doesn't mean you're not nuts, though. I just want to point that out."

"How's she doing anyway?"

"The girl? There've been some bumps along the way, but I hear she's getting along okay. Trying a little college these days."

"You look pleased with yourself."

"More like satisfied it wasn't all for nothing."

Jeep nodded again. "And that's just the way you are, but there's always a downside. You're a tough guy, Slim, and in a pinch there's no one I'd rather have around, but you've got a lonely man's heart and you always will."

"Lonely? What's lonely got to do with doing the right thing?"

Jeep shrugged. "It's a tough old world. To be honest, you must live outside the law."

"You got the line backward, I think."

Jeep said, "Whichever. Works both ways. Anyway, good people are always kinda lonely, because almost everyone else is either full of wickedness or just full of shit. And that's your fate."

"There's a happy thought."

"I didn't bring it up."

"Fair enough," I said, but I didn't feel particularly good or virtuous. "Maybe I'll change the subject now."

"Fine by me."

"How's Opal?"

At this mention of his wife, Jeep smiled as much as Jeep ever smiles, which is not much. He said, "Beautiful. Mean. Beautiful."

"You said beautiful twice."

"I did."

"Couldn't help noticing the mean, either."

He nodded, but didn't say anything. We sat there a moment. Finally, I said, "Peggy's fine, too."

"Who?"

"Whatshername."

Jeep grunted. I never knew why, but Jeep and Peggy didn't like each other. Not that they didn't get along, really. And they'd never come to blows or anything like that, but there was ice between them that had never melted. It was just one of those things: two people you love don't love each other, but you're never sure why and neither of them will, or can, explain. We went out into the parking lot and shook hands.

He said, "You want to borrow Betsy?"

"I'm hoping that won't be necessary."

"Might as well, though," he said. "I brought her."

"I had a feeling you might."

He went to his truck and opened the door and brought out Betsy. He put her walnut stock in my hand, and I felt the cross-hatching on the grip rub my thumb and palm. She felt solid and powerful. I felt more like an American. I broke her in half and stowed her and some ammo in the saddlebag on the bike.

Jeep asked, "You need a lift home?"

"No," I said. "My head's clear now, and the doc says my eyes are working okay. Besides, I don't want to leave the bike anywhere up here overnight."

Jeep shook his head disgustedly and said, "You know, didn't used to be folks had to worry about stuff like that. You could leave your car up here with the keys in the switch and the doors unlocked, and when you came back the next day the most that would have happened is someone had washed it and filled your tires."

"I don't know about that," I said. "I remember correctly, there was a lot of crime back then, too. Maybe even more than now. Plus a lot of other awful stuff that maybe wasn't illegal at the time, but sure as hell was uncivilized. I'm not sure any generation has a monopoly on lawlessness or general assholism."

"Maybe not, but look, man, back then there was at least some kind of wall between folks and the assholes. Look at that building across the street there. It used to be a restaurant. Nothing fancy, but a local family owned it. Italians. It was there for thirty years. Say you're there one night, having a nice meal inside, and some shithead thinks to try to make off with your wheels. You caught him, you could shoot his ass, and that was that. Nobody would turn you in, and you couldn't even pay the local cops to look at you cross-eyed. Guys like Luster and Galligan, we had the unions to push back against them, keep them in line, and maybe even stop them killing a few of their employees. Nowadays, though, that place across the street is a pawnshop. Does better business than the restaurant ever did. You shoot the guy stealing your car, you'll not only go to jail, the car thief will probably sue you and win. He'll get emotional damages, too, all the harm you did him. He can't sleep at night. Has nightmares, like that. And Luster and Galligan? We kowtow to them because they're all we have left, and when they go there's not one of us knows what'll keep these towns from drying up and blowing away for good, pawnshops and all."

"You paint a pretty picture."

"But you know I'm right."

"I don't know," I said again, but the truth was I wasn't so sure he wasn't.

Jeep tipped his hand and climbed in his truck and roared away. I stood watching him a moment, then climbed on the bike and rode home toward a royal chewing-out.

I'll ask you again."

"Okay."

"Are you out of your goddamned *mind*?"

"Hey, there's a child present."

"No," Anci said. Surprisingly, she ignored my remark about the child and forked some potatoes into her mouth. They were the way she liked them, extra creamy with chopped scallions sprinkled on top. She was the only one eating. "She's right. Are you out of your goddamned mind?"

My food was getting cold. And warm. Besides the potatoes, I'd made pork chops and fried okra and green salad. There was ice cream in the fridge, too, and some of Anci's favorite orange soda. Also, a box of those fancy lemon cookies Peggy liked so much. I was overcompensating.

"Why on earth would you ever do anything so . . ." Peggy paused, searching for the exact word. " . . . *asinine*?"

Anci said, "What's that?"

This was a teaching moment. Peggy hit pause on her lecture and put her hand on Anci's shoulder. "It's a bad word that means stupid."

Anci nodded. She liked bad words fine. She said, "Assnine. That works."

"That's good, darling, but it's not *ass-nine*. It's *ass-i-nine*. There's an extra little stop in the middle."

"Ass-i-nine," she said, trying it out. She looked at me. "You are *asinine*."

Peggy said, "That's it."

I said, "You two are something else."

"Don't change the subject," Peggy said. She turned back to me. Her eyebrows bunched, and she had that little knot between her eyes she got when confronted with unacceptable levels of idiocy. "You could have been hurt. *Seriously* hurt."

"I know."

"And for what?" she said, waving her hands. "Because you wanted to ride your bike in the rain?"

"I like the rain," I said. "It reminds me of your beautiful . . ."

"Darlin', don't press your luck."

"Sorry. Anyway, it wasn't really raining when I left. I thought I could beat it in."

"Well, you didn't," Peggy said. "It beat you. You lost control of your bike on a slick road and went into a ditch. And without your helmet, too."

"Yup," I said. "Pretty stupid, huh?"

"Stupid doesn't cover it. It's . . ."

She paused. Anci said, "Asinine."

I turned to Anci. "Guilty as charged. Never do anything like that, squirt."

"I won't."

"I'm serious now. Ever."

"Okay."

Peggy wasn't satisfied, not by a good distance, but after a while she gave it up and turned her attention to her food. The rest of the meal was fairly calm, if not exactly gladsome.

Peggy didn't sleep over that night. She was still upset with me, so there was that, but something else seemed to be bothering her. There was no reason she'd know I'd lied to her, but her mood darkened throughout the rest of the evening until it turned itchy and nervous, and pretty soon it was even getting to Anci. When she announced she was leaving, I think we were all a little relieved.

I spent the rest of that evening reading *To Kill a Mockingbird* with Anci for school and making phone calls to what must have been every hospital in the tristate. No one had logged anyone claiming to be Guy Beckett, and I wasn't able to locate any anonymous victims of violence or John Does matching Beckett's description. I called an ex-miner buddy with the Williamson County sheriffs to ask whether anyone had used Guy Beckett's cell phone or one of his credit cards, but that came up empty too, and cost me a valuable favor for nothing. Really, I don't know why I was doing it. I'd already decided to let the whole thing go. On the other hand, it was like poking a dead snake with a stick. Something about you just didn't want to stop.

After a while, I gave up idly playing private detective. I went to bed and lay there worrying over everything, aching in my head and neck and missing Peggy. By the time I was drifting off to sleep an hour or so later, I'd resolved to talk to Luster in the morning and quit. After that, things could shake out however fate or the disappointment of a rich old man wanted them to shake out. I could always get another job. Maybe. I fell asleep with Betsy on the pillow beside me and visions of the phony round-faced cop sliding through the wet grass in my brain. Let me tell you, sleeping next to a loaded gun will do wonders for your restfulness.

In the morning, my thoughts were clearer. I'd come to peace with my decision and wherever it might lead. I got out of bed, went into the kitchen, scooped some coffee into the pot, and got out some breakfast stuff for Anci. The weather was rumbling again, the gray winds switching the branches and spitting noisily against the windowpanes. The spine of stiltgrass along the sandstone monument overlooking the Vale brandished and billowed. It was a day full of threat.

After a while, Anci came down and ate. She had an appetite but not much to say, so instead of talking we listened to a radio program she liked. When she went back up to shower, I thought about giving Peggy a ring, but I changed my mind suddenly and instead screwed up my resolve and dialed Luster. The phone rang and rang, but no one answered, so I called the mine and spoke to the lady with the dog on her head.

"He's home today, Slam," she said.

"Slim."

"No, honey, Slim's dead. We talked about this."

"I guess I forgot," I said. "May his beautiful soul rest in peace. Anyway, I just called up there to the house and nobody answered."

"Well, that place is roughly the size of Soldier Field. Sometimes they miss the phone. I know for a fact he's there today, though. He's got a meeting with the police this morning and he insisted on having it at the residence."

I told her again how sorry I was about Slim and hung up. I knew what I had to do: go up to his house and resign in person. That was the adult thing to do. I rounded up Anci and, much against her will, set her off to wait for the bus. This was one of her least favorite things. Even for rural parts, we live in an out-of-the-way spot, and the way these county buses run you could basically go to the Oort Cloud and back in the time it takes them to drop you off at home. I drove her to school myself when I could, or Peggy did. I promised to pick Anci up later, save her the agony of the bus ride home. She seemed to think I'd forget, so I put in a call to Peggy. I was almost relieved when it went through to voicemail and I was able to leave a message. If I wasn't there, Peggy would run Anci back to the Vale. Whether Peggy would stick around long enough to see me was a question I couldn't yet answer. I didn't have time to answer it anyway.

I had a job to quit, and maybe two.

FIVE

Luster's place was east of the Vale on a pleasant cut of land between the Little Grassy and Devil's Kitchen lakes called Baker's Crossroads. The house sat atop a low hummock surrounded by crown vetch and big bur oaks at the edge of a narrow track of road called Knight Hawk. I guess a county commissioner owed a favor. At the bottom of the hummock was a lagoon, now nearly black with algae, and some knots of paling knotweed and loosestrife. A family of hackberries surrendered their mottled leaves and the autumn gusts caught them and tossed them around like ticker tape.

I left the bike at the bottom of the hill and got off and walked up. Some underemployed birds lifted off the road and fluttered southward on spotted wings, but otherwise nothing stirred. The lady at the mine was right: the house was as big as Soldier, with a little left over. You could have stuffed our place at Indian Vale into the little left over and still had room for a head or two of cattle. There was a car in the drive, a white Lincoln shining under coats of wax. There was a fountain with a statue of a naked lady and some neatly coiffed box hedges. There were some of those solar lights you stake in the ground to form a path to the front door, but a couple of the lights had been kicked over, and one of them had been stepped on and busted. Neither Jonathan nor the old man struck me as especially clumsy, and the sight of this small disorder made my throat tighten in an unhappy way.

I went up to the door and tried the bell and heard it

chime prettily behind the thickness of the wooden frame. I waited a moment, then checked my watch, rocking on my heels a little in an attempt to be casual. Then I knocked and tried the handle and the unlocked door swung open, the expensive weather stripping releasing its hold with a swoosh. I stopped being casual. I could smell what was inside immediately: a hint of smoke and the sharp tang of cordite. A house that big, maybe there was a shooting range inside. With the One Percenters, you never knew.

I went in to find it. I called out Luster's name and Jonathan's but nobody answered. I took a day or so to search the downstairs part of the house before I found the kitchen, where I slid a knife out from a wooden block on the counter. I was coming down with an anxious feeling, and a knife made me feel a little better about things. I went back to the front and climbed some thickly carpeted stairs into the upper reaches of the house and walked down a wide hallway and finally into a bedroom, last door on the left. It was a big, bright space with an odd kind of industrial Bandraster ceiling of exposed metal beams. There was a chifforobe and dresser and a closet that might have doubled as a hangar. There was a long gun mounted on the wall, an A. H. Fox double-barrel with scrolled engraving and an inspector's cartouche stamped 1906. A beautiful weapon. On the south wall was a wooden frame, and in the frame a chunk of coal the size of a derby hat. A bay window overlooked the oaky woodland spreading west and the rocky spine of the hills nearer the horizon. All that was interesting, but Luster was more interesting.

He was on the bed, on top of the sheets. On one of the acorn newels was a beaver-pelt Stetson. On the other was a six-shooter in a patent leather holster. None of it had done him any good. He was in his boxers and shirtless, on his back, facing the ceiling with his feet and arms spread, and there were holes in the top of his chest and holes and blood spatters on the beams and ceiling directly above. Part of the ceiling had broken away, and the bedspread and Luster were covered in a thin white dust. Here and there, his blood and the powder had mingled to form a kind of plaster on his naked chest.

I checked his vitals but there wasn't any doubt about it. The skies had fallen. Matthew Luster was dead.

I called the cops, and the cops came. Not just cops—*all* the cops. They surrounded the property: radio cars and county sheriffs' prowlers and evidence vans and Illinois State Police unmarkeds. They overran the cobbled driveway until the later cops were forced to park all the way down the steeply sloped lawn, so far out that technically they weren't even in Baker's Crossroads. An ambulance was grudgingly permitted to park in the grass near the front door.

Then they questioned me, up one side and down another. They wanted to know about me and what I was doing snooping around at the residence. They wanted to know about the knife I was holding. I told them knives didn't fire bullets. When they were finally satisfied I hadn't done anything bloody they started to ignore me, distracted by the crime scene and trying to contain the chaos they themselves had created. I put the knife back in its block and wandered around a little, listening in on some of their talk. Then I slipped outside and wandered around the back of the house to see what I could see. No one stopped me or even seemed to notice my presence. There were too many cops for anyone to think of policing anything. Every cop in the tricounties must have been there. There were cops in the grass. There were cops on the roof. The garage door lifted on its arm and a crowd of cops came burping out, as though the house had swallowed too many to keep down.

After a while, Jonathan arrived. His arms were full of groceries. The big cop with soft eyes from that first day at the Knight Hawk appeared out of nowhere to explain what had happened, and the groceries dropped from the boy's arms and some of the items rolled out of their bags and down the hill and into a ditch. A can of creamed corn floated away. Jonathan wept into his hands. Some things they don't prepare you for at business school. As I approached, both men looked up at me.

Jonathan said, "Thank God you're here."

"I'm here," I said. "I'm afraid I'm the one who found him. But I don't know what good I can do."

The big cop stuck out his hand.

"You must be Slim," he said. "I'm Sheriff Wince. Now that they've taken your statement, son, I'm eager we speak."

On account of his name kept coming up, I'd asked my buddy in the Williamson County sheriff's about this Ben Wince. The story of how he'd attained office was a pretty good one, and here it is:

Wince was a local boy with a reputation for honesty, but it'd taken a botched suicide to win him his star. For twenty years, he'd languished away as deputy, and then one day Sheriff Edelson, who'd held the office so long almost no one could remember the last guy, began slipping into dementia.

And when I say "dementia," I don't mean he left the house without shoes or forgot his Social Security number. This was the real deal. Edelson launched drug sweeps of churches, social groups, and preschools. He developed insane conspiracies and let them mushroom into office-wide investigations. When the federal government started spreading around some of that post-9/11 money, he used Randolph County's share to buy an armored antiriot vehicle. Got his office written up in the Chicago papers for that one, and not in a good way. Before long, even the major crimes unit of the Illinois State Police stopped returning his calls. Innocent citizens were harassed, and one night a high school boy was pulled from his car on a lonely county road and beaten nearly to death in front of his date. But even crazy behavior behind the county shield wasn't enough to stop the law-and-order crowd from voting him back into office.

Then, one morning not long before election day, Edelson was refilling his coffee at the station house when suddenly he paused to stare squint-eyed out the window. There was a squirrel on the sill, staring back. Edelson scowled at the squirrel. The squirrel scratched his nut. Edelson couldn't abide that. It was too much to endure, these derisive squirrels freely roaming the countryside. All his efforts at law enforcement had come to naught. He did the honorable thing: he unholstered his service weapon and shot himself in the head.

In one of those freak things, the bullet didn't kill him, but it did complete the job of scrambling his brains, turning him into a vegetable. The public took in the sad news, reflected soberly on what it all meant, and again returned Edelson to office. In a landslide. Only when a civil case was launched by the parents of the assaulted boy, and a settlement quietly reached, was Felix Edelson shuffled quietly out of office for reason of mental incapacity, pension intact. Wince had been sheriff ever since, though a statistically significant portion of county voters apparently viewed his rise as opportunistic and he was reelected only by the slimmest margins.

We went into the house. Wince asked Jonathan to join us, but he refused and instead stayed outside, collecting his fallen groceries and shivering against the cold and an unfolding nightmare. A plainclothesman came huffing down the grand staircase, followed by a nervous-looking guy with no hair and a patent leather bag like in the movies.

Wince said, "Well?"

"He's dead."

"Is there anything science *can't* do?"

The little guy ignored him. "With prejudice, too. I don't think I've seen one like this before."

Wince said, "And here I thought you'd seen everything."

The little guy didn't like that. He was one of those folks who wore his exasperation like a sign on his head. He rubbed his mustache with his thumb in a funny way and sneered and said, "Go on up. See for yourself."

Wince looked at me. "You've already been up there, so you might as well come up with me. Besides, I want a word with you, just the two of us."

I didn't want to—I didn't need to see any of that again— but this seemed like more than a polite request. Up we went, back down the hall and into the bedroom. The body was where I'd left it and the blood and its smell.

Wince said, "Holy shit."

"That's understating things a little."

Wince nodded agreement. He crouched down to take a look beneath the bed. There were shallow indentations in the carpet and numbered tents here and there to mark them. At last, he sighed and rose heavily again to his feet. There was a copy of the ME's notes on the bedside table. Wince picked them up, and looked at them a moment, and said, "Shooter under the bed, waited for him to lie down. Probably worried he'd be armed. Probably good thinking, too. There are more guns in the house than spoons. You saw the Fox over there?"

"I saw it. Thing's worth more than my house."

"Both our houses added together." He looked at the report some more and then looked at Luster. "Five in the chest, closely grouped, no misses. Pretty good work. Or pretty lucky."

"Depends on which end of the barrel you were on."

"That's a point," he said.

"There's something else," I said. "A burn mark on his upper lip."

He stood over the bed and looked closely and didn't see it at first, but then he said, "Goddamn, you know what, I think you're right."

"It wasn't there when I saw him yesterday."

Wince snapped on a glove and carefully opened Luster's mouth and looked inside. Then he looked up at me.

"He's been shot in the mouth."

"Head's intact, though."

"Looks like small caliber. Little twenty-two, maybe. Basically a pellet gun. Not the gun that killed him, that's for sure. Killer scorched his lip with the barrel," he said. "That's a good eye you got on you, son."

I said, "Dwayne Mays was shot in the ear. Luster in the mouth."

"After he was dead."

I nodded. "After he was dead. Some kind of message? Dwayne listened to the wrong people, Luster talked to the wrong people? Or talked too much?"

"Could be," Wince said. "Except Dwayne's wound was fatal, not an afterthought. And he was a newspaper reporter, not a broadcaster. You wanted to send a message, wouldn't you cut off his fingers or something instead?"

"Hell, I don't know. It was just an idea."

Wince said, "My experience, things don't go down like that. The killer doesn't leave behind a playing card or a miniature dollhouse version of the crime scene or whatever they do in the movies. You wish maybe they would sometimes. It'd be easy to narrow a list of suspects down to, say, the guy with all the antique pocket watches."

"Probably."

"Well, don't feel bad. It's a common mistake. And look at the bright side, you've given me something to rub in that little shit Dunphy's face. He completely missed this business with the bullet in the mouth," Wince said. He thought it over for a moment and then turned back to look at Luster's body and said, "You got any sense of what it's all about?"

"Me? Why would I?"

"Boy downstairs says you were working for the old man, poking around looking for this photographer went missing."

I said, "Looking and looking badly. Truth is, I was on my way this morning to turn in my resignation. I'm not even sure what they thought I could do for them."

"Me, either," he said. "Least not yet. One thing, though, you've had yourself one hell of a day."

"More like hell of an afternoon. Whatever's happening here is happening fast. Somebody's working with a sense of urgency."

"Seems that way."

"Maybe this is the part where you read me the riot act for mucking around in police business?"

He shrugged and said, "Maybe it is. And I guess I ought to. But way I see it is this—and let me know if I've got anything wrong here—Luster basically made you an offer you couldn't walk away from. The boy out there filled me in on the details. I don't know you'd find many cops would sneer at you for grabbing that deal, way our own pensions are going these days."

"Thanks."

"Don't thank me yet," he said. "I'm not saying you were entirely above-board on this, either. Fact is, I think you weren't crazy about the assignment, but you went along anyway, thinking you could maybe ask a few questions and do a little light lifting and basically fart around until the police cleared the case or Beckett came home on his own or Luster came to his senses and called the whole thing off."

"That's pretty close."

He said, "I have my moments. Maybe I'm getting soft in my old age, but I'm inclined to let you off the hook here, mostly because Luster should have known better than to try a foolish stunt like this." He looked at the body on the bed. "What the hell was he thinking?"

"I was wondering the same thing," I said. "He didn't seem confident of a good outcome from the police. And he did ask me to bring Beckett to him first, assuming I ever found him."

Wince sucked around on that one some, looking me in the face.

"Way the boy downstairs tells it, too," he said. "He says he doesn't know for what, though. Claims Luster never told him."

"You believe him?"

"You asking private detective questions again?"

"Nope."

"Good. You're learning. Consider your knuckles rapped. Head on back into the policeman's reunion."

"There is a cop or two down there."

"A lot of them, this is their first red ball. I didn't know better, I'd think some of them are actually happy about it."

"Everybody likes to feel useful."

"I guess, but their usefulness is a pain in my ass. I'm tripping over three shades of uniform down there, and that's before the press and the local pols even show their faces. I don't even want to think about scene contamination."

I said, "Then I won't mention that your ambulance parked right where an intruder might have left footprints in all this new mud."

He smiled, a little sadly, and rubbed a leathery hand at his pelt of gray hair. "I said I don't want to think about it. Go on down now."

I started for the door. Then I turned and said, "One last thing. I think Beckett and Mays might have been working on a story about the meth trade at the Knight Hawk."

Wince looked at me, but his face was noncommittal. You get more out of Sheetrock. He said, "Lot of that in the mines these days. Sad business."

"Yeah, but this might have been something bigger. Knight Hawk's tanks of anhydrous ammonia have been under assault lately. The company's posted armed guards and everything. If you've ever seen those tanks, you know how much ingredient they're holding."

Wince tried to maintain his neutral expression, but his right eyebrow flicked softly, and I knew I'd told him something he didn't know. Money in the bank, I hoped, if I ever needed it.

"Anyway," I said, waving my hand and heading back downstairs. He followed after a while, but didn't hang around for more chat. The cops gathered around the stairs, and the ME and his team went up again and came back shortly with Luster's covered body. I waited for them to go out, then went to look for Jonathan but didn't see him anywhere, and his car was gone from the drive. I tried his cell but it went to voicemail, and I clicked off without saying anything. He'd talk when he was able to, I guessed. I walked past the funeral procession and down the hill to my bike. My phone rang. It wasn't Jonathan's number, but I answered it anyway. I shouldn't have. That phone was leading to nothing but woe, and if I'd had any sense I'd have tied it to a brick and thrown it in the lake.

Temple. Of course. "I need to see you right away."

"Mrs. Beckett—Temple—I'm just as sorry as I can be for your loss. Really I am. But that's a bad idea," I said. "Actually, it's a terrible one. The police have asked me to steer clear, and from here on that's what I mean to do."

That failed to make an impression. "Listen to me," she said, her voice dropping. "The people who killed my father and may have killed my husband—they know about you."

"Mrs. Beckett . . ."

"Slim, goddamn it. Listen to me. They don't care who you are or what your story is. They don't care that you aren't a private investigator. They don't care what you told the police, and they don't care that you're steering clear. Trust me. You've got a daughter, don't you?"

I froze for a minute. I said, "I've got a daughter."

She said, "Then they've got a target."

SIX

Susan opened the door. She was in street clothes again. I don't know why I expected some kind of uniform, but I admit to a degree of disappointment. This time, she had no wordplay for me. She nodded at me and I at her and then she stepped aside silently and I headed into the big sitting room where Temple was waiting, her face in her hands. I stood there until she looked up at me. She'd been crying, but now her face was composed and angry. Her hair was loose on her shoulders, and her blouse was torn a little at the right sleeve and the skin was torn, too, and bleeding. The way the light was, for the first time I saw that the black stone on her finger was a slice of coal, cut into a disk and stamped with an elegant cursive "L." There might not have been any pictures of the old man in the room, but he was there with us nevertheless, along with the evidence of Temple's grief. There was a mess in the corner, broken glass and an overturned tray and what I guessed were the remains of breakfast. A few of the curtains were torn down.

Temple looked torn down, too. She said, "It wasn't supposed to turn out like this."

"I can't think of anything that is."

"Do you want a drink?"

"I sure don't."

She slapped the tops of her legs twice and stood suddenly and walked to a mini bar I hadn't noticed before. It was roughly the size of a small yacht, so I'm not sure how I missed it. She took down two heavy crystal glasses and a bottle of something brown and filled them, neat. She drank one of them and refilled it. She picked up both glasses and walked over and set one in front of me and returned to her seat with the other.

"You don't have to drink it," she said. "But at least now I'm not drinking alone."

"Maybe you could have one with Susan instead."

"Susan doesn't drink."

I sighed and pushed the glass a little farther away. I didn't want to get too close to it. "Mrs. Beckett, where is your husband?"

"Temple," she said, "I want to be called Temple. And I honestly don't know."

"Dammit, if you're playing some kind of game . . ."

She said again, "I honestly don't know." She sat there a moment, quite still, taking in her new reality. It had closed up around her all of a sudden, like a steel trap. Life had a way of doing that. You can plan for it, plan against it, hoard your shekels, stockpile bullets or bombs or quivers of arrow. And then life happens, and you blunder right into it like a dope. Temple shuddered and drained her second drink and said, "You . . . You saw him?"

I'd seen him. She nodded her head in jerks.

"You think I should be crying, don't you?" she said.

"I don't think anything," I said. "People mourn in their own way."

"That's just something to say."

"Sure."

She said, "My relationship with my father wasn't good. I guess you noticed."

"I don't know."

She thought I was just being polite and she didn't like it.

She frowned at me but pressed on. "I don't think he thought much of me. I'm pretty sure he didn't. And I know I often didn't think much of him. He was more or less a stranger to me when I was a girl, and after my mom died . . ." She looked up at me and shrugged and left it at that. She said, "Your father was something once, wasn't he?"

"I guess he was."

"Did you get along with him?"

"You have to know a person first to find that out, and I never did."

"He was distant?"

"He was a sonofabitch."

She didn't have anything else to ask about my father. Just as well. She turned her eyes to look at the door. "The police left just before I called you. They're going to post a patrol around the house, day and night. Cops with guns. They think I'm in danger."

"You might be," I said. "Maybe it'd be best if you went somewhere else. Stayed with family or friends for a while."

"They seemed to think so, too," she said. "But I'm not going. Besides, there isn't anybody."

"What about Jonathan?"

"You're kidding, right?"

"A hotel then?"

"You're kidding, ri—"

"Or maybe just get out of town."

"I'm not going."

That was that. I wanted to argue with her about the wisdom of sticking around, but I'll be honest, I was weary and in no mood for arguing. Trouble does that to you, I was finding.

"And you say you've had no word from Guy?"

"None."

"But you know what he was working on before he disappeared. You knew before and didn't say anything," I said. "I wish you had."

"I know."

"You told me that he and Mays were working on a piece about the meth trade?"

"I think so."

I threw up my hands. "Temple . . ."

"Dammit, I *think* so. I don't know for sure. Guy and I . . . Guy and I didn't talk much about his work. I'll be honest with you . . ."

"Never too late to try something new."

She ignored me.

"I'll be honest with you. Guy wasn't actually living here when he disappeared."

"He wasn't living here?"

"Not actually."

"Not actually?"

"No."

I thought about it. I said, "With Mays?"

"How did you know?"

"Just a guess. He doesn't have any family, and if it were another woman I doubt you'd be mentioning it now at all."

"Probably not."

I said, "Their story, the meth story. Who were they looking at?"

"First, I need you to understand something. The pension. Your pension. My father was killed before he could secure it. That kind of thing takes time, and he didn't have the time."

I just stood there looking at her. I knew what was coming. I could feel it in the pit of my stomach. It was like blundering onto the tracks and turning around and realizing the train was bearing down on you, too late.

I said, "But you do."

She stepped to me and pressed her hands on me and said, "But I do. And I will, Slim. You've got to believe me. I do and I can and I will. I own the Knight Hawk now. And there's only one thing I want."

"Let me guess."

"Find who did this."

"You know," I said, "funny thing is, I was on my way to your father's to resign."

"I don't blame you. But you won't quit now. You don't strike me as the type who likes getting jerked around."

I said, "Oh, I don't know." But damned if she wasn't right. I was involved and that's all there was to it. I thought for the hundredth time of Round-Face and his promises of violence. I thought for the millionth time of that pension. If there were going to be dead bodies, the least that could happen is I could get that damn pension. I said, "Before I can press forward—assuming I can—you'll have to tell me who your husband and Mays were looking at."

"A lot of people, at least at first, but one name kept coming up. Jump. Jump something. Something like that."

"Jump Down?"

She said, "That's it. You know him?"

"Yeah, I know him. Everybody knows him. And once again I'm changing my mind about this mess. Jump Down, he's a vampire. Actually, he's worse than a vampire because he's real. Mrs. Beckett . . ."

"Temple."

"Temple, I'm not sure what you want from me. Even if I did know, I'm not sure there's anything I could do to help you. Fact is, I'm pretty sure there's not. I can tell you this, though. If your husband and Mays were looking to tangle with Jump Down and his crew, you really are in danger. Those people are killers. They're the kind of killers that other killers are afraid of. You should tell the police everything you know and let them handle it, because now that I know what's going on here I am taking my family and running for the hills."

I got up and turned to go.

"Wait, Slim," she said. "It's worse than that."

I shook my head.

She lifted one of her eyebrows. She said, "No?"

"No. Because nothing's worse than that."

"It is. It's worse," she insisted. "Do you know a man named Roy Galligan?"

"I know of him. His name's coming up a lot these days."

"He's . . . he was my father's greatest business rival."

"I know all that," I said. "He owns the derelict mine up the hill there above your house."

"And the working mine across the gap from it."

"The King Coal," I said. I knew it. My pal Jeep Mabry worked there.

Temple looked at me with a grim mouth and said, "Galligan's involved."

"Involved? What do you mean? Involved in what?"

She said, "Slim, Roy Galligan has got his hand in the meth trade at the Knight Hawk. He's in it up to his scrawny neck. That's what Guy and Dwayne were working on—the connection between Jump Down and Galligan. I think my father found out what was going on and confronted Galligan, and Galligan had him murdered."

Like the late Matthew Luster, Roy Galligan was an Illinois native and a true son of Little Egypt. It makes a man proud, having homegrown villains like that. His grandfather founded the first coking plant in Stotler County, and his father was such a big shot that he turned down pleas from both political parties to run for governor. On his twenty-first birthday, Roy's daddy had given him his first coal mine, a Union County scratchback, and he'd been in mining ever since.

Sometime in the early sixties, at the height of his industry, Galligan managed to cobble together a six-outfit string; it was too small to compete with the big conglomerates but more than enough to keep himself on the map. In '78, he made a bundle selling out to Amax, OBC, and Zeigler. He kept the King Coal and one or two of the smaller shops where he could mine coal and be left alone to run things his way without anyone paying him much mind. It was a hobby, I guess, or more likely it was just in his blood.

Those were good days for Galligan, but lately the pendulum of his happy fortune had swung the other way. Mounting operational costs and environmental laws, which guys like Roy hated more than they hated labor unions, were slowly bleeding him out of the business. The King Coal wasn't the last small outfit in Little Egypt, but in the past twenty years or so its breed had become increasingly rare. Pretty soon they'd be extinct, and then the mining would be done by remote control, by faraway people who wouldn't give two shits how they left the land, people who knew how to use the federal courts to their best advantage. Even with the sorts of restrictions most outfits had to work under, a federal suit could be tied up until all the complainants were in the cold, hard ground, and their problems passed on to a younger, less refractory generation, one that'd been taught to live with disappointment.

So he was something of a wounded animal, and if he really was involved in this business, I thought, I'd have to run a lot farther than the hills until I felt safe.

It was just past noon when I left Temple's house. I'll tell you, I was hoping never to see it again. Or her. I knew it wouldn't be that easy, but that's where my head was at. The morning's events had shaken me to my socks. Actually, it had turned my socks back into raw wool and the raw wool back into a sheep, and the sheep had bitten me on the ass.

It wasn't raining for a change, but now it was cold. A front had bullied its way in from the north, and a wintry change had overtaken the weather. I zipped up my jacket and changed to the heavier gloves I keep in the saddlebag just in case. Cold on a motorcycle is something you don't want to mess with. Even moderately cool air will slice right through you, and in wintertime hypothermia sets in so fast you'll still be wondering what the fuss is all about when they're cutting off your fingers and putting them in a jar of formaldehyde. Still, I needed some time and space to think, so I rode east to Wolf Creek Road and then south around the edge of the swollen lake until I found old Hampton Cemetery.

It's a quiet place, very small, and surrounded on all sides by red oaks and a few crooked silver maples. I got off the bike and walked through their shadows and fallen leaves until I found a familiar grave and sat down near it, not knowing what to think.

I don't think I'd ever been so confused or out of sorts. I didn't know where to turn or where to run or even whether running was an option. That was a lot of not knowing, I'll grant you. At least one thing was sure, though—guys like me didn't go up against people like Roy Galligan, and when we tried, we usually found ourselves buried in earthen dams or filling out a bag of dog food in some backwoods general store. It wasn't a happy thought, but it was the one that stuck with me.

After a while, I said good-bye, apologized for not visiting enough, and got back on the bike and rode away. I was up the road a few miles when I pulled over again and took out my cell. I called Jeep Mabry first. That was a terrible call to have to make, but it was maybe more pleasant than the one I made next, to Peggy. Then I rode into Herrin and pulled in at Hungry's on Main. I went inside and sat at the counter with some coffee. After a while, Peggy came in.

She sat next to me and ordered a coffee for herself. I asked for a refill. Neither of us spoke while we waited. After a long while the waitress came back carrying the dirty carafe, explaining that she'd had to put on a fresh pot. After she left, Peggy looked at me.

"Well?"

"Coffee sucks."

"Now's really not a time to be funny."

"Sorry."

She sighed. "So let's have it."

We had it.

When I was finished, she said, "Jesus fried eggs."

"That's one way to say it."

"They killed Matt Luster."

"Someone did."

"Well, that'll lead tonight's news."

I said, "I didn't know you knew him."

"Of course I know him. Know his reputation anyway," she said. "Anyone who gives a damn about local environmental business knows that."

"I honestly didn't know you did," I said. "Give a damn, I mean."

"It's something I try not to talk about around you, darling. I don't want it to come between us. It's your job, after all, and it was your father's job, too."

"Could we not mention him, please? Everyone wants to talk about the old man these days. It's like I can't get away from him."

"Sorry. But, yeah, I do give a damn—a damn about the planet, Slim. A great big hollering damn. You saw what happened down in the Gulf a while back. Or what about Martin County?"

"Martin County? The sludge pen? I'd almost forgotten."

Peggy looked regretfully at me and shook her head. "One of the worst environmental disasters in the history of this country, and everybody's forgotten."

I had to give her that one: it was a lulu, more than three hundred million gallons of coal sludge released into the Tug Fork and surrounding area when a Massey Energy impoundment pen failed. And this was no ordinary failure: there was an abandoned coal mine underneath the pen. Somehow they'd missed it during the land survey. Or maybe they hadn't missed it; maybe they just didn't think it would be a problem. It *was* a problem. One fine morning, the ground in the impoundment gave way, and the sludge emptied into the mine, and eventually flowed out the entries and into the world. As disasters go, it was like Rube Goldberg had started doing gags for hell. And, the thing is, three hundred million gallons was a bargain. The company's Brushy Fork impoundment pond in West Virginia is built to hold between eight and nine *billion*. In a rogues' gallery of reckless industrial actors, it's hard to select a chief villain, but the ratfuckers who ran Massey might just have captured the prize. Even their corporate logo—a black capital letter M, aflame, like a basalt altar—betrayed a satanic worldview. They'd changed their name of late—after the public at large began finally to catch on to their dirty dealings—but the players were more or less the same and the institutionalized contempt for humankind and natural places remained intact.

She looked at me suddenly. "But let's not stray too far off topic."

"I wasn't trying to."

"I recall, I was reading you the riot act."

"Just getting started, probably."

"Keen as always," she said. "Let's get the obvious thing out of the way. You lied to me about what happened to you the other day. Your injuries."

"I did, and I feel bad about it, too. I felt bad while I was doing it. But I didn't want you to worry, and I didn't want you to think I was crazy."

"And now I'm doing both."

"Well, it's a fail then."

"Pretty much," she said. She sighed and thought a while. Then her head snapped up and her eyes widened.

"Oh my God. Anci."

"Is safe," I said. "Jeep's keeping an eye on her."

She cocked her head. "Jeep?"

"Yes."

"Jeep *Mabry*?"

"Yes."

"The *psychopathic* Jeep Mabry?"

"He is not," I said. I shrugged. "Borderline, maybe . . ."

"And what do you mean, looking after her? You sent him into the school?"

She was aghast, so I said quickly, "No, no. Not inside. He's, you know, outside, watching over everything."

Well, that just made things worse. Peggy said, "Oh, dear God in merciful heaven. He's outside, lurking in the bushes?"

"I had to guess, I'd say he's in the empty field across the street. Better cover there."

"Not helping."

"Right. Sorry."

She put her face in her hands. "Tell me he's not armed."

I sat quietly for a spell. At last I said, "I won't tell you."

"This gets better and better. I don't guess you geniuses gave any thought to what'll happen if he gets caught out there? People are a little paranoid these days about men with guns lurking around schools."

I shook my head. "He won't get caught." She was right, of course. Neither of us had thought of it.

Peggy looked at me for a long time. A small change was happening in her eyes, a fleck of dark light, like a flaw in the iris, and it was a change I didn't like. I could almost hear her starting to think of me as another of those adult mistakes we'd been talking about a couple nights earlier. What I was going to do, I'd have to do as quickly as possible.

Peggy was impatient for a resolution, too. She said, "I'm waiting to hear your plan, Bubba. And, for your sake, I hope it's a good one."

"Maybe not good, but it might be the only way through this mess. Way I see it, if this Temple Beckett is right, and Roy Galligan really has dealt himself into the meth racket in some of these local mines, then none of us is safe until I convince him I'm out of his way and out of it for good. If he's dealt himself in with Jump Down and his team, convincing them is going to be tough and dangerous. These are the kind of people who deal with the discovery of mouse droppings by burning down the house. Measured steps are not their thing." I paused and drank some coffee. Its general awfulness seemed to fit the occasion. "On the other hand, I can't go to Galligan just yet. There are too many unanswered questions, and Temple's suspicions aren't any kind of proof anyway. Accusing him of being a meth dealer without hard evidence is almost as dangerous as anything else. So basically I'm in the worst position of all. Everyone thinks I know *something*, when the truth is I don't know *anything*. I need more. I need something to trade. What is it you schoolteachers say? Knowledge is power."

"Now you're just sucking up."

"I thought it couldn't hurt."

She said, "You're actually going to do it, aren't you? You are. You're out of your mind, you know that?"

"Maybe I am, but I don't think I have any choice. There's only one person who knows the truth about what's happening here, assuming he's still alive," I said. "I've got to do what I was hired to do in the first place. I've got to find out what happened to Guy Beckett."

PART TWO

RECLAMATION

SEVEN

The kitchen door banged open, and the snowbank moon-light came in, followed by men with guns. There were four of them, two big, two smaller. The big guys had shotguns. One of the little guys had a pistol, the other a hunting rifle. Even without the hardware, they looked like they meant business. I was eight years old. I'd had trouble sleeping in my bed of late, and had taken to stuffing myself between the pantry door and the radiator, where there was a warm little cubbyhole, when I couldn't sleep. I happened to be there that night, and it was dark in the kitchen so no one noticed me. The men waited there a moment and someone whispered and someone else shushed and then my father appeared in his robe.

"You're not here," he told them. His anger was subdued, and I wondered whether the men were even able to hear it in his voice, but it jumped across the room and ran at me like a panther. I felt my knees draw tighter against my chest.

One of the big men moved closer to him, and close enough that I could see: it was my father's work partner, Cheezie Bruzetti. His head was stuffed into a hat too small, and his plump face was red from the bitter cold outside. His mittened hands wrapped thickly around what looked like a .410 bore lever-action with the loop cock, but the barrel of the gun was broken and rested at a lazy angle over his fat right shoulder.

He didn't respond directly to my father. He just said, "He says he's not the one."

"He says that?"

"Yeah."

"Well, he would, wouldn't he?"

"We kinda believe him, though."

My father said, "You didn't bring him here."

There was a silence. One of the men coughed.

Finally, Cheezie said, "Outside."

"Outside?"

"In the trunk."

My father watched them a moment. He didn't move and they didn't move, but I could feel their fear swirling in the silver light, and then my father turned suddenly and went out of the room. One of the men farted nervously, and Cheezie snarled at him and said, "Christ, would you get yourself together?"

The man tried to get himself together, I guess. I don't know. I still couldn't see him very well. After a moment, my father came back, still in his robe, wearing rubber boots.

He said, "Okay."

They went out. I don't know how long they were gone or how long I sat there, and I guess I should have snuck back up to my room, but moving seemed impossible, and so I stayed with my thoughts buzzing in my head until the door opened again and my father and Cheezie came back in with snow clumped on their feet and melting on their heads.

Cheezie said, "See?"

My father shook his head. He replied, "No, I don't see. Someone told them where we'd be and what we were doing, and it was him. You can be sure of it."

"You're some kind of detective now?"

My father ignored him. "It was him. Probably they

promised him something Job security. Or his pension. They like to hold that pension out there, see who bites. And he bit. The strike will last another six months because of him. People's children will go hungry. Take him where we talked about and leave him there. Throw your guns in the quarry. It's deep enough it won't be frozen tonight. Make sure they all throw them. I know Sacks won't want to."

"It was his daddy's gun."

"I don't care if it was his daddy himself. He throws it in or he goes in."

Cheezie said, "I'll make sure."

"Don't ever bring anyone to my home again. Not like that. My daughters are upstairs in their beds. Now get the hell out of here."

Even after these hard words, they hugged each other briefly. This was war, but they were brothers and always would be. Cheezie turned and went out of the house again, leaving behind little silver pools of melt, and my father waited for him to go, then started back to bed. He paused in the doorway and sighed and, after a moment's reflection, turned and looked directly at me in my cubbyhole, and I was frozen.

He said, "It's a hard old world for some folks, boy. Don't ever forget."

He went out and I heard his footfalls on the stairs and that's the last thing I remember.

The night Anci and I left Indian Vale, the first snow of the new season appeared. The moon showed its bright face over the edge of the cliff, but was quickly overtaken, and the sky soon turned silver and bright. The wind came up and yelped at the world, and it was so cold even the grass shivered with it. That wind had come from someplace else, I thought, some place where they weren't having a spate of murders and missing photographers. I wanted to go there. Then again, maybe the wind came from the Missouri Bootheel. If that was the choice, I'd take the murders. You have to have standards.

We threw some things in our bags: clothes, shoes, books. Anci packed snacks and a few orange sodas. I packed Betsy. We loaded up the truck as quickly as possible and headed out. It wasn't exactly a full-on retreat, but it felt like sneaking away. I thought again of my father and of how the man named Deaton came to our house and how my father had refused to budge, and I even thought of Temple Beckett and how she'd declined to run. I told myself I was doing it for Anci, and mostly I was, but I'll admit, I was scared. I didn't feel safe until we were on the road and the Vale was being swallowed up by the night behind us.

Along the way, I explained what I could of it to Anci. Leaving her in the dark didn't seem fair, but I wanted to worry her as little as possible, so I trimmed off the sharp edges, at least best I was able.

She sat quietly listening as the dark miles blurred by. She turned it over quietly for a time, then said, "So it's got to do with your work?"

"I'm afraid so."

"And you did this for me?"

"Well, a lot of it, yeah, but I also did it for me and even for Peggy, too."

"Because we're family," she said, with a certainty and determination that made me proud.

"That's right. And family has to stick together when the times get tough."

She nodded. I could just feel her thinking about family, and I knew where her mind was going even before she spoke again. "You know, if you're in trouble you could always . . ."

"No."

"Well, you could if you wanted to."

"Not in this lifetime, sweat pea. Besides, Peggy will help. And your Uncle Jeep and Aunt Opal. There's no need to bring anyone else into it. He wouldn't want to help anyway."

"How long's it been since you went to see him?"

"Since the last time he told me to stop coming."

Anci shook her head. She looked at the spider shapes the cold was making on the window glass.

She said, "Some people just don't want to be happy." But I wasn't sure anymore who she meant.

That was a tough night. We spent the next several hours fighting actual spiders at the Pin Oak Lodge on 13. You'd think the cold would have killed them, but the Pin Oak is a special place—terrible but inside our budget—and apparently the conditions there bred some kind of super bug. Neither of us slept soundly, and after a while I gave up trying. I lay there listening to the sound of my own thoughts as long as I could stand them, then got up quietly and dug around in Anci's bag until I found one of her books. I climbed back into bed to follow the further adventures of the virgin vampire club. Except there were werewolves, too. Everything but a Karloff mummy, but maybe he showed up in the sequel. Anci and I had read a good piece of this one together a while ago. Back then I couldn't stand the thing, but at one in the morning pretty much anything is entertaining, and I ended up finishing the story and worrying over how the sequel was going to turn out. Maybe Anci had already read it. I couldn't remember.

I returned to her bag and dug around some more. In a zipper pocket were some letters from her mother I didn't know about, and I took them out and held them, and even the sight of her handwriting made me wince a bit. The return address was roughly where I figured it'd be, and the paper looked homemade. The fact that they were paper letters in the first place made me think she was some place off the grid, some place where smartphones and computers and the like aren't tolerated or just don't work. I don't think I'm an intrusive parent or much of a snoop, but I admit I thought about reading them. I wondered why I spent so much time searching for the missing. The abandoned are always searching for something, maybe.

Finally, I put the letters away again and zipped shut the pocket. We'd talk about it later, maybe, or I'd wait for Anci to mention it to me. I went back to digging in the bag and was surprised again to find some Nevada Barr novels I didn't know she had. Anci grunted and rolled over to face me, and I tried to be happy about my discovery to her, but she didn't want happy and instead said a dirty word at me and threw a shoe. I took *Winter Study* and the feel of those letters in my hand back to my bed to wait out the dark, which somehow seemed deeper and more lonesome than before.

Sometime around 3:30, Anci woke up screaming. I thought at first it was a nightmare, but she said she'd felt something crawling on her leg.

"Another spider?" I asked.

"Not unless it was a spider as big as your hat."

I thought it had to be a rodent of some kind, but, sure enough, it was a spider as big as your hat. A real monster. I swatted at it, but it was too quick for me. It skittered off the bed and onto the wall. Anci screamed again, louder this time, and the shitkicker in the next unit pounded on the connecting door and said some pretty raw stuff. Well, I was tired and out of sorts, and pretty soon I was talking back, and then we were in the parking lot face-to-face, like a manager and umpire in a baseball game. The poor dope who lived on-site got dragged into it, and finally someone offered to call the police. Rather than risk another run-in with Wince, I checked us out and got on out of there.

"Lovely," Anci said, but she was too mad at me to say more.

I offered to take us someplace else, but by then we were both awake and hungry, so we drove up Interstate 57 to a truck stop I knew to be open at that hour and grabbed some food and coffee. Anyway, I had coffee. Anci had juice. We both shoveled down big plates of scrambled eggs covered in Day-Glo cheese and slices of toast that seemed to have been salvaged from a fire. Still, we were grateful and finished our plates.

When the sun finally came up, it broke through the silver sky, and the snow vanished like a passing memory. Anci cleaned up in the truck stop bathroom, and I drove her to school. I kissed her and promised to be waiting when she got out. I watched her go inside. I dialed Jeep Mabry and made our arrangements. Then I started the truck and headed off to find the house that Mays built.

Crainville is just north of Crab Orchard Lake, but Mays's place was north and east of that a piece, off County Road 16 in a spot near Hurricane Cemetery. It was a lonely plot in a lonely patch near a lonely stretch of road where most of the motor traffic belonged to the little farms down the hill. I drove out that way and found a quiet place to park. I got out and unlocked the case I'd stowed Betsy in and walked the half mile or so to the house. If the cops were still there, I'd stuff Betsy up my shirt and just keep strolling on by. If by some odd chance Wince was there and spotted me, I'd probably get to take a ride in a squad car.

The cops weren't there. No one was there. Maybe they'd all gotten depressed and gone home. This was a sorrowful sight, though "sorrowful" might not capture the sense of it. Stephen King would have rejected it as implausibly dreary and ominous. The little bungalow nestled down inside a swampy little hollow, like a tick buried in an armpit. It was basically a pile of concrete blocks and dirt. Mostly dirt. Rust had eaten the flashing, and the roof sagged like a wet paper towel. You could have knocked the whole thing over with a dirty look and a hard word. There was a motorcycle there—parts of a motorcycle, anyway—but it had fallen against one of the porch posts and partially collapsed the overhang. There was a dead possum in the yard. Someone had shot him and left him there, and the rains had washed his bloody spot pale pink. I didn't have the first idea what to make of that. I'd brought along some tools from the Vale—thinking to dismantle a lock, if need be—but I've had harder times opening bags of bread, and the door opened easily and let me inside.

Inside . . . oh, boy. The cramped living room stank like a cesspool of stale beer, two troubled lifetimes of cigarette smoke, and almost enough mildew to cover both. Someone had left open the western-facing window for, I don't know, four or five years, and some brittle-looking vines had grown through and curled up on the floor to die. The short-haired brown carpets were filthy and worn through to the subfloor, and the mismatched furniture was draped with months' worth of dust. Had I gotten the address wrong? I took out my phone and dialed Temple's number.

"You're sure this is the place?" I asked Susan when she answered. I gave her the house number.

"I tried to warn you," she said. "It's something, isn't it?"

"It's like home design by William Castle."

"Mays's ethics were the only spotless thing about him. The man was a pig."

"Question is, why would Beckett agree to stay in a place like this?"

"Some people could live in anything."

"There you go with the past tense again."

"I'm a past-tense kind of person," she said, and she hung up on me.

I gave the living room a good going-over. I didn't know what I was looking for, exactly, but on television they were always searching rooms for clues. I looked under the throw rug but found only some flattened dust bunnies and tragic palmetto bugs. I searched the pressboard shelves but turned up nothing but porno DVDs and a few trashy thrillers. Finally, in a fit of desperation, I reached under the couch and came out with a handful of dirty underwear. I spent a long moment contemplating amputating that hand.

I screwed up my courage a little and decided to have a go at the kitchen. If this was like most neglected houses, the kitchen would be in worse shape than the living areas, and the bathrooms would be worse than that. I resolved to stay away from the bathrooms. Beckett could be lying helpless in the tub, and I wouldn't go in after him alone. My insurance wasn't that good.

But Guy Beckett wasn't in the kitchen. Or in the refrigerator. There was nothing in the fridge at all, not even food. I kept searching and found what must have been Beckett's guest room. On the floor was a mattress that looked like a damp sponge, no doubt used for all kinds of illicit acts. But the shelves were overflowing with books—and not just any books, but volumes on the history of photography, collections of work by Robert Capa and Henri Cartier-Bresson, and an esoteric-looking survey of something called steganography. The only thing of even slight interest was a signed photograph of the former St. Louis Cardinals quarterback Jim Hart. At the bottom of the action shot was a graphic box with some of Hart's career stats: pass attempts, completions, touchdowns, like that. The photo was inscribed to Beckett personally; Hart had been athletics director at Southern Illinois University for a while, so maybe he and Beckett had met there. I took apart the framed picture of Hart, wondering if Beckett had stashed anything behind it, but all I found was disappointment. Maybe Wince was right about life not being like the movies. I put the picture and frame back and went back into the living room, and it was then that I heard the bedroom closet slide open.

I'd forgotten to look inside it, I guess. And maybe that was for the best, if someone was squirreled away in there, waiting. I could feel my heart hammering. I nearly peeled myself like a banana and went screaming out of the house, but somehow I kept it together and came up with a plan. I slid along the wall until I made the front door, opened it, breathed once, and closed it again loudly, as if I'd just left. Then I slipped off my shoes and made my way quietly back to a spot at the edge of the hallway, where I could wait unseen. It wasn't much of a plan, maybe, but it was what I had. Whoever it was worked quickly. The closet door must have come off its runner because it shut noisily and then banged itself against its frame; then I heard footsteps across the floor and a long moment of silence. When the footsteps came up the hall and walked past me, I cleared my throat, and whoever it was turned around, and I once again found myself looking at Round-Face.

I don't know which of us was more surprised. Me, probably. My nerves had basically had it. He wasn't wearing the ridiculous deputy's costume this time. Or the wide-panel shades. Halloween was over, I guess. Instead, he was wearing a checked sports jacket—glen plaid, I think it was—and dark slacks with a sharp crease. Everything fit just fine. He looked at me. I looked at him. He had the photograph of Jim Hart in his hand. He licked his lips.

He said, "Slim?"

I nodded. I said, "Yup. Slim."

He said, "Well, this is unfortunate," and his hand went quickly to the back pocket of his slacks.

I agreed that it was. I raised Betsy and shot him square in the chest.

EIGHT

The beanbag inside the sawed-off twelve gauge moved at a rate of roughly three hundred feet per second, so it was like Round-Face got hit in the sternum by a very small high-speed train. He grunted and left his feet. He pitched over backward and banged his head hard on the coffee table, which split in half with a sickening, mildewy crack. Then he lay there without moving.

I waited a moment for the ringing in my ears to subside, then checked Round-Face's vitals. He was breathing, and his heartbeat seemed strong and steady. When he came to, he'd feel like he'd gone under the wheels of a convoy of diesel trucks. But he'd be okay. The thing he'd been reaching for in his pocket was a spring-loaded sap. I couldn't believe it. He was going to sap me, like in an old detective book. I looked for a wallet but found only pocket lint and a folding knife. The lack of ID wasn't much of a surprise, but after my carelessness with the closet I wanted to be thorough. I went into the kitchen and looked around until I found a bit of rope under the sink, and I used the rope to tie him up. He didn't so much as fart the whole time. I'd like to have talked to him, asked him what it was all about, but the guy was really out. I tossed the pocketknife into a corner across the room, then used the landline to call the cops and report an intruder. I gave the address and hung up as the operator was asking my name. They could do with him what they wanted, assuming he ever woke up from his nap. On the way out the door, I stopped and picked up the picture of Jim Hart.

A what?" Temple.

"You heard me."

"A round-faced man?"

"Yup. Mean little bastard, too. He and I have run into one another before. Technically, more than once. And technically, he ran into Betsy. Well, technically, Betsy ran into . . ."

She stopped me. "This is getting complicated," she said. "Tell me, he wouldn't be a certain someone responsible for your cuts and bruises you had the other day, would he?"

"He might be," I admitted. "And I'd like nothing more than to learn his story, but I think finding Guy is more important. For all of us."

"Agreed," she said. "But how?"

"Working on it."

"And you say he was stealing a photograph?"

"That's right," I said. "Anyway, that's what he was doing when I met him. I don't know what else he might have been after. Any ideas?"

"I honestly don't know. A friend of Guy's?"

"Friend?"

"One of Galligan's men, then."

"Assuming he really is involved."

"I told you . . ."

"I know," I said. "One of the richest men in the downstate is risking dying in a prison hospital to make a few bucks in the local meth trade. I got to be honest, this is making less and less sense to me."

"All I can tell you is what I know," she said. The line was quiet for a moment while she thought. "Is it worth anything?"

"The photo? I can't imagine."

"Anyway, bring it to me right away," she said. "As soon as you can. Maybe something will occur to me."

"Meantime, watch yourself."

"Believe me, I never stop."

Well, if Guy Beckett wasn't at home—any of his homes—maybe he was hiding out with friends. I drove into the little town of Herrin and booked us a new room at the Park Avenue Motel. It was nicer than the Pin Oak—anything was nicer than the Pin Oak—and I was promised that no spiders or other pests lived on the residence. I checked in and went up to the room and put our stuff away. I put the photo of Jim Hart on the bedside table. I didn't know why I was carrying it around, except that it was my first official clue, and I was proud of it. I put my clothes and socks and stuff in one dresser, Anci's in the other. There weren't any bugs or rodent nests in either drawer, and that picked me up a little. I began to feel confident about things again, so confident that I decided I needed taken down a peg or two. I phoned Susan.

"I thought you'd have given up by now," she said.

"A desire to keep breathing has convinced me to press on with this mess," I said. "Sorry to disappoint you."

"Believe me, that's impossible," she said. "What is it this time?"

"Beckett's women."

"You looking for a date?"

"More like information. I should have asked you the other day, but I left my private eye manual at home. Anyway, I thought you might be able to point me in the right direction."

"Then you're sniffing up the wrong tree," she said.

"I'm sniffing, but I think the tree is just fine," I said.

"That doesn't really make any sense."

We could worry about my private eye patter another time. I said, "I'm guessing that you kept pretty close tabs on Beckett. I think you like to keep on top of things, and one way to do that would be to know what Beckett was doing when he was doing it and who he was doing it with."

"That's a lot of knowing."

"Tell me I'm wrong, though. Go ahead, I dare you."

I could hear her grit her teeth. She said, "You ever think about doing this kind of thing professionally?"

"Not on your life."

"Mary-Kay Connor and Carla Shepherd," she said after a moment. "Guy had an ongoing thing with both of them."

"Had one going or has one?"

"Don't know, really. Given recent events, I've lost track. I'll tell you this, though, Guy Beckett would date a warm hole in a motel room pillow, but he wouldn't date it for long, so I guess they might be history by now."

"Any chance Temple knows about them?"

"If she does, she doesn't know about them from me."

"Saving them for later?"

She sighed. "Two things I've learned in life: always having an escape route, and always keep a silver bullet or two lying around."

"You're an interesting person."

"Buddy, it's a curse."

I scratched down the names and other info. I thanked her for the help, and she told me where to put my gratitude and hung up on me. Our relationship was as healthy as ever.

Before long, I was on my way to the tiny village of Johnston City. There used to be coal mines and cash in Johnston City, but when the mines went west, toward so-called cleaner coal and a union-free horizon, the cash packed up and followed. There'd been other stuff, too, nice stuff. A movie theater and hotels and fancy nightclubs. There'd been a park and a band shell and rows of fancy houses. The American dream, all that. Bit by bit, though, it'd all gone away. Up and down the country—whatever direction you're facing—the story's the same. And there's always some guy on the TV or in Washington to explain why those jobs aren't ever coming back or some such, as though the idea of paying folks a decent wage to make things were some kind of impossible fantasy, like turning the earth inside out. Meanwhile, these little towns watch themselves dwindle away to a few empty streets and a lot of confused faces. These days, fewer than four thousand folks call Johnston City home. The old movie palace is a whiskey den, the band shell collapsed twenty years ago, and the hottest businesses in town are the churches and the jails.

Mary-Kay Connor's house was a small cottage—modest but neatly kept—but her street had gone outlaw. The house next door was basically a ruin. Its windows had all been busted and its front door was missing. Maybe they'd hocked it. Some skeletal teens lingered on the front porch, sipping bottles of beer and seemingly not bothered by the odor of ammonia so heavy in the air. Meth house, I guess it was.

I went up to the door and knocked, and after a moment a young woman answered.

"Mary Connor?"

"Mary-Kay, please," she replied. "You Slim?"

I'm Slim. I followed her inside. The place was as neatly kept as your grandmama's Hummel collection, and with all the native domestic trappings, too: a big, ratty armchair from the Ford administration, some right-wing millionaire blowhard blathering away about "regular Americans" on the tube, and a pair of lanky tomcats sleeping near a gun case in the corner. A little boy, seven or eight maybe, was playing with some kid stuff on the floor by the TV. I looked at him a moment and thought I saw something familiar.

"Thank you for calling," she said, her eyes following mine. "The boy is mine. The cats, too. The guns belonged to my pop."

"FOP?" I asked, noticing the plaques on the wall.

"Was. Thirty years in the uniform. He was killed last year in a liquor store holdup. Wasn't even on duty. Kid shot him three times in the chest through a bottle of Johnny Walker Blue. He was the first cop to get killed in JC since 1965. Some days I'm almost glad he didn't live to see what's happened to this street. I guess you noticed the place next door."

"I noticed," I said. "No luck getting them run off?"

"You know how it is. Cops come by every couple of months and clear them out. Pretty soon they're back. Like shower mold. I've got to where I don't let Eric here play outside so much anymore. We'd like to move someplace where the air won't kill you, but this place is paid for."

She led me to the kitchen. It was nicer than Mays's. You

could have raised Hampshire hogs in a corner of it for a year, and it still would have been nicer than Mays's. It was bright and warm, and there was a big window overlooking a fenced yard with a tire swing hanging from a silver maple. Someone had set up a hay bale to take shots at with a bow and arrow. Mary-Kay put on coffee.

She said, "I got to tell you, I wasn't sure at first I wanted to talk to you, seeing as how you're working for Beckett's wife."

"I understand," I said. "But the truth is, if I'm working for anyone, I'm working for myself, though her father was the one who got the ball rolling downhill."

"I heard about what happened," she said. "I won't lie to you and say that I was tore up, exactly. That old man rode Guy pretty hard. Twenty-two years of treating him like a rented mule, making him feel worthless, unworthy of the princess. Made Guy just miserable, and I hated him for it. Still, I don't like to hear anyone come to violence like that."

"Me, neither," I said. "So why did you agree to see me?"

"Didn't know that I would, really. But I want Guy found and brought home, and I'm a big enough girl to not care who does it or why. Besides, you had a nice phone voice, and I figured I should at least get a look at you. And now that I see you, I see that you've got an honest face. You're kinda cute, too."

"Thanks."

"Except maybe them black eyes. You in some kind of accident?"

"Some kind. Do you mind telling me when was the last time you saw Beckett?"

"About a week ago. It was Eric's birthday. Guy took him to one of those pizza places with the singing animals."

"You met Guy through some kind of work?"

She nodded. "Through the land reclamation project, yeah."

"I didn't know he worked with them."

"Only from time to time," she said. "When Dwayne or the newspaper didn't have an assignment for him, or when he needed a little extra scratch. We were looking at a violator near Boskydell, a Big Eagle mine that was eating houses and road for miles around, and we brought on Guy to take pictures of it."

I didn't know the case, but I'd been around plenty like it. Mine subsidence, they call it. You're going about your business, easy as you please, then wake up one day to find your house sinking into the earth. It was such a common peril in southern Illinois that people bought insurance against it, like other folks insured against rising waters in a floodplain.

I said, "Let me ask you, what's your impression of this Beckett character? Everyone seems to have a different opinion of the man." It didn't seem charitable to add that everyone seemed to have a different bad opinion.

"Well, I don't know. I sometimes have different opinions of him, too. Let's just say I've had some long nights."

I took a chance. I said, "Love does funny things to people."

She looked at me. Her eyes were like stabs. "It sure does."

"You ever meet this Dwayne Mays?"

"Couple times. Didn't care for him much, I'll be honest." She looked up at me suddenly and made a gesture and frowned a little. "I keep speaking ill of the dead."

"It's okay."

"He was always dragging Guy into one kind of crusade

or another. A bit of a do-gooder, too, and not ashamed to let you know it. I'll be honest, I prefer my homilies in church. Anyway, you know the kind."

"I think I do."

"And this latest business . . ."

"The meth story?"

"That. I warned Guy that getting wrapped up in that would lead to nothing but misery, but he wouldn't listen."

"You don't happen to know of anyone making threats at him, do you?"

"Not directly, no. I think he tried to keep me out of it. He seemed worried and anxious, though, and that was before he took to carrying a gun around in his car."

"Well, that could be perceived as a sign of something."

"Yeah," she said. "That's the way I took it, too. This wasn't a peashooter, either. You ever seen one of these Taurus Raging Judge Magnum things?"

"Can't say as I have."

"I know it sounds like a gas station prophylactic, but let me tell you, it's enough gun to kill the Lincoln on Mount Rushmore. I don't like to think what would have happened if Guy ever fired it."

"When did he start carrying around the cannon?"

"Couple few days after he got into it with someone outside the house here. Car just pulled up out of nowhere, and Guy was out the door like a bat out of hell, and he and another guy were screaming at each other out there on the street. I'll tell you, I was plenty worried about it, but Guy told me it was all just a misunderstanding."

"A misunderstanding?"

"I know. Weak, right? But I guess that was something I

wanted to believe, because I believed it until all this other business went down."

I said, "Did you get a look at this person?"

She nodded. "Hell, I'm human. I admit I peeked. Guy told me to stay in the back of the house, but I squared Eric away in his room and came back and watched through the curtains. Big dude, with a head like a muck bucket and a beard. Any ideas?"

"Doesn't ring any gongs," I said. "Way I see it, there are a couple of possibilities here."

"Okay. Let's hear them."

I said, "Number one, Guy ran into trouble while researching this story with Dwayne Mays. His wife tells me he'd gotten tangled up with a guy who calls himself Jump Down."

"Jump Down? That's ridiculous," she said, interrupting.

"I think so, too, but that's his coal mine nickname."

"As in, he jumps down from high places?"

I shook my head. "More like he jumps down your throat. Anyway, he's one of the bad ones."

"You're starting to worry me here."

"I don't mean to," I said. "Means anything, my suspicion is that Guy is hiding, not hurt. Whoever killed Dwayne Mays and Luster left them out in the open for everyone and his Aunt Mabel to inspect their handiwork. The cops disagree, but I think someone is sending someone else a message. If someone did hurt Guy, I think they'd want us to know it."

She nodded at that without looking too convinced. She said, "You said there was another possibility."

"Maybe more than one. But the likeliest I can think of is that Guy's run away from something completely unrelated."

"Or someone."

"Or someone," I agreed. "You have any idea who or what that might have been?"

She knew, and she knew I knew. Or guessed that I knew. She didn't look too thrilled about it, either. "I got a pretty good idea."

"Is he eight years old and not allowed outside much these days?"

"You're a pretty good detective."

"Not really," I said. "He and Beckett share a resemblance."

"I guess he does. Why do they always look like the one you'd like to forget?"

And I couldn't help but think of Anci and how my bottomless love for her was forever mingled with painful reminders. "I honestly don't know," I said. "Except life is hard and hell is hot."

"Who said that?"

"My daddy."

"Sounds tough."

"Tough as old boots," I said. "And—much as it pains me to admit—a good man to have nearby when the chips were down. I once saw him stand down a herd of anti-union thugs with nothing more than rolled-up sleeves and grit."

"Folks aren't tough like that anymore, even the ones who are pretty strong. And Guy isn't even that. His mother was a tiger but his father was a squish, and Guy took after him. I love him, and I'd like to have him around, but he's the kind of guy you'd spend your whole life worrying about breaking."

"Let me ask you this: how'd he seem the last time you saw him?"

"That's what's been bothering me. Something was on his mind. You can always tell when Guy has something on his mind. But he wouldn't say what."

"You ever get any sense of what it might have been?"

"Don't know. I asked him. Pestered, really, but I couldn't squeeze it out of him," she said. "Let me tell you, that was uncharacteristic. This is a person who likes his chatter. A billboard keeps better secrets. My best guess is it had something to do with this story he was working on with Dwayne. Or maybe it was these idiots he's fallen in with."

"What idiots?"

"A group of liberal wackos he'd hooked up, probably to chase skirts. They call themselves the Friends of Crab Orchard, I think, but as far as I can tell they're just a bunch of new age fruitcakes who want a little attention."

That rang a distant bell. And then I remembered: Susan had mentioned them. Beckett's environmental club. "You ever run into any of them?"

"The only way I'd do that is with the Ford," she said. She must have seen my raised eyebrows. "Safe to say I don't favor their view of the world."

"I guess not," I said. "Any idea who was in the group, besides Guy?"

"Nope."

"He never mentioned any of them?"

"He never did," she said. She shrugged her shoulders. "Well, Tony, I guess."

"That sounds like a person to me," I said. "Tony who?"

"Pelzer. Friend of Guy's from way back." She stabbed her palm twice with a forefinger. "Ass. Hole. But Guy thought he was a hoot. Tony used to do some private security work. At least that's what he called it. Frankly, Tony's office was out of his place at Bluegill Point, and there wasn't much to it other than the occasional strong-arm job or mall security gig. But all of a sudden Guy had him around more and more, and he even followed Guy into this group of his. Well, that didn't register. Tony Pelzer thinks the EPA ought to be turned into an empty office suite. I asked Guy if he was paying Tony to keep an eye on him. Bodyguard him, I mean, but he got angry and went off on a rant about what a great friend Tony was, which I took to mean that Tony was soaking him good." She rolled her eyes. "Why do so many men have terrible friends?"

"I guess I don't know," I said. "Sympathy, maybe?"

She looked at me with pity. "Oh, honey."

"Okay, maybe not," I said. "You say Pelzer is out at Bluegill Point?"

"Round those parts, yeah."

"Everything's happening out at the lake," I said.

"Well, the lake's where things happen."

I got up and thanked her for her time and the coffee, and she walked me to the door. Outside, the boys were still lingering on the front porch. One of them was flipping around a butterfly knife.

"Hey, one last thing," Mary-Kay said as I made my way down the steps. "When you find Beckett, would you deliver a message for me?"

"Sure, anything."

"Tell him there's more to life than running away."

That depended on who or what was doing the chasing, I thought but didn't say. I walked back to the truck, thinking of all the people in my life who could stand to hear that same message.

NINE

Tony Pelzer was in the book. I phoned and left a message asking him to call me back as soon as possible. I didn't want him to think it was a sales call or some other foolishness, so I mentioned Guy Beckett's name. If he failed to call back after that, I figured that'd tell me something. What, I couldn't yet guess. Next, I called Peggy. She had a free hour between 12:30 and 1:30, and that's what time it was. She wasn't as gruff as we'd left it before, but she wasn't exactly friendly, either.

She said, "Well, at least you're not dead yet."

"There's that."

"You're not, are you?"

"I don't think so," I said. "But I did shoot someone with a beanbag today."

"Come again?"

"Nothing," I said. "How's Anci?"

"Checked in on her just a few minutes ago over lunch," she said. "She wants you to know that she harbors a grievous dislike for John Knowles, but she's otherwise fine."

"Who?"

"The *Separate Peace* guy," Peggy said. "The kids are reading it this year, and Anci's not the least bit happy about it."

"I'll have a chat with her," I said, but secretly I was proud. Like all good-hearted young people, I'd hated *A Separate Peace*, too. "And how about you?"

"Me? I'm nervous as the sacrificial goat at the GOP convention."

"Me, too."

"Not helping matters is knowing that, somewhere out there, Jeep Mabry . . ."

"Now that I think of it, maybe we should be careful what we say on the open line," I said, interrupting her.

"What?"

"It's something you hear people say, you watch enough television thrillers."

"You're kidding?"

"Only half," I said, but maybe it was less than that. "And I'd say Jeep is maybe preferable to Jump Down or one of his gang sniffing around. Or Round-Face."

"Assuming he or they have anything to do with it in the first place."

"Assuming that, yes."

"I got to tell you, darling, the more I sit with it, the more the whole thing sounds like a stretch to me."

"Me, too," I said. "Someone killed Dwayne Mays, and I don't think what happened to Matthew Luster was a suicide, but it does feel like we're missing a pretty big piece of the pie here somewhere."

"We? Who's this 'we' you speak of, white man?"

"Okay, okay. Fair enough. You're not ready yet to join our firm."

"Speaking of firm."

"That's one of my favorite benefits, too."

"That and a full pension."

"Hopefully, anyway. See you tonight?"

That was the question I'd been waiting to ask. Nervously, too, like that goat.

Peggy thought about it for a moment and then said, "I'll

bring Anci around after work, see what we can work out for dinner that doesn't involve you two idiots eating Velveeta over scrambled eggs."

"All right."

"Someone's got to look after you, after all."

"They sure do."

"It's just no good leaving you to your own devices."

"It's just really not."

"I love you, stupid."

"I love you," I said. "Should I call you a name now, too?"

"Not unless you want to wake up looking straight up at the bottom of your own feet. How about just call me beautiful?"

"You are that."

"Well, I already knew it."

There was a moment of silence on the line. Then Peggy said, "Okay, maybe we can stop acting like blushing teenagers now."

"That would be a relief. I had a hard enough time the first time around."

"Me, too. And I'm not sure I ever learned my lesson. Probably I didn't. Where are you off to now, Sherlock?"

"Believe me, you don't want to know," I said.

"Believe me," she said, "you're right."

Indian Vale was along the way to my next stop, so I ducked in to check on the house. I had to feed the animals, one, but I also wanted to lay eyes on it again, even if we'd only been away a few hours. Everything seemed fine at first. The clouds had pushed off, and the sun had come out, and the Vale was bright and clear in the cool air. The wind pushed leaves around in the yard to swirl and rattle like they do. I parked the truck and walked around the house, and it took me a while to realize that someone had broken in.

It took me a while because they were good. They were awfully damn good. There was a measured calmness and professionalism about the thing that I found both terrifying and impressive. They hadn't kicked down the door or smashed a window. They hadn't sawed a creep-shaped hole in the outer wall and gone in that way. The southward-facing kitchen window had always had a loose lock, and someone had discovered it and prized it open and gone in, leaving behind just the barest hints of chipped windowpane. I didn't follow suit. I went back around front and unlocked the door with my key and went inside to look around. Everything was perfectly still, and nothing seemed the least out of place, and let me tell you, that was disconcerting as hell.

After a while, I went upstairs and found the cats. Usually we were at odds, but for a change they seemed happy to see me, so I pet them and put down food and water before realizing that I wouldn't be able to leave them to their own devices like that, even for a few hours at a time, as I'd been planning. I felt ashamed of myself and my species, and not for the last time, either. I called a vet's office in Marion that also did boarding, then put the cats in their boxes and drove them into town, where I dropped them off and generally began to feel better about my human virtues. Funny how little it takes.

On my way back through, I had an idea. I returned to the Vale and went inside and upstairs to Anci's room. I brought down her old computer and put it on a table in the living room, facing the front of the house. Jeep had showed me a program once that you could download to turn your computer into a surveillance camera—a kind of motion-activated thing—and I used it now to do just that. I opened the lid and switched on the little camera and set it to record. I put a big vase on one side of the computer and a framed photograph on the other side, hoping to camouflage it somewhat. It wasn't a great job, to say the least, but maybe it would do.

After that, I dialed Jeep Mabry's number and told his voicemail about the break-in. Then I went back to where all my troubles had started.

When I rolled into Coulterville, the Knight Hawk's tipple was catching the sunlight and burning like a beacon. The mine's flags were out and whipping around noisily in the air, and the afternoon shift-horn blasted over the little town and echoed around and up the wooded slopes and into space. I felt a little like a knight of old, ready to storm some mysterious citadel. I decided I was hungry.

I stopped for a bite of lunch at the town's only cafeteria. As I was walking in, an old man with bright blond hair was coming out. He was a sight, too—dressed fancy, as though for a funeral he was happy to attend, with a wide-brimmed fedora on his head. A side of beef in an orange ball cap sneered at me as he and the old man made their way toward one of those great old Town Cars that ought to have their own zip codes. The boy opened the back door, and the old man smiled thinly at me and swiped a finger across the tip of his nose twice. He climbed inside, and after a moment they drove away. I didn't know what in the hell that was all about, so I went in for my chili.

Inside was crowded, and the service was slow—more

chatty than slow, really—but the chili was pretty good, and I ate a big bowl with crackers and generous splashes of hot sauce and washed it down with coffee and rumor. Luster wasn't even in the ground yet, but word was already swirling about the impending sale of the mine. Most of it was idle talk, but when I heard Roy Galligan mentioned as the most likely buyer, I did sit up and take note. Then some dipshit said he'd heard a helicopter full of Chinese businessmen had landed at the mine, intent on inspecting a prospective investment, and I knew we'd arrived at the end of useful information.

"Quite a day in here," the old man at the cash register said. I recognized him as a fire boss I'd worked with years ago without ever really getting to know. "Sorry about your wait."

"It's nothing," I said.

"Bit of a fuss, what with old man Galligan stopping in."

"That was him? The old coot with the blond hair?"

"That was him," he said. "Kinda think he's sniffing around that mine over yonder, given the current circumstances. You up to that Knight Hawk mine, aren't you?"

I said, "I'm up to that Knight Hawk."

"Few years now, too, I recall."

"Four this winter," I said.

He nodded. "I was there twenty-five, myself. You might not remember me. They called me Sappy back then."

"Of course I remember you, Sappy," I said. "Slim."

We shook hands.

"I remember."

"We lie like helium," I said, and he laughed.

"We really do," he said. "I do remember you some now,

though. Besides just your face, I mean. I remember some of the guys making a fuss about your daddy."

"Sure."

"I guess you heard about Luster."

"I heard about it."

He nodded. He had a big burn scar on the left side of his face. Not a pretty sight. The skin was pink and raw and had that pearlescent shine that burned flesh gets. His hair was cropped short—on the burned side, it looked a little like scorched grass—and his left eye was rheumy and a slightly different shade of blue than the other. His left ear was a knot of flesh, like puckered lips, and I noticed him turning his right toward conversation to make up for whatever hearing he'd lost.

"It's all anyone's talking about in here."

"I bet."

"I'll be honest, I ain't shed much tears over it. I guess you noticed my face."

"I barely noticed," I said.

"Oh, people always feel a need to lie about it, but I don't take offense," he said. "Not anymore, anyway. Folks see something like that, they look. You can't hardly blame them."

I didn't know what to say, so I said, "That's a good attitude to have about it."

He shrugged. "It wasn't always like that. Few years back, when it happened, I was mad as hell. Boy, was I mad. Took me a couple years to get over it, too. Hard years. Lost my wife. Started drinking more than was wise. Fell out with my kids. Like that."

"What happened?" I asked, because I could tell he wanted me to.

"Fire on the line. Coal fire. Somehow, we had combustion on the conveyor right off the longwall pan. So the crew called me and my team in, and we evacuated the area and switched on the fire suppressors, and guess what happened."

"I'm thinking nothing."

"Damn things were bust. Or never worked in the first place. Never found out. New units, too. Luster had taken out the old ones and put in these things. Gave the contract to a personal friend. The old ones worked fine. Those new things were just for show, I guess. You could have picked me off the floor. You ever been in a fire down there?"

"I never have."

He said, "Well, don't. The walls close in and the smoke fills everything so fast you don't have time to shit your pants or pray. Coal smoke, too, so this is the real deal. It's like the world just goes away. Everybody started screaming and running this way and that. I gathered the remainder of my team, and we tried to do it old school, with hoses. They kept them in a metal cabinet right there off the face. They were new, too, replaced at the same time as the suppressors and by the same outfit, and we grabbed those, and guess what happened then."

"I can't even begin to."

"Couplings didn't match. They had the one spigot and the one hose, and they didn't fit. We kept trying to screw them together—probably a little longer than good sense dictated, but under those conditions you don't really trust what you're seeing. Time we figured out what was going on, the fire was fully out of control, and I'd lost three men and got this new face. When it was all over, they dumped the whole thing on me. I tried to convince them what had happened, but someone had to take the fall, and in the end they went after the guy with the most empty space in his pockets. Luster went right along with it, too. For a while, I crossed the road to work at a Galligan outfit, but his shop made Luster's look almost civilized when it came to safety. So I lost my job. Both jobs. I lost my family. I had my dark night and found the Lord, and the Lord told me I liked the chili business better than the coal mine business anyway, and here I am today. Listen, Slim, I try to be a good man and a better Christian. I pray every day and ask for guidance, and I try to forgive my enemies and even love them a little, like the Book tells us to, but I confess that when I heard what happened to Matthew J. Luster my dick got a little hard."

Half an hour later, I arrived at the Knight Hawk. It was still there, and the lot was full of the day shift. No *For Sale* signs or Chinese investors anywhere in sight. No helicopters. You could have knocked me over with a blown kiss. I crossed the colliery and checked in at the main office. Billy Bear was back from his daughter's Rock Island wedding, and he heard my voice and rumbled out to see me.

"Hey, Slim. I guess you heard."

"Even the chili guy up the road knows about it."

"Sappy?" he said. He waved a hand at me. "Sappy hears everything. Even with just the one ear. Word is, you're mixed up in it somehow, and I tell you what, I can't have it. Consider yourself on leave until further notice."

"That so?"

"As in, not currently an employee at this coal mine."

"Not an employee?"

"Not until further notice. Least until I'm satisfied no trouble's going to follow you down in that hole."

I said, "In that case, as a private citizen I want to tell you that you can go fuck yourself, Bear."

We nodded at each other. I started out, then turned back around and asked, "By the way, how was your daughter's wedding?"

He shrugged, "Beautiful. I wept like a baby."

I nodded at him again and went out. I walked across to the equipment locker, picked up a helmet, and went down into the mine. Bear could come get me, if he wanted. Some reason, the drop felt longer than I remembered, and the blackness blacker. I'd only been away for a couple of days, and already I was starting to forget what it was like. I walked to the eastern-most work section and searched around, but he wasn't there and no one knew where he was or wouldn't say. Probably the latter. I crossed back to the other side and looked some more until after a while I found Jump Down hanging around and smoking grass with his crew near the ventilation brattices. He was a pale thing, Jump, tall and as lean as a skinned rabbit, a six-foot-eight redneck shitweed. He had a long face, with cavernous cheeks and a shaved head and what I took to be an expensive set of false teeth bought after his originals had been eaten away by meth-induced bruxism and hyposalivation. Horrible thing they called meth mouth.

As I approached, he spied me, and his eyes brightened, and he used his elbows to press himself off the brattices. His boys shuffled nervously, and one of them starting pacing like a caged gorilla, ready for the door to open, but Jump just showed me his perfect teeth, friendly as you please, and he and they winked at me in the sodium spots screwed to the ribs of the mine.

He said, "Hey, hey, there he is."

An hour later, the two of us were sitting at a back table at a little place up the road called Steamy's. Jump Down sucked the glass neck of a light beer. I had coffee. I made the mistake of taking the keys out of my pocket and putting them on the table. No one at the mine cared that we'd left to hit a bar. I was officially on leave until further notice. No one told Jump Down where to go or what to do, not the bosses or the ghost of Matt Luster. We were quite a pair.

It was early yet, but Steamy's was crowded and noisy. As usual, the ladies were dressed up and the guys were dressed down. Most of these good old boys, the greatest effort they'd put out was scraping off whatever was clinging to the bottom of their boots and making sure the can of chew in their back pocket was still a nice circle. A haze of cigarette smoke floated above the layer of ball caps and heavily sprayed do's. You weren't supposed to be able to light up in bars in Illinois anymore, but it was a rule most of these backwoods places just ignored, and it's a wonder all that hairspray didn't combust and burn the place to the ground.

Jump Down said, "I've been coming to this dump since I was a kid, you know? My old man used to bring me. I'd sit on the floor, by his stool, with my back against the bar, and wait for him to finish his shot. In the day, there was a kind of whorehouse in the back room."

"A whorehouse?"

"Where whores work," he explained.

"I know what it is," I said. "I never heard about it, is all."

"I don't think that's what they called it, but that's what it was. Cash for pussy, it's a whorehouse. Anyway, the old man would leave me with Steamy, back when Steamy was alive, and go back and bang some cunt, and then he and she'd come out and she'd give me some kind of little gift—candy or spare change or whatever she had—and we'd head on home to Mom. One time, though, she didn't have anything. I pestered her, and she ended up giving me a condom. Bright green. I guess she thought I'd blow it up and play with it like a balloon. I don't know what she thought. Anyway, the old man didn't notice what she'd done, and when we got home I went into the kitchen with mom and started playing with that green condom, right there in front of her, and that was pretty much the longest night of my life."

"Sad story."

"It's not sad. It's not anything. It's just how it was." He leaned against the back legs of his chair. "I knew you'd be coming to see me, man. Knew it was just a matter of time. Only question is, what you think coming to see me will get you."

"A truce," I said.

He just stared at me.

I said, "For me and my family."

"You got a family?"

"Yeah."

"A kid?"

"A daughter. Beautiful. Smart as a whip, too. But as long as I'm tied up in this, she's tied up in it. I got a feeling that everyone involved in this lovely mess thinks I know more than I do. And now I've had to leave my home like a fugitive, my woman is watching my every move like a Catholic school sister ready with her ruler, and I've basically been fired from my job. And all that in three days. I'll tell you, I've had better stretches."

"Things can always get worse. Ain't that what they say?"

"It's one thing they say. But here's what I want: you call off your boys. I don't care what you do or what your deal down there is in the Knight Hawk. I don't care if you're tied up in the Mays killing or with this business with Luster or Galligan."

He smiled at me, but it wasn't a pleasant look, and I suddenly felt my asshole trying to escape into my body. The boy had cooked enough shit, or done enough of it his own self, that he'd fried his circuits. He had a twitchy feel about him, and when he talked his eyes bulged and his lips overworked his words, like they had too much energy, and his mouth was doing its part to use some of it up.

"Galligan?" he said. "What's this about Galligan?"

I shrugged and said, "Idle talk, mostly. Just something I've heard on the vine. But the main thing is, I don't care. That's what I want you to walk out of here with. If nothing else, that. You could be mixed up with the ghost of the czar, or Shoeless Joe, and it'd still make me no never mind whatsoever."

"What outfit does Shoeless Joe work at, man?"

"Never mind."

"Wait, you think Mays was working on something to do with business inside the Hawk?"

I said, "I've heard that's one possibility, yes."

"Well you, or whoever you heard it from, is wrong."

"They are?"

He sniffed. His eyes wobbled slightly in his head, like out-of-tune television screens. "Yeah. I mean, don't get me wrong," he said. "I think that's what he might have been up to at first. He was sniffing around for weeks, man. Around the edges. Tell the truth, I thought someone was going to have to do something about it, but then all of a sudden he changed course."

"Changed course? Changed course to what?"

"Someone hit the Hawk's ammonia tank at the cold-storage shed."

"And for some reason Mays and Beckett thought it wasn't you or your crew?"

Jump Down shook his head. "I don't have a crew, man, and I don't cook or sell product."

"Look, I know you're being careful in what you say, but I'm not wearing a wire."

"I don't have a crew, man, and I don't cook or sell product."

"Fine," I said. "Hypothetically."

Jump looked at me for a long moment and then finally nodded and said, "You don't shit where you eat. Hypothetically. And you don't let anyone *else* shit where you eat, either. So there's that. Let's just say that no one who might be engaged in that activity at the Knight Hawk would be so goddamn stupid as to tap the Hawk's tanks, and if someone *was* that stupid they'd either get made un-stupid or dead real quick."

"Okay."

"Also, the tank."

"What about it?"

"The ammonia tank. It's a sixty-one-hundred-gallon capacity," he said. "You've seen it. That's a lot of cookie dough."

"More than you . . . than some hypothetical someone might reasonably need?"

"More than that, yeah. Enough to take the entire down-state on one hell of a ride."

"So someone with big ambitions," I said.

"Or someone who doesn't know what the fuck he's doing," he said. "Like I say, that's a lot of ingredient. You'd need a truck and bobtail to tap it, and you'd need a tank to store it in, and a thing like that will attract attention, Slim. So I hear anyway."

"I'm not wearing a wire."

"I don't care," he said. "You're thinking Galligan?"

I didn't know yet. I didn't know yet for sure, but a picture was beginning to take shape, too cloudy yet to bring into focus, but it was there and nagging at the darkest parts of my waking mind. I had the Mays and Luster murders and Beckett's disappearance and Round-Face and Temple Luster Beckett and Tony Pelzer and Roy Galligan. And I had the lake, Crab Orchard Lake, and a group called Friends of Crab Orchard that Guy Beckett and Pelzer had apparently joined to chase tail. I put some money on the table and rose to go. Jump Down smiled and raised his drink and winked again at me, not as meanly this time.

"I can't go home again yet," I said, to no one in particular, and saying the words hurt like a kick in the nuts. I looked at the boy. I wasn't any better disposed to him than before, but I have to admit to being surprised that it hadn't all ended in gunfire and tears. I asked, "By the way, why in the hell did you ever agree to sit here talking to me?"

He smiled and said, "I used to have a daughter, too."

TEN

I had a couple hours left in the day. I dialed Jeep Mabry and learned that Peggy and Anci had left school on time and without fuss. Since then he'd gotten the stink-eye from a crow a couple of times, but that was the extent of the day's activity. I thanked him for the hundredth time and received only an irritated grunt in reply. He was off to his shift at the King Coal. I dialed Peggy next but ended up leaving a message saying I'd come to the hotel as soon as my errands permitted. Then I dialed Tony Pelzer's number again. Nothing. That nothing was getting a bit nettlesome, I confess.

Then I drove back out to the Crab Orchard preserve. There are three manmade lakes out there, and Devil's Kitchen is one of them. It covers almost eight hundred acres, is ninety feet deep at its deepest point, and has earned the fealty of local fisherman for some of the best bluegill and trout fishing in the state. Pelzer's place was just outside the park near Devil's Kitchen, north a bit of the preserve, in a tiny nothing of a place called Bluegill Point. I stopped in at a shade-tree bait store for a pack of smokes and some snacks, just in case it turned out I was in for a wait.

And wait I did, but nothing came of it. I knocked on the door but no one answered, and I hung around for a while but no one ever showed up. A sign in the yard said *Pelzer Security*. A beat-up red and black GMC van sat in the driveway, its crumpled hood secured with bright yellow bungee cord and a concrete block, but it didn't go anywhere, either.

It didn't look like it could go anywhere if you hitched it to a team of elephants. When I finally grew bored of listening to the honking of the local geese, I fired up the truck and headed home, or whatever was passing for home that night.

When I got back to the Park Avenue and went upstairs to the room, I found Anci and Peggy arguing over one of Anci's video games. Scary thing, set on a zombie island. I didn't like her playing it, but this was one of those battles I ended up giving ground on. You do that sometimes to keep the peace, and you do it sometimes because it's okay for a kid to win every now and again, but mostly you do it out of sheer exhaustion. Anyway, the two of them had attached the console to the hotel room TV, and I was in the bathroom over the sink with the water running and a brush in my mouth when I figured out what that meant.

I swung back into the bedroom and said to Peggy, "You went to the Vale."

She glanced up at me briefly over her remote control and then looked back at the set.

"You'll have to take that thing out of your mouth and rinse, darling, because otherwise it sounds like you're drowning in mashed potatoes."

I went and rinsed and came back and said it again.

"That's better."

"Stop avoiding the subject."

"Anci needed some things," Peggy said. "Necessary things. You only packed her one pair of shoes, for one."

"We were in a bit of rush, I recall."

"She also needed something to keep her from going bananas while her daddy runs around playing Philip Marlowe."

"It's true, I do," Anci said. She was good enough to kick zombie butt and have a conversation without missing a beat.

"I'll tell you," I said, "I'm not happy about this. You might have run into trouble."

"And I'm a big girl."

"Me, too," said Anci.

My nerves were fried, and I wanted to holler at both of them, but instead I sat on the edge of the other bed and watched them kill zombies for a while. They were pretty good at it, though I noticed Anci saving Peggy's bacon on more than a couple of occasions. When they were done, we walked up into town and had dinner at a little café that probably didn't know it was catering to three people on the lam from meth pirates. Despite what should have been our bad nerves, we had an appetite. Peggy ate a giant salad, and Anci and I had burgers so big they nearly filled our plates. We ate without talking much and then I paid our check and we went back out onto the street.

It was a quiet night in town. I guess every night in that town was quiet, but that one was almost unseemly in its silence. Up the sidewalk, two guys were loading a television as big as a movie screen into the bed of a pickup truck, and the streetlamps were flickering and buzzing. A black sedan moved slowly up the street, turned right against the red light, and disappeared around the corner. The wind pushed around a few candy bar wrappers. That was pretty much the extent of the nightlife. The evening had come on cool, so Anci slipped on her pink gloves, and Peggy shrugged deeper into her jacket. I started wishing I had a hat or a fur-lined turban or something to bottle in the heat.

Peggy and I were walking side by side, Anci just a pace

or two behind us but keeping up, because she was a long-legged critter like her old man.

Peggy said, "I've been thinking. You two really should come stay at my place for a while. You'd be a hell of a lot more comfortable. Anci could have her own room. And frankly, that hotel is kinda low-rung."

"It's better than the last place," I said.

"Hard to believe."

"It's better than the last place," Anci said.

I said, "I appreciate the offer, but anywhere I go is likely to become a target. I think it's probably safe to take Anci, though."

I knew that would cause a ruckus, and it did. Anci stopped in her tracks. We were next to a storefront Tae Kwon Do school, but the idiot posing on the poster in the window wasn't nearly as scary as my twelve-year-old. She gave me a look that would have frozen the balls off a bronze statue of Charles Manson and folded her arms across her chest. "Only if you're going to haul me off, kicking and screaming," she said.

"Not a debate," I said.

"What does that mean? You don't just get to decide what's a debate and what's not."

"The hell I don't. I'm your father."

"Fine, and I'm your daughter. We're related. What's that got to do with anything?"

We kept at it for another moment, arguing on the sidewalk, when another car came by. For an instant, I almost didn't pay it any mind—it was just a car on the street—but then I recognized it as the black sedan from before. He was circling the block again, and his windows were tinted so black you couldn't see inside the cabin. As he passed us, he slowed way down, then suddenly sped up again a little as he went by—but not before I noticed the Knight Hawk parking sticker on his bumper, and then it hit me like a ton of frozen bricks.

"Oh, Sam Hell," I said aloud. "My keys."

Peggy was confused. "Your what?"

"My keys. I put them on the table. At Steamy's. It had my hotel key on the chain with the name of the hotel. That sneaky little motherfucker."

"Darling, I don't know what you're saying."

The black sedan slid up the block and again neared the corner. But this time, instead of rounding it, he pulled to the curb and stopped. The brake lights flashed bright red and died.

I turned to Peggy. "Take Anci, right now, and run back to the café."

"Slim . . ."

"Goddamn it, do it now."

Everything froze for one awful instant, and then everything jumped up like a terrified cat and screamed. Peggy grabbed Anci by the arm. She was scared and did it too hard, and Anci cried out a little and fell. The doors of the sedan flew open and two dudes got out, one from either side. One was a fat guy with a beard and a ball cap. His head was like a muck bucket, and I wondered whether he was the man Mary-Kay Connor had seen arguing with Guy Beckett that day in Johnston City. The other was a thin guy in a denim jacket. They were killers. You could tell it by looking at them. That, and the fact that they were both holding guns down by their legs. The fat guy skirted the back of the sedan and stepped up on the sidewalk to join his buddy, and the two of them came toward me in a fast walk. They walked shoulder to shoulder, with just a bit of room between them, in perfect lockstep, and generally gave off an impression of having worked together on this kind of project before.

For just a second, my feverish brain grabbed hold of some distant idea about chivalry—or maybe it was something I'd picked up watching late-night westerns—and I imagined they might wait for Anci and Peggy to round the corner before opening fire. Then the thin dude raised his pistol and snapped off three quick rounds. So much for Gary Cooper. The sound of the little automatic was a light pop, like a bottle of flat champagne. I felt one of the bullets rip the air beside my head. The others went wild, one of them blowing out the window of the Tae Kwon Do school. Peggy screamed, and when I looked back Anci was struggling to drag her into a doorway and out of sight. That was some kid.

They came at us. I jumped and hit the curb and street with my shoulder and rolled and came up behind the pickup truck. The dudes with the TV dropped it and ran in two directions, and the big set hit the ground flat-faced and broke with a sound like a cannon shot. Bullets hit the truck and there was a flash of light that blinded me for a second or two. The fat guy fired, and the truck's passenger-side mirror left its post and went whirling down the street. The front windshield exploded, and then the back, showering me with glass. Suddenly, the truck lurched forward on one side, and I realized that one of them had shot out the right front tire.

"You're wasting ammo, dipshit," I heard the thin guy say.

"Well, it's mine to waste, cock-knocker."

"Don't make me take that thing from you."

"I'd like to see you try. Go on."

"Oh, shut up."

It was one thing to be murdered on the street. It was another thing to be murdered by an old married couple. That didn't sit right at all. Lots of things didn't sit right. These bastards had fired bullets at my daughter. I should have been frightened—and I was—but my fear had been overtaken by an anger like a whirlwind. I wanted to kill them both and drink their blood. Unfortunately for me, the only thing I had on me was a pocketknife, and against firearms that wasn't much. I inspected the pickup truck, and found it to be the only one in southern Illinois with an empty gun rack.

I could feel them coming at me, still fast, from either side of the truck. Their plan was to arrive at the truck bed at the same instant and catch me between them, but the fat guy stepped on something and fell, and the thin guy got a step or two ahead of him. I seized the moment. I pushed left, toward the street side, and met the thin guy head-on. I'd timed it well, and I managed to catch him with his right foot in mid-step, so he was slightly off-balance. His left leg was forward and presenting itself as a target, so I kicked hard at the knee and got lucky. The bone cracked with a sound like wet corn snapping and went the wrong way. Some of it broke through the fabric of his pants. The dude dropped his gun and moaned and went down on his good leg. He reached for his piece, desperate, but I kneed him in the face and lunged for it too and was just a hair quicker.

He looked up at me and said quietly, "Goddamn."

I staggered a half step past him. I meant to shoot him in the shoulder, put him down that way, but he twisted his body at the last moment and tried to stand up. The bullet hit him in the side of the head, and his brains shot out and splattered against the side of the truck.

The fat guy came around the bed and tailgate, stepping over the busted TV. He saw what had happened, roared a curse at me, and fired off twice, hitting the buildings across the street. He had a bigger gun, and the sound of it echoed around the little downtown. We were on either side of the truck now. I fired back but missed. I'd shot a gun a little, of course—I'm a son of the country, after all—but I'm not much of a marksman, and I missed the fat guy badly and ended up shooting the Tae Kwon Do champion in the head.

"Motherfucker," fat dude said. He got impatient and charged. Thinking to bull-rush me, I guess. I backpedaled fast and lost my footing in the other dude's blood and brains and went over hard on my tailbone. The fat boy loomed over and raised his gun.

"Motherfucker," he said again. He couldn't think of anything else, maybe. He raised the gun and the gun jerked and there was an eruption like a belch of hellfire and some smoke. But then something weird happened: the fat guy's head blew right off his neck and jumped into the truck bed with a hollow metal bang. The rest of him slumped, smoking, onto the street. Two men down.

I looked up to find Jeep Mabry standing there with a sawed-off. He said, "I'm thinking now that coming to look in on you was the right call." Or words to that effect.

I started puking my guts out, and Peggy kept screaming, and those were the last sounds I heard for a while.

The cop who took us to the station was named Willard. He was a stump of a guy with a flat nose and some unfortunate pattern baldness that maybe didn't make him the happiest camper in the world. He arrested me and Jeep, read us our rights, cuffed us, and drove us to the station house, where he put us in separate interrogation rooms. I asked to see Anci and Peggy, and was told I couldn't, not yet, but that they were okay, badly shaken up but intact. No injuries. They'd seen a medic, and they were together. Then he went away again and left me for about an hour. I sat there twiddling my thumbs and trying not to think too much about the man I'd killed. I didn't even know his name or his story. I didn't know whether he'd been paid to do what he tried to do, or whether he did it because he liked it or what. Came down to it, I guess I felt okay about what I'd done. He'd tried to hurt my family, after all. But you were never going to love a thing like that, at least a healthy person wasn't.

After a while, some cops came in: Willard and Ben Wince and one of the state cops I'd seen before at Luster's house. I stood up, and Willard raised a hand and said, "Don't do that, please. I ain't a priest, and this ain't church. You don't have to stand up when I come in a room. Besides, it makes me nervous."

He and the others sat. I sat back down.

I said, "I'm a little nervous myself."

"I would be, too. You just blew a man's brains out on the streets of my fair city, and that's nothing to be too relaxed about."

"They shot first," I pointed out. "And I'm guessing that if you check their histories you might find a story of violent crimes and other nefarious doings."

Wince grunted and Willard showed his teeth. He said, "That we did. And that they had, but that don't exactly clear the slate. Dead bodies have a way of complicating matters. You want to tell me your story? I already got a pretty good one from your boy in the other room."

I shook my head.

Willard said, "No? You don't think I did?"

"Not unless you cut his tongue out and used it to write a story yourselves," I said. "I don't mean to make a fuss. I know how this looks, and I'll cooperate fully, but this was a case of self-defense, pure and simple. Those bastards shot at my daughter. You worked some kind of miracle, brought them back to life, I'd shoot them again right here. Twice."

Willard sucked that around for a moment. His eyes lost their hard glint and he traced a shape on the tabletop with a finger.

"Well, there is that," he said. "The fact that the ladies were there goes a long way to corroborate your story. Plus those guys with the TV."

"I felt bad about that. It looked like a pretty fancy setup."

Willard ignored that. "I'm thinking only a stone lunatic would drag his kid into a firefight like that."

"Thanks."

"I didn't say you weren't one, though. Let's not get too far ahead of ourselves here."

"Less thanks."

He thought some more and finally shrugged. "Again, that isn't going to open any cell doors, but I admit there's a few points here in your favor. Your girlfriend tells it that they just came out of nowhere, and started shooting up the place."

"That's pretty much it."

"You ever seen either of them before?"

I said, "I've been trying to place them. One of them might match a description given me by one of Guy Beckett's girlfriends. There was a Knight Hawk parking pass on the car, but I guess the car might belong to someone else. I don't know who the dead guy was, but I don't think he worked at the Hawk."

"So you're thinking this has something to do with the Beckett disappearance?"

"I'm thinking it's likely. I've fallen behind a bit on some bills lately, but I don't think I'm behind enough for anyone to resort to this kind of thing."

Willard nodded. "Okay. Let me ask you this then. And I caution you to think carefully before answering."

"I'll try."

"Any chance you get tangled up with a guy named Clay Reeves earlier today?"

"Jump Down?"

"I believe that's the name he goes by, yeah. Kinda silly, you ask me."

"A little."

"What is it with you guys and those nicknames, anyway?" Willard said. "I go to the hospital, ain't everybody calling someone 'Trauma Ward' or 'Crash Cart' or any such foolishness."

"'Crash Cart'd be a pretty good nickname."

"Now you're just trying my patience."

I said, "Hell, I don't know what it is. Something in the air down there makes people act like dummies, maybe. I'm not a psychologist or a scientist. All I know is, once a miner gets a nickname, it sticks with him . . ."

"Or her," Wince said.

Willard looked at him.

"You running for office?"

"As it happens," Wince said. "Year from now. But this thing, my sister's a miner."

"Or her," I said, nodding at Wince, "It sticks with him or her pretty much forever. I've known people who basically stopped responding to their given names in favor of their mine names. A lot of them even have them on their gravestones."

"Now that's deep."

"Sure is."

The state cop said, "This is a waste of time."

This was a young guy with carefully combed hair and a face like a carnival prize. His shirt was tucked in, and his tie had a knot as tight as a hooker's fist, so I gathered he was a pretty fancy cop. Willard didn't appear to think much of him, either.

He said, "You got somewhere else to be?"

"As a matter of fact . . ."

Willard groaned and rubbed his face and said, "I recall correctly, you're at our disposal for the duration, Dave, so please, dispose."

Dave disposed. He sat there like an angry bump. Wince chuckled.

Willard said to me, "Jump Down."

"I saw him earlier today at the Knight Hawk. We had a little chat over beer and coffee. He drank the beer. Surprisingly friendly, he was, actually. He told me the story of the green condom, and I tried to talk him out of killing me and my family."

"I don't known about any green rubber, but it looks like he didn't really take the rest of it to heart."

"Looks that way, yes."

"When'd you leave him?"

"About three this afternoon. Little earlier maybe. We were at Steamy's."

"Anything come of it? Anything physical, I mean."

I shook my head. "Not even hard words. I'll tell you, that surprised me a bit. The boy's a buzz saw in a world of forest. I thought it'd go hard, but he seemed eager to let the whole thing slide."

Willard sighed. He turned to Wince and Wince shrugged. He didn't look at Dave. He didn't care what Dave thought, I guess. Dave noticed it, too, and sulked it up something fierce. Finally, Willard looked at me again.

"Well, that's a problem then. You say you left Reeves this afternoon, and apparently some time between then and around four thirty or five he must have dispatched his boys to pay you a visit."

"Or later, possibly," I said. "I didn't see them until tonight."

"Or possibly later," he agreed. "Funny thing is, we've spent the last couple of hours trying to run him to ground, but we've come up empty. No one seems to know where he's at. You got any sense of why that might be?"

We sat there for a long moment. If this were a crappy novel, there'd be a line here about a dog barking in the distance.

Finally, I said, "You think something's happened to him?"

"I think that's possible, yes. Maybe he's run off from something. Something threatening, if you follow me. Another possibility is, he's already cold as a crate of Russian hammers."

"Or maybe he just doesn't keep regular hours. He's in that kind of business."

"He is," Willard said. "Problem is, someone torched one of the kid's flops this evening. One of those of those awful places at the trailer park outside Carbondale. Obvious arson job, and now no sign of Reeves, so you can see how this looks to us."

"I was with Peggy and Anci all night," I said.

"Your buddy wasn't, though, and he's got something of a reputation for getting into scrapes. Oddly enough, he's refusing to alibi himself right now. Now why you think that is?"

"He couldn't have done it," I said, hoping I sounded more confident than I felt. In fact, he *could* have done it, and if he thought that Jump was a real threat to me or Anci he probably would have. But I thought he would have asked me first, or told me after. I said, "I need to talk to him."

"Not right now, you can't."

"When?"

"When we decide to let you. *If* we decide."

He stood up. I remembered his lesson and remained seated. Dave smirked at me. The two of them went out. Wince lingered behind just a moment.

"I told you to stay out of this mess, Slim," he said.

"Wish I'd listened."

"If you don't wish it yet, you will soon," he said, and then he was gone, too.

They kept us until morning, then kicked us loose. Neither Jeep nor I had a lawyer, and neither of us had any real money to speak of, so we ended up sharing a public defender. The guy turned out to be a real goober. He showed up late, read slow, talked slower, and was covered more in food stains than clothes. I hate to sound like that—the public defender system is a good thing—but you got the feeling that, in this guy's hands, you could walk in to donate to the policemen's fund and end up tied to a metal table. Anyway, the sense was that they wanted to charge us, but our self-defense story kept getting in the way. The goober warned us not to enjoy fresh air much, because charges were probably forthcoming.

That was something to ask about, but Willard didn't make an appearance, and no one else really spoke to us except the guy at the properties desk, who just grunted and gave us back our things. I had a few bucks missing, and I think Jeep lost his Timex, but neither of us raised a fuss. Outside, the day was cool and bright. The two of us were underground coal miners, so the physical effect of a few hours in a holding tank was pretty small, but it still felt good to be outside again, and we paused a moment to stretch in the sun. There's nothing like an overnight in jail to convince you of the wisdom of the righteous life.

"I'd rather not spend any more time in there," I said. "I shared a cell with a drunk who kept time by farting."

"Not my favorite experience, either," Jeep said. "Some time around midnight, they tossed in a first-timer who wanted to be King of the Cell, and for some reason he chose me as his target."

"Sometimes they'll choose the biggest guy, thinking it sends a message. How'd it go?"

"For him? Not well, but after that everyone left me alone. One guy even offered to make my bed."

"I'm hoping you didn't take him up on it," I said. "They already think you killed Jump Down."

Jeep didn't say anything.

"You didn't, did you?" I said.

Jeep didn't say anything.

"Because, the thing is," I said, "he's missing. One of his places was burned, too, which feels like revenge to me. You were supposed to be at work last night, but instead you showed up to shotgun one bad man a few hours after another bad man mysteriously vanished."

Jeep said, "You think I did it?"

"I don't know for sure that anything *was* done. Jump Down probably isn't the easiest guy to get in touch with. Maybe the place burned on its own. If that's where he kept his meth kitchen, my understanding is they burn easier than birthday candles. I'm just saying that if anything did happen, now might be a good time to come clean."

"In front of the police station?" he said. "You really are new at this."

"Well, maybe you can tell me all about it later," I said, but instead of answering he trailed off to phone his wife.

Anci and Peggy had left the station house the night before, and I wasn't sure exactly where they'd gone. Back to the hotel, maybe, but more likely to Peggy's place. Wherever they were, I wouldn't feel completely comfortable until we were all together again. Willard had promised me there'd be some kind of police protection, but I got the feeling that was the kind of arrangement that would keep away the honest but not much else. I punched in Peggy's number. Anci picked up. Like I thought, they'd gone to Peggy's.

"She's out, by the way," Anci said. "As in, like a light. You've never seen a person sleep so hard. I tried waking her a while ago, but it's like trying to rouse a tree stump. I'll try again in a while. Maybe tomorrow morning."

"She had quite a start," I said. "We all did. It kinda takes it out of you. How are you holding up?"

Anci shrugged with her voice. "I'm okay. That's never happened to me before, and I hope it never happens again."

"It won't, I have anything to do with it. To that end, I've got to talk to your Uncle Jeep about a few things. Then I'm going to see about finding us a new hotel. Might be time to move again, given the circumstances."

"Maybe back to the Pin Oak."

"Maybe not."

"Peggy's house is okay, though. She gave me my own room. It's small, but it'll be nice sleeping in a room where the only snoring you have to hear is your own."

"Sorry."

"You can make it up to me by making it so we can go home again," she said.

"Well, that'll be soon, I hope. It's not safe yet, exactly, but most of the people I was worried about have been accounted for. I've got one or two more small things to look after this morning, and then hopefully things will start to fall into place."

"Sounds like a plan. Pick me up from school today?"

"You got it."

"On the bike?"

"Right on."

I hung up and was heading back to meet Jeep when the phone buzzed again. I looked at the screen. There was a text from Anci, which she must have sent as soon as we'd parted: "Don't forget your meeting." But I was all about that incoming phone call. My heart lifted, and I wished I had a pocketful of confetti to throw. The number was Tony Pelzer's.

"You've been calling me?" a voice said. It was an odd creature, this voice, rough and high at the same time. Also, there was something distantly familiar about it, though maybe that was just my imagination.

I said, "Once or twice. I think it's time we meet."

"I think so, too. I'm here at the house. You know where it is?"

"I know where it is."

"Okay. Come out. But, listen, I want you to be cool, okay? I want you to be very cool. Can you remember that?"

"Cool is my middle name."

"I'm guessing it ain't."

"I know."

"But I want you to. Be cool, I mean, because it's not always easy."

"You sound anxious, Mr. Pelzer."

"I'm very anxious," he said. "And it's Tony. And fuck you."

"I'll be there as soon as I can."

"Twenty minutes?"

"More like forty."

"Fine. But don't dawdle. Forty-five and I'm gone. And for the love of Mike, don't bring a piece."

I rolled again toward Bluegill Point. Along the way, I stopped by the Vale and swapped the truck for the bike, because I'd promised to give Anci a ride on it later. I checked the kitchen window lock, but it was the same as before, and I went inside and looked at Anci's computer, but all I saw on the makeshift security feed was Peggy stopping by to pick up some of the Anci's things. I collected my helmet and Anci's and my jacket and gloves and went out again. The weather was still cool, but the clouds had pushed off, and the sky was clear and blue and beautiful. You'd never think all this strife was going on under that sky. I strapped Anci's helmet to the rack on the back of the bike and took off.

It was just after nine o'clock when I found myself back on Tony Pelzer's doorstep. The GMC was still there, but in a different spot, so either Pelzer had gotten it running or gotten that team of elephants. The sign with his name was still there, so the elephants hadn't stepped on it. I went up on the porch and knocked and after a short moment there he was, shirtless, with a soft belly and a bruise the size of a grapefruit on his furry chest. I felt a shock of recognition and a few things sliding into place. I remembered the weird things he'd said on the phone, and I remembered what Mary-Kay Connor had told me about him and his job. I'd thought maybe the badge and police uniform were pieces of a costume. That they might have been part of a security job hadn't occurred to me. I tried to be cool, but he was right, being cool wasn't easy.

Tony Pelzer was Round-Face.

ELEVEN

I've never been shot with one of those things before," he said. He touched the bruise gently but winced and sucked a stuttering breath. "Got tased once. No, twice. And maced unconscious. That ain't my favorite memory. And this one time, I got hit with a cattle prod pretty good."

"A cattle prod?"

"It's a long story," he said and nipped at his can of beer. We were sitting on his back deck not far from the banks of Grassy Creek. "But I ain't never been shot with one of them beanbag guns."

"Betsy."

"That what you call her?"

"Yup."

"I got my heart broken by a Betsy once, so that hurts double."

"I bet."

"I kinda thought you'd say you're sorry."

"You were kinda wrong. You kicked me so hard I thought I'd wake up surrounded by a gang of bowling munchkins."

"I actually am a little regretful about that. I'm a tough guy, and I tend to overdo it sometimes. I wouldn't have been after you at all, except Beckett's wife asked me to back you off."

"Temple?"

"She does love to hear her own name. What's with that anyway? Who in the hell names their kid Temple?"

"Redneck *telenovela*," I said.

"What?"

"A flair for the dramatic married to a certain kind of taste. She pretended not to recognize your description, by the way."

Pelzer said, "Can you blame her? At first, she's thinking you're just the old man's crazy idea. She wants you gone, but she's afraid to tell her father no, so she calls me. Then a couple of days later, shit gets real, and suddenly she starts to need you. Not exactly a great time to admit she had you roughed up. 'Nother beer?"

"Sure."

He left the deck and went inside for a pair of fresh ones. I didn't figure he planned to murder me in his own house— the deck furniture looked new, for one thing, and murder would probably risk staining it—but I sat in my chair with the hand in my right jacket pocket around the grip of the unregistered Beretta 9000S I'd borrowed from Jeep Mabry. Came to it, I could shoot Pelzer out of his chest hair before he cleared the sliding door. Least I hoped I could. Probably the shot would go wild and clip a gas main and blow us both to Terre Haute. If I was going to keep at this business, I was going to have to find a weapon I was more comfortable with. Alligator on a leash, maybe.

It didn't come to that, though. Guns or gas mains or angry reptiles. Pelzer came back with two fresh ones. I'd had one, and didn't want the second, but having it in front of me might calm him down some, so I accepted the cold can and set it on the patio table.

"This is a little awkward," he said, slugging his.

"Putting it mildly," I said. "Last twenty minutes or so,

I've been trying to think up a polite way to ask you for my co-pay back."

"Mine was bigger, probably. That is, if I had a co-pay, which I don't, being self-employed. I woke up on the floor feeling like I'd been run over by a football team. You didn't tie me so tight, but I gave myself some pretty good burns wiggling free of the ropes, and by the time I got out of there I could hear sirens on their way. You called the cops?"

"Seemed like the best thing to do at the time."

He shrugged. "I don't blame you. I guess I might have done the same. I mean, I blame you a little. I might have been willing to talk, but you didn't give me a chance."

"You didn't give the chance before. Plus, you were reaching for a weapon."

"That's fair. I'm a fair person, and that sounds fair to me. So where are we here?"

I said, "I'm more interested in where Guy Beckett is."

"Wish I knew. Truly. I've been running all over the place for days looking for him. I even looked in Texas, believe it or not. He and Temple have a place there. Well, Temple has a place there, and Beckett was allowed a room. I got a buddy down that way. He looked in for me. Nada. Beckett and I spoke the night before Dwayne Mays got pulled off the count, and I've not heard a peep from him since."

"He asked you to look after him?"

Pelzer shrugged. "He asked me to babysit, yeah. Couple weeks earlier. We're buds from way back, and I do this kind of work these days, so it seemed like a good fit. Dwayne was against me coming in, though. He thought I'd step on this story he and Beckett were working on. Serious shit. Meth dealers in the mine. I'm sure you know. The two of them were haunting the Knight Hawk for weeks. It has a rep. Lot of shit moves in and out of there. Then one night, they staked-out the whatdoyoucallit tanks."

"The ammonia tanks."

"That's the stuff. I can never remember," he said. He shook his head. "Ammonia. Jesus God. How in the hell do people use that shit?"

"It makes them feel good for a while," I said. "People like to feel good."

"Yeah, but this kind of feeling good rots their teeth and boils their brain. It turns them into the walking dead. I knew a lady once carried a kid to term in a meth house, and when the thing was born it came out looking like a melted candle. I'm not guessing that felt too good."

"Probably not."

"Anyway, after that night, Dwayne had a flash, and he and Beckett stopped pestering the small fries and started working on something else."

"Galligan."

Pelzer raised his eyebrows. His soft face moved around a little like when you're working wet bread dough.

"Not bad, Hawkshaw. Galligan. Least that's what I figured. Dwayne was pretty tight about the whole thing, and I think Beckett was scared out of his wits. That wife of his had tossed him out during one of their frequent bouts of marital distress, and Guy was living with Mays and feeling like a bird on a wire."

"He could have run," I said.

"From Galligan? And gone where? The moon?"

"Good point," I said. Money had long arms. "So Dwayne thought Galligan had dealt himself into the local meth business? I got to tell you, I've heard this one a couple times now, and it just doesn't sit right with me."

"Me, neither. He's an old guy, for one, and kind of an old-school hard-ass. It's hard to imagine him getting in bed with these young dirtbags. Two, add it up, it's a lot of risk for not much reward. At least that's what I told Beckett."

"What'd he say?"

"Well, the night of the stakeout, they were watching that tank, the big one, way down the hill at the cold-storage hut."

"I know the one."

Pelzer said, "I think Beckett expected some kids to show up with gas cans or something, but instead it was a tanker truck and bobtail. The entire tank got tapped. More than six thousand gallons of whatdoyoucallit."

"Ammonia."

He shook his head. "Got a mental block about that. Nasty shit. Beckett said they'd painted the sides of the tanker, but someone had done a shitty job, and you could still make out some of the letters. It was a Galligan mine truck, all right."

"Which one?"

"King Coal. One up the hill above the lake."

"Next to the Grendel."

"What?"

I said, "It's an abandoned coal mine across the gap from the King Coal. Not important."

"I don't like being left in the dark."

"You're in the wrong story then," I said.

"Brother, you said it. Anyway, from what I gather, Dwayne got this flash. He started thinking Galligan wasn't selling the shit. He started thinking maybe Galligan was actually giving the shit away."

"Giving it away? Why?"

Pelzer said, "Juice the mine's numbers. Dwayne read it in a book somewhere, I think. Mines in Africa or Asia, some godawful place, they used to juice the workers secretly, or against their will, or whatever. Gives the guys a serious buzz and keeps them working harder and longer. Production goes up, tonnage goes up, mine stays open longer. The money flows."

"That sounds more far-fetched than the first idea."

"What I told Beckett," he said. "But you got to admit, these are desperate times. A lot of these old guys are watching their fortunes disappear. They're watching their *fathers'* fortunes disappear. And now they got to think about what they're leaving behind for their kids and grandkids or whatever. A lot of them are just egotistical assholes, too, and willing to do almost anything not to lose the game. So I guess you never know."

"I'm not sure," I said. "You'd think a thing like that would be hard to keep a lid on. They might get lucky for a while, but eventually something would go wrong. Even if they kept the dose super light, someone would notice. They'd give someone a heart attack, or guys would start tearing out their own eyeballs down there. You never know how someone's going to react to amphetamine use."

Pelzer said, "I'm not saying it's perfect. I ain't even saying I bought it, though knowing what I know about Roy Galligan I wouldn't automatically rule it out. I'm just saying it's what Mays was starting to believe."

"What about Beckett?"

"I think he just wanted off the roller coaster," Pelzer said. "Mays was one of these guys gets hold of something, he hangs on like a pit bull. I admit, this wasn't my favorite guy, but you had to admire that in him anyway. He led with his dick a lot, but he was a pro and completely unafraid to be hated. Impressive shit for a puffer."

"So Beckett felt like he was just along for the ride?"

"More or less, yeah. I mean, the guy's a fucking shutterbug. It's not even really his thing. Galligan gets busted, he's there popping his flash in the old man's face, then it's his thing. Until then, he's just someone for Mays to bounce ideas off."

"Mays's Dr. Watson," I said. I still didn't like it, but it made a kind of sense. And it might explain Beckett's disappearance. He thought he was just a tagalong to catch stray bullets, he might have made a break for it. And that was to say nothing of his relationship with his wife. Or his kid in Johnston City. Add it up, he might feel like he was running away from a world of headaches. The bastard.

I said, "Okay. So who killed Luster? I'm thinking we're down to Galligan. Mays starts working Galligan. Galligan starts feeling heat and starts working back on Mays."

Pelzer nodded. "At which point, Beckett is beginning to feel like the only whore in camp on payday. Repeatedly fucked. He goes to his father-in-law, Luster, and asks for help. The old man sends him packing—this is not his favorite relative—but then starts digging on his own. Maybe at a certain point he goes to Galligan and starts making accusations."

"I hate to say it," I said, "but it's not completely farfetched. At least that part. No one ever mentioned any of this to me. Luster included."

"Yeah, but why would he? See, he gets you looking for

Beckett. He's got Galligan sweating it out on the other side. Dead body in the coal mine, private eye looking for his missing son-in-law. There's no reason to tell you more than he did, because if he tells you too much and things go south then he's got to decide whether to pay you off or pop you."

"Nice."

"These ain't nice people, Slim."

I said, "So what's the story on the picture?"

"The picture?"

"The picture of Jim Hart. You were taking it from Mays's house when I introduced you to Betsy."

Pelzer leaned back in his chair and showed me his teeth. He sucked on his can some more, but it was mostly empty sound now, very little liquid. He was really pounding them.

"I don't know as I like that," he said. "You bringing that up over and over."

"I don't know as I care," I said.

He smiled some more and said, "You looking to start something?"

"Not really. But I'm okay with it if you are. I guess we're one to one, so maybe we need that tiebreaker. Other hand, I don't think there's a reason for this to turn confrontational, if you don't want it to."

He thought about that some. Maybe he wanted it to, maybe he didn't. His face had this way of eating his expressions and making him hard to get a read on. At last, he sighed and got up and went into the house. I took the 9000S out of my pocket and put it on the table next to my beer. After a moment, Pelzer came back out with a fresh can. None for me. He sat down and took a long pull and put his beer down in front of him and only then noticed the pistol.

"Goddamn it, I asked you not to bring one of those," he said.

"And then neglected to pat me down before you let me in," I said. "Damn, man, how long have you been in security work? 'Cause to me that's an easy one."

He actually looked a little ashamed.

"What can I say? I'm an earthmover. Sometimes I let things slide. Sometimes I forget to do things, but you need a door opened I'm your guy." He took a long drink. It must have been about half the can. He wiped his mouth with his arm and belched loudly and said, "So what now? You shoot me?"

"Hell, no. I just wanted you to know where we stand," I said. "Now about Jim Hart."

I could see his wheels turning, and not quickly, either. He could let me shove him around on his own patio deck or he could get shot. It wasn't clear which one he was going to choose. After another moment's reflection, he let it go.

He said, "You ever heard of steganography?"

"Some kind of dinosaur?"

"Cute. No. It's a process of hiding pictures inside of pictures. Like in spy books or whatever."

"Like microdots?"

"Yeah, like that, but with lots of detail. Way I understand it, you can hide all kinds of things inside a simple photograph."

Something in my brain started buzzing. A hazy memory from the other day.

"Wait a minute. Beckett had a book about it in his room at Mays's place. Stega-whatever."

Pelzer nodded. "Steganography. That's right. Guy hated

computers. Almost had a phobia about them, though I think maybe part of it was put on. You know, the old-school artist bit. Doesn't want anything getting between him and his *vision* or whatever. Anyway, Beckett didn't want to keep evidence against Galligan on a machine, and he didn't. Least ways, not on any machine I can find. But he leaves his wife—or gets tossed out—and he doesn't take anything with him, except that photograph."

"You're thinking there's something encoded on it."

"I'm thinking it's not outside the realm of possibility."

"Okay," I said, "but what?"

"No idea. Best guess, numbers. Money or tonnage or whatever, but numbers. If they started zooming upward around the time Mays thought they would, it might go a ways toward proving their theory. Or maybe it's a photograph. Like a picture hidden inside a picture, something incriminating. Long story short, I need that photograph and I need it yesterday."

I nodded. I didn't want to give it to him, but there wasn't any reason to further provoke him.

"I'll get it to you, and we can get it looked at together. Maybe the university photo lab?"

"You say so."

"Okay," I said. "I got to tell you, though, I've been around and around with this whole clue business, and everyone I talk to says that mysteries don't get solved when the detective discovers a microdot on an autographed picture of a quarterback."

"Not usually, I guess. But you never know. For example, Mays was found with a notepad in his mouth."

"I know."

"Yeah, I know you know. But I bet you didn't know this: Pad was blank, almost blank. There were two words written on it. Buddy with the sheriffs gave me the scoop."

"What two words?"

He smiled a little. I'd put him back on his heels a while back, but now he was feeling more in charge. He had a superior streak in him. He didn't like being out of the driver's seat, and when he was back in it, he enjoyed it with the subtlety of a bull in a stable of virgin cows. He said, "Funny thing. You seen Galligan lately?"

"I've seen Galligan lately."

"Yeah, well, then you've seen that blond hair. Had it when he was a boy, and the vain little shit's been dying it blond ever since he hit his silver years. It looks ridiculous, but that's what he does. Behind his back, his guys call him Yellow Boy."

"And that's what was written on the pad?"

Pelzer said, "Yup. That's what was written on the pad. *Yellow Boy.*"

PART THREE

YELLOW BOY

TWELVE

My father came in and sat at the table. He was forty but looked ten years older; I was twelve but felt ten years younger. After months of quiet tension, the old house at Indian Vale had lapsed into a different kind of quiet, the dull exhaustion of a final, sorrowful resignation. It was like the sound of nothing that fills your ears when you sink to the bottom of a lake. He looked across the table at me, then took off his wristwatch and started fiddling with the stem, as he often did when he was choosing his words.

"This is only good-bye for now," he said at last. "Your mother and I have a few things yet to work out, grownup things, but I won't be around for a few days."

"Okay."

"It's for the best," he said. Somewhere along the line, he'd become a man who told you how to feel instead of asking how you felt or trying to convince you of anything. He just told you, and whether or not you agreed, in his mind that was what it would be until he changed his mind again. "I'll need you to look after your sisters."

"I'll look after them," I said. "All of them. Mom included. Someone has to."

"You taking a tone with me?"

"Yup."

He put the watch back on his wrist and tied the little buckle.

"I'm still big enough to knock you out of that chair."

I shrugged. He was.

He drummed the table with his fingers, blew out a breath. "Is there anything you want to ask me?" he said.

"Not really," I said, but then I asked him some things anyway. "You'll be staying with Cheezie?"

"For a few days, maybe. Maybe a few days longer than that. Then I'm not sure. I've got options."

"And I can reach you there? At his place?"

"For a few days, yes."

I said, "You've left us some money?"

He took out his wallet, pulled out some bills, and put them on the table between us. I didn't move to touch them.

"There's more upstairs on the dresser, and I gave your mother a little, too. You think I'd abandon you like that? Leave you penniless?"

I said, "I think you'll do whatever it is you decide to do."

We sat there a moment. After what seemed a long time, he stood and pushed his chair back neatly under the table and walked to the door and slipped into his coat. It was fall and the air was cool. He opened the door, then stopped and looked back halfway over his shoulder, in my direction but not at me.

"I won't say I'm sorry," he said. "I'll see you soon."

Then he was gone. I didn't see him again for nearly three years.

I separated myself from Pelzer. That wasn't easy—he wanted to tag along—but I promised to call later that evening, and we shook hands and went our separate ways without further damage. There was one more place Beckett might be, at least one more place that I could think of, and I meant to check it before the day was out.

First, though, I rang Peggy. I caught her at home and in bed.

"Still in your jammies?"

She said, "Jammies and a robe and some slippers from college. Even found an old teddy bear, and I've nearly hugged the stuffing out of him. I feel like I've had the wind ripped right out of me." She sounded like it, too. Her voice was hollow and kinda weak, like she'd been fighting a crud and the crud was finally getting her down. "I've slept something like fourteen straight hours now, and I still don't feel like I can get out of bed."

"Sleep fourteen more if you have to," I said. "Maybe I can come by with some food later."

"If you're able," she said. "Bring Anci, too, if she'll come."

"Of course she'll come."

"I feel silly," she said, but she sounded more sad than silly. "Acting this way. I imagined I was tougher."

"You're plenty tough."

"I don't know. Few minutes before it happened, there I was, fighting zombies and bragging about what a big girl I am. Now look at me."

"Everybody has a line," I said. "I'm betting that a lot of people's involve flying lead."

She was quiet for a moment, and, not being able to see her face, I couldn't tell how she was registering that. Then she said, "You killed a man last night."

"Mostly on accident," I said. "But just between us, I'm not overly upset about how it shook out. I guess he might have tuckered out and decided he'd had enough. Maybe he'd have put down his guns and taken up a life of good deeds for orphans and war widows, but usually bad men don't go in that direction. Once you have someone in that position, on his knees and at your mercy, chances are he's eventually going to come back at you. Might not be the next day or the next month even, but he'll do it. If only because he can't live with the fact that you had him dead to rights like that and let him off the hook."

"I don't know," she said. "I know there's plenty of evil in the world. I know you can't always hold its hand and give it a hanky for its tears. I'm just not sure violence is the best way to solve problems."

"It's surely not, but sometimes it's the only way we've got lying around."

"And someone taught you that, Slim."

"That's a low blow."

"Yes, it is," she said. "I also can't help thinking how much this looks like you obsessively searching for someone else's runaway spouse instead of your own."

"That's an even lower blow."

"Okay, I'll cop to that one. And I'm sorry. Could be I'm not being fair. But you can maybe see how this looks from the outside."

"I can maybe see it," I said, "but I think you're drawing the wrong conclusion."

"I'm in good company then. Sugar, I'm not sure how much more of this I can take. Whatever you have to do to get away from this thing, do it."

"I'll try," I said. "Meantime, hang in there."

"I'm not sure I can," she said, and for the first time I wasn't so sure she was wrong.

I still needed to find Guy Beckett, though. Someone had killed Dwayne Mays and Matt Luster. And someone had either killed Beckett or chased him away, whether Jump Down or Roy Galligan or both. They'd done it for money or for jobs and the survival of their way of life, or all of that rolled up in a giant ball. But only Beckett would be able to answer my questions and put the whole thing to bed.

I stopped in at the Herrin library and used one of the computers to search for Carla Shepherd, the other woman Susan had mentioned a day or so ago. Found her on a public list of donors for some environmental project or other, and gave myself a private eye gold star for it, too. She was listed as living in Pomona, a tiny place deep inside the Shawnee National Forest, some forty minutes south of the Crab Orchard Lake and preserve. On my way back through town I stopped in at the school, hoping to catch Anci for lunch, maybe talk her into a slice of pizza and an orange soda, but when I roared up I instead found her standing around outside the school with a bunch of other kids.

Anci said, "There you are."

"Don't tell me," I said. "They decided you were unteachable."

"Maybe after you get done playing around at mystery-solving," she said, "you can go into comedy. I bet you'd go far."

"I'll give it some thought. Really, though, what gives?"

"I told you earlier. It's a half-day today. Teachers' conferences, and you're up."

"You told me all this?"

"I sure did. You don't remember, do you?"

"I do." I didn't. "When's my appointment?"

"This morning. Right now. I even texted you a reminder," she said. "Now shoo. I'll wait here for you."

She waited. I went to park the bike. I checked my phone and, sure enough, there was her reminder. I went inside the school and found Anci's classroom. It was regulation: There was an American flag and a blackboard. There were books piled on a long table beneath a bank of windows and some computers. There was a decorated bulletin board with some student papers pinned to it, some class project about the environment, and I was briefly reminded of the Friends of Crab Orchard. I didn't have time to dwell on it, though. The teacher was waiting for me with a smile on her face you wouldn't break your brain to imagine as impatient. She couldn't have been older than twenty or twenty-one, still just a kid herself, but you could tell she was used to dealing with young bullheads and their ilk, and she took charge immediately and forced me to sit in that little desk. They always make you sit in that thing. I don't know why, but I figure they must have a whole college course about making adult people sit in that tiny desk.

We shook hands, and she smiled a bit more warmly and called me by my given name. I told her to please call me Slim; that other name was what they called my father.

She said, "Well, you can relax . . ."

"I'm relaxed."

She ignored me and pressed on.

"I've got nothing but praise. Your daughter is an amazing young woman."

"Ain't she, though?"

"And *smart*."

"She's a clever little monkey, all right. Sometimes a little too much so. It's vexatious. Example: I'm told she's been talking lately about becoming a lawyer."

"That's wonderful."

"The hell it is."

I laughed a little, but she didn't, and the rest of our meeting wasn't quite as warm and fuzzy as it otherwise might have been. We went over Anci's grades and her recent test results, and then she closed her score books and said, "There's just one little thing I'd like to speak to you about."

"Do tell."

"Your daughter—how to put this?" She thought about how to put it. I could tell she'd already thought how to put it, but I didn't want to discourage her professional development, so I just sat there quietly. She said, "Along with acting a bit more like an adult than her classmates, your daughter sometimes . . . talks a bit more like an adult. If you follow my drift."

"Stock tips?"

"Profanity."

"Oh."

"Now, don't be alarmed."

I wasn't especially alarmed. Or surprised.

"It's not always," she said. "Just sometimes, but I've noticed some of the other students are starting to pick it up."

"Well, hell."

She nodded sternly at this. "I think I'm beginning to see the source of the problem."

Our meeting ended, and I went out and found Anci. I knew that somewhere nearby Jeep was watching over her like a hell's angel turned loose on earth, and if anyone so much as took a suspicious step toward her he might just have an instant to contemplate the pretty cloud of red he'd somehow walked into. I waved a hand in what I guessed was his general direction and then turned my attention to Anci. I couldn't leave her to her own devices, of course, and Peggy wasn't in a state to watch over her. She'd have to come with me. With Jump Down either dead or hiding out, and at least two of his men in the morgue, I didn't figure we were in much danger of being shot at again. I hoped that wasn't wishful thinking.

Anci strapped on her helmet and we climbed on the bike and rode out of town toward Pomona. That time of day, traffic was slow moving, so we were able to holler at each other a bit over the noise of the bike. I tried to talk to her about what the teacher had said. She didn't deny the charges—in fact, she owned up to the whole thing—and I was so proud of her honesty that it took me a moment to recognize that she'd managed to get out of trouble without promising she wouldn't do it again, and I knew I'd been had.

Anyway, the day was turning out warmer than it had been lately. Another front was moving in, and the day was rumbly. The sky churned a little, and far away to the west was a dark line of clouds like a slit throat. Eventually, we made our way through the Shawnee and into the empty streets of Pomona, where I managed to get us turned around on North Railroad Street, named that, I guess, after the only moving object in town. Seriously, the atmosphere out here is pretty laid back: even the town mutts could barely be bothered to lift their heads as we rolled by.

Finally, Anci said, "I think we're lost. Maybe we should pull over and ask."

We did, walking up the way some and taking in the sights, of which there were none. Really, Pomona was more of a village than a town—half a village, even—with most of its folk living in the hills surrounding a little valley. End to end, the main drag might have run all of a hundred yards, but I doubt it. There was a post office that served as the entire town's mail pickup because Pomona was too rural for the mail carrier to do door-to-door delivery. There was a coffee shop that closed a few years back after the proprietor finally figured out that having no client base is a poor business model, and there was a bar that had been there for fifty years, though it never seemed to have more than two customers at a time, one of them a cat. There was a used bookstore that also sold live fishing bait, so that customers were always taking home stowaway crickets with their copies of *The Da Vinci Code* or *The Girl Who Kicked the Shithouse* or whatever. It was a place where the village constable might run you in for smoking grass in public, if the constable wasn't the one smoking grass in public in the first place, which she often was.

It was also a place where everybody knew everybody, so it was a snap getting directions to Carla's place from a dude in the town's hundred-year-old general store, one of those cheerful, pot-bellied hippie bears with more facial hair than head, and who smell like a quarter-ton of smoldering incense.

"Carla lives up the road," he said—shy or sly, I couldn't tell—as he worked the brass fittings of the countertop with an oily rag. "Split-level cabin. You couldn't miss it double-blindfolded."

"Any idea if she's up there now?"

"Carla in some kind of scrape?" he wondered, voice low despite the empty store. I knew the habit. In small towns, the secrets tell themselves.

"Not as I know of. I just wanted to talk to her about a mutual friend."

More appraisals. At last, he nodded and said, "Likely she's there. Carla mostly works out of the house these days. Watch out, though. She's got herself a torpedo of a mastiff bitch."

"Thanks for the warning. Dogs usually like me, though."

The dude laughed a little. He said, "This one don't like anyone but Carla. And Patty. And even that sometimes seems like an uneasy truce."

"Up the road" ended up being ten miles north, through broad-back hill country shot through with mockernut hickories and slender bur oaks and little creeks that overswam their banks and flooded the asphalt. A couple of times the road dwindled down to something not much wider than a deer path, and I worried we'd taken a wrong turn. Even at their widest the lanes were perilous, and the bike rocked and bucked along their cragged edges like a mechanical bull. Anci laughed and enjoyed the ride and pretty soon I was laughing, too, glad we weren't pulled over by some county mountie out looking for joyriding lunatics. By the time we found the cabin, nestled in a dark patch of sweet-gum trees down a quarter-mile gravel drive, my ass hurt like I'd been dragged up the hill.

The Shepherd household was a log cabin with a wraparound porch and beech-wood planks radiating soft yellow beneath the rustle of the autumn canopy. The pegged wood looked as smooth as polished elk bones, and the place generally had a pleasant air about it. You could imagine it making a pretty good hideout, too, secluded spot like that.

"Little luck, he'll be in there," I said. "Beckett. Maybe this'll be the end of this business, and you and I can go someplace fun together. Like a vacation."

"Where?"

"I don't know. Anyplace. I ain't ever been to Memphis. Maybe we can go there, make fun of Elvis's bathroom."

"Maybe we can take grandpa."

"I don't think so, sweet pea."

She thought about that for a moment, a serious expression on her face. Finally, she said, "I visit him sometimes, you know?"

"I know."

"Peggy takes me."

"I know that, too."

"And I know he's done bad things," she said. "He never says so directly, but I know it. I can tell, way he talks about things. The past. Grandma. You. I just wish there was a way."

"I guess I do, too. At least I used to. Listen, though, what happened between him and me, you know that isn't ever going to happen between the two of us. Not ever."

"I know," she said, but I could tell it made her happy to hear it out loud.

I asked her to wait on the bike, and I climbed off and walked to the porch and knocked on the door. No answer. I looked through the front window but couldn't make out anyone inside. Well, I'd come a long way and didn't want to leave empty-handed, so I stepped around back of the house to see what there was to see. Fence. Big one, too. Ten feet, maybe. There wasn't anything else to do. I fought my way up and over. I'll say this, you cross the forty-year line, that kind of climbing gets a little less graceful. I got up okay, but I came down hard and tweaked my ankle and landed on my butt. I glanced around, hoping no one had seen. I was glad Anci was around front and out of sight.

The backyard was a broad, sloping space spotted with more sweet-gum trees and a few stony outcroppings stippled with brown moss. There was a good-size garden, now tangled with winter vegetables, and a jakes with one of those composting toilets. There was a doghouse filled with nice clean straw but nothing else. I was glad about that. I wasn't ready to meet the family pooch. I didn't anticipate trouble, but I put my hand in my jacket and took hold of the rubber grip of the 9000S. It was a confidence thing.

Everything was still. There was a steep grade behind the house, and a finger of water trickled down a stony moraine, but that was it. I kept near the fence line and hobbled purposefully on my hurt ankle toward the house, and I was nearly there when things suddenly came unglued and got un-still. A dark blur flashed through my peripheral vision. There was a whipcrack of sound like muscles unclenching and a flash of animal heat, and something hit me so hard in the back that I left my feet and did a flop that would have made Dick Fosbury burn with envy. I fell forward and to the side, hitting the fence on my way down. I wondered when they'd started running trains through people's backyards and how I'd managed to stray onto the tracks. Worse, I landed with the 9000S balled up underneath me. It's a wonder I didn't blow my own guts out. I made to roll over, but before I could something heavy hopped onto my back and grabbed the ruff of my neck in its jaws. Spools of hot slobber sluiced down my open collar. So much for the dog lover in me.

"Word of warning," a woman's voice said in a growl that for a moment I mistook for the dog talking. "You move, or I give her the signal, she takes your head off."

"That seems like a useful warning."

"What's your handle?"

"Call me Slim."

"I'm pretty close to calling you an ambulance. What's your story?"

"It's a tale," I said. I choked back a mouthful of wet dirt and just a hint of dog shit. They must have been building dogs heavier; this one weighed as much as a wood stove. "I'm looking for Guy Beckett."

"You're not a cop. Whaddya want with him?"

"Like I said. It's a story. Long one, too," I said. "Short version is, I'm just doing a job for Beckett's father-in-law."

"Luster? He's dead, case you haven't heard."

"I've heard. Do you mind if I get up? I'm lying on a piece here, and it's got a hair trigger."

"Don't we all," she said. "Okay, get up, but leave the gun in your pocket. I think for a minute you're pulling my chain, buddy, you'll find yourself right back on the ground, and this time maybe with holes in you."

The dog lifted off me and padded away.

"No need for holes," I said. I looked up. A pretty brunette in a wheelchair looked down at me. The mastiff was crouched at her side. She was covering me with one of those .45 Long Colt things. The woman, not the dog. The gun was big enough she had to hold it with both hands, and heaven only knew what would happen if she fired it. Probably she'd go racing down the hill and through the valley and on back toward civilization.

She said, "I kinda thought when someone finally came out here, they'd look like Frankenstein's ugly cousin, but you just look lost."

"Thanks," I said. "And I'm sorry to bust in on you with the hand-cannon. It's just I've had a wild couple days, and I'm getting tired of little surprises."

"Well, I'm going to say you just had another one."

"I have." I slapped some of the mud off my clothes. I figured there were muddy paw prints on my back, too. "I don't guess I have to ask how you knew I was on my way, do I, Carla?"

"How do you know I'm Carla?"

"You're either Carla or Patty. I'm just guessing which."

"Petey phoned me, said you'd been in the store asking questions."

"It's gotten so you can't even trust a hippie," I said. "It's dispiriting."

"Depends on who you are," she said. "I trust them fine. You want to come inside?"

I wanted to come inside. The place was lodge-warm against the cooling afternoon. The kitchen was big and shiny, with exposed wood and glazed brick and an oven mounted with cast-iron hooks for the pots and pans. Everything smelled faintly of freshly baked bread and crushed herbs, and a bowl over-piled with windfall apples on the butcher-block counter radiated a soft sweetness, like an organic censer. We sat around an oaken farm table with high-backed chairs on one side, a long bench on the other, sipping mugs of coffee while Carla's live-in girlfriend Patty, a wiry, camo-clad blonde, poured hot chocolate for Anci.

Carla said, "She's adorable." She tousled Anci's hair and gave me a playful look. "And a polite young lady. So don't even tell me she belongs to you, Scruff."

"I belong to him," Anci said. She looked at me. "Scruff." And she and I dapped and blew it up.

"Partners in crime?" Carla asked.

"You have no idea."

"What ship did he get you off of, girl?" Patty asked. "Tell the truth."

"Ship of fools, most like," she answered.

Carla raised her eyebrows at me.

"Genius," I explained. "Well, criminal genius, but we're working on it."

Carla said, "I don't guess I have to ask what this is about, do I? You said you're here about Guy, but you mean you're here about Guy's disappearance."

I said, "That's right. I tell you, I've spent the past three days chasing his trail all over the tricounties without turning up so much as a whisper. He's the most thoroughly disappeared person I've ever heard of."

Patty sat with us, glowering. She had that look about her, like getting her to glower wouldn't take much effort, and now Guy Beckett's name had jumped out of nowhere and slapped her in the Chapstick and she was glowering up a squall. If she'd actually had a green-eyed monster wrapped around her neck, the meaning couldn't have been clearer.

Carla looked at her and me. She touched Patty on the arm and said, "I know. We've been waiting word from him, too, and hoping he'll reappear, but I'll be honest, we think he's come to evil."

"You sure he'd have gotten in touch?"

"I'm almost certain of it. We were close. Our group, I mean."

"Your group?"

Carla nodded. "How we all met. Couple years ago, Patty and I got wind of a plan to build an industrial incinerator out there near the wildlife refuge at Crab Orchard. You know the one."

"Sure do."

"Anyway, some dope at EPA was behind it all, and he'd gotten the park's industrial clients behind it. See, the park leases big chunks of land to business and industry types. Has since the war. Back then, they actually built munitions out there."

"And coal mines."

"Yeah. Those, too. Hell of a place for all that, a wildlife refuge. Add it up, you've got a mess, so EPA was saying the park needed an incinerator, but they wanted to build it right next door to one of the bird and fish habitats. We put up some flyers around campus to drum up opposition. Anyway, the whole thing made enough noise that Dwayne Mays and Guy eventually picked up the story and ran with it, and when it was over Guy stuck around."

"Oh, holy shit."

"What?"

"You're the Friends of Crab Orchard."

"That's what we called ourselves, yeah. You've heard of us?"

"You might say that. Who else was in the group?"

"Mostly, it was me, Patty, Beckett, and one or two others. Plus, a couple of students from the college. We tend to let our members out themselves, seeing as how our projects aren't always the most popular things in the world. I'll be honest, I'm not sure Guy's heart was always fully committed to them, either. Though I guess it depends on what the project was."

Patty glowered some more. She went noisily to the stove and poured herself some more coffee, then came back and took a seat one over from Carla. Carla looked like someone'd just peed in her boot.

I said, "What about this Dwayne Mays? Did he stick around with your group, too?"

"Naw, but we'd have liked to have him. Dwayne was a good man, and he cared more than Guy did. But joining us would have been a conflict of interest, and that was something Dwayne shied away from."

"I've heard tell."

At this point, Anci slid out of her seat and looked at Carla and said, "May I use your bathroom, please?"

"So polite," Carla said.

"Oh, she's a polite one, all right."

"Down the hall, left."

Anci nodded thanks, then stuck her tongue out at me and went out of the room.

I said to Carla, "I got to tell you, I was kinda hoping Beckett was hiding out here with you."

Carla said, "No."

Patty said, "Hell, no."

I said to Carla, "Okay, I was getting that sense of it. When was the last time you spoke to him?"

"Few days ago. Right before he vanished. He called late, or early. Four thirty in the morning. Patty answered."

"So you didn't talk to him personally?"

"No. Would have, but wasn't given the chance."

She refused to look at Patty. Patty refused to look at her. They both stared at me. Tolstoy wrote that all unhappy families are unhappy in their own way. He should have met these two.

I said, "Okay, and what about Tony Pelzer? I've heard he was part of your crew also."

"Not really. Less so even than Guy, really, and that's saying something. Tony thinks climate change is a big liberal conspiracy, so he certainly wasn't inclined to believe anything we said. Frankly, we couldn't stand him. Guy was a person enjoyed putting on airs, though, and Tony was like a bodyguard. Made Guy feel important. Made the rest of us pretty damn nervous."

"I've met him, and he makes me nervous, too," I said. "Let me ask you this: Has anyone made any threats at you lately, or come up here looking for Beckett?"

They sat there a moment without talking. They finally looked at each other and back at me, and Patty grunted a little like something had crawled inside her nose, and then they were quiet again.

I said, "I promise not to yell."

They looked at each other again, and Carla nodded. Patty said, "Two days before Guy disappeared. After dinner. Carla was in the house. I was walking the dog down the hill and having a smoke. It was just before sundown, or near then, but it gets dark up here that time of day, under the trees. Well, we get a few hundred yards from the house, and the dog here starts growling and carrying on, and at first I think maybe she's spotted a deer or maybe just a squirrel or whatever, but she keeps at it so I go to get a closer look."

"Not a squirrel, I'm thinking."

Patty shook her head. "A man. And then two of them. Maybe three. I don't know. Like I said, it was kinda hard to tell in that light."

"Any idea who they were?"

"No."

"So what happened?"

"Well, I did what you'd ordinarily do. I called out to them, but no one would answer. So I opened fire."

"Come again?" I said.

Carla looked sad again. Or weary. She said, "I've tried talking to her."

Patty was indignant. "Hey, I'm sorry, but you come creeping around in the undergrowth up here, you're asking for trouble. I gave them a chance to come out, and got nothing back in return, so I pulled my piece and fired off a couple of rounds."

"Warning shots?"

"Bad shots," she said. "I missed."

"Could have been hunters," I said. "Or maybe someone just got turned around."

"These parts? Not unless they fell out of an airplane."

"Okay, maybe not. So what happened then?"

Patty shrugged.

"Nothing. I turned the dog loose and checked the bushes, but whoever it was had gone. Run off, I guess. I didn't see any blood spatter, so I reckon I missed them pretty good, but I tell you I spend a little while on the porch every night now with one of our long guns."

I looked at Carla. "I'm glad you're the one who found me."

Patty said, "You should be, too."

Anci came back in the room and took her seat. I smiled at her and patted her hand, but she didn't smile back. She looked a little wan and I worried she'd overheard that last bit about the shooting.

"Everything okay?"

"Something I ate at school isn't sitting right," she said. "I'm fine."

"We're almost out of here." I turned again to Carla, said, "Any way you can think of to get a message to Beckett?"

"I'm sorry. I really am. I just don't know. And that's assuming he's still alive."

"I've taken up enough of your time, then."

"We're glad to help."

We got up and shook hands all around, Anci even. I left them my number in case Beckett reappeared or got in touch, and then they both walked us to the door, Carla smiling tightly, Patty glowering.

Anci and I stepped off the porch and walked to the bike. Carla rolled back into the house. Patty kept following us.

"This is some courtesy now," I said.

"Just keep walking, dammit," she said beneath her breath.

I kept walking, dammit. We made our way down the hill a bit, and I climbed on the bike and hauled her off her stand and waited for Anci to saddle up behind me. She did this with expertise and grace, I am proud to say.

Patty said, "You really let her on that thing with you?"

"Well, we're not a shooting-randomly-at-strangers kinda family, but we do what we can."

She didn't like that. She said, "Hey, I explained that. Tried to, anyway, but I guess I didn't get my message through. I protect what's mine, and I'm pretty damn good at it, too."

"You don't say. And just how good is that, exactly?"

"I got nothing to do with Guy getting lost, if that's what you mean."

"Well, that's what I mean," I said. "And I'm guessing you didn't follow me out here to tell me something so obvious a blind haint would trip over it. So give me what you've got or kindly step the hell away from my wheels, please."

She went pale and then red-faced and her mouth opened but nothing came out. If she could have she would have crumpled the bike into a ball and kicked the ball down the hill into a lagoon. Instead, she took a folded paper from her shirt pocket and held it toward me.

"Beckett," she said.

I unfolded it. A coupon for baking powder. Expired, too. I turned it over. The backside was better. Words had been scribbled on the page above, now missing, but someone had brought out their ghosts with firm pencil rubs. I looked at Patty.

I said, "Where'd you get this?" But I knew the answer to that one already. She'd been in Mays's house, just like I had, and she'd taken one of my clues. "It's all right, Patty," I told her. "You aren't the world's first jealous lover."

"Maybe just the meanest."

"If you want to convince me you had nothing to do with Beckett's disappearance, you're not helping your case. Anyway, why give this to me?"

"Because I think Beckett came to harm through something he was tied up in, and I want her to see it. The sooner she sees him for what he really is, the better."

"For you, you mean?"

"And her."

"And what is he, exactly?"

"Trouble off its leash."

She said this last almost sadly, and I confess my heart went out to her. I didn't know her or Carla, really, and I didn't know anything about what their relationship was like, but I knew what it was to lose someone you loved more than anything in the world and the hurt that followed. I nodded and again looked at the coupon.

"I'll be damned," I said. "It says Yellow Boy."

"Yes, it does. Any idea what it means?"

"Not really," I said.

But I'm getting there, I didn't say.

Outskirts of town, we pulled into a Texaco for gasoline and soda pop. Anci sat quietly in her seat while I filled up the tank. Usually, she took the opportunity to move up the saddle and play around with the throttle, but this time she stayed put. When I was done filling, I picked up some colas and snacks. Orange soda for Anci, clear soda for me. I got some cookies for Anci. I gave the boy at the counter some money. He gave me back some change. It was the least complicated exchange I'd had in days. It felt good. I thanked the boy and shook his hand.

Anci was still sitting quietly when I got back. I handed her a soda, but she refused it with a wag of her head.

"Okay," I said. "Enough of this foolishness. Give."

"Give what? I told you . . ."

"Yeah, you told me you ate something at school that didn't agree with you, but I happen to know that you have an unturnable stomach. I once watched you eat an entire jar of jalapeño peppers without so much as changing color. And now you're refusing orange soda, which I've never seen you do under any circumstance. So give."

She sat there, stubbornly I thought at first, but then I realized she was fighting tears. She was such a precocious kid, sometimes I forgot that she really was just a kid. I leaned against my saddle and put my arm on her and softened my voice.

"Whatever it is . . ." I said.

She snuffled a little and rubbed her eyes and looked at me and said, "When we were at the house."

"Carla and Patty's, you mean?"

She nodded.

"And I went to the bathroom."

"Okay."

"Well, I didn't really have to go. But I needed an excuse to get out of there a moment and do some poking around."

"Poking around? For what?"

"Guy Beckett. If he really was there, probably the last people who'd tell you would be Carla and Patty."

I said, "Why, you sneaky little fox."

"Tell me I'm wrong, though."

"I admit, it's pretty good thinking. Maybe you should take up the detective work, and I can sit back and learn a few things."

"Well, I didn't find him. Beckett, I mean. I looked in a bedroom and in a closet."

"Bad men often hide in closets," I said, but she ignored me.

"There's another bedroom back of the house, but he

wasn't there, either, and there weren't any clothes or luggage or anything anywhere."

"Seems like you were pretty thorough. And fast. You couldn't have been gone more than a few moments."

"There was a picture in the hallway, though."

"A picture?"

"Photograph. Looked new to me. Recent, I mean."

"How could you tell something like that?"

"Patty's shoes. She was wearing those boots with the red toes in the picture. She was wearing them today in the kitchen and they still looked new, so I figured the picture wasn't taken too long ago."

"You're a genius."

"It must have been their group. They were standing outside, in a park maybe, holding a sign."

"Friends of Crab Orchard?"

"Right. Patty and Carla were in it. And a balding guy."

"Beckett, probably. I wish I'd seen it."

"A couple other people, too."

"The college students Carla mentioned, maybe."

Anci nodded. She said, "And Peggy."

THIRTEEN

You should have told me."

Peggy hugged her teddy bear tight. The black button eyes bulged. She was squeezing the life out of him. We were in the bedroom at her house in Zeigler. She didn't look so happy. Still beautiful, but wrung out. Her eyes were puffy where she'd been crying, and her face looked tired and scared. I wanted to tell her it was all going to be all right. Only problem, I didn't know what "it" was. Not yet. She was on the bed, and she'd backed herself flush against the painted headboard like she meant to push through it and the wall into the yard. I was leaning on a chair, still feeling faintly stunned. The lights were turned out, but sunlight leaked through the blinds and gave the room an unearthly orange glow.

She said, "I tried to. Wanted to. Really I did. The night of Anci's birthday party."

"So that's what it was."

"That's what it was. The right time never presented itself, though. Or, hell, probably I was just chicken."

"But I don't understand," I said. "Why keep it a secret in the first place?"

"Well, darlin', I figured my admitting that I was trying to put you out of a job might not exactly throw a log on our romantic flame. A lot of people don't like what we do. Think we're anti-union or anti-American, even. Trying to steal the bread from their kids' mouths. Things can get kinda ugly."

"I can see that," I said, "But I'm not one of those people, and you still should have told me."

"I know that. But listen, Slim, the truth is, I'd already walked away from that. I didn't like lying to you, even by omission, and I didn't want some secret to wreck our life together. I quit a while back, but then this business with Dwayne happened, and it was like I got dragged back into it. It was too late to quit."

"Too late why?"

Peggy said, "Because everyone in the group who'd been in contact with Mays and Beckett at any point was in danger. No one was going to care that I'd turned in my resignation. Too late because Dwayne was dead and Guy really was missing. We thought at first he was just hiding out after Dwayne was killed, and would come home again when the coast looked clear."

"But he didn't."

"That's right," she said. "And now he's dead."

That sucked a little of the air out of the room.

"You think so?"

"I really do," she said. "For about a year there, we were what you'd call a tight-knit group. Especially after that business with the incinerator. If Beckett was alive, he'd have found a way to get in touch."

"That's what Carla and Patty said, too. I'm guessing you might also be the reason they didn't open fire as soon as they saw me today."

Peggy nodded. She said, "I called up there, told them you might be along one day. I figured no harm would come to you, but . . ."

"But Patty is nervous."

"Nervous and jealous as a jilted rattlesnake. I don't know

that anything ever happened between Carla and Guy, but Beckett did everything but bring out the violins."

"This is quite a fella I've been busting my ass to find."

She said, "He wasn't without his charms."

"Not you, too?"

She almost got hot about that, but then she remembered where we were. "No. Not me. Not that he didn't try."

"I bet. Dammit, I had Anci with me today."

"I know, Slim. I . . ."

Just then Anci came into the room and went to the top of the bed and sat down. Peggy rubbed her head and kissed her hair.

"Maybe not the best time, squirt," I said.

Peggy said, "No, let her stay. Please."

Anci looked at me. "Okay?"

I nodded.

"Okay."

Peggy said, "Good. She's part of this, too, and she should hear it. It's because of me she was in danger the other night."

"Those men on the street," I said. "They didn't belong to Jump Down."

"No," Peggy said. "They were Galligan's. And they weren't shooting at you, Slim. They were shooting at me."

A little more of the air went out. I had to sit down. I sat down.

"That's not funny," I said.

"It's not, no. But it is the truth."

"My God, it's true then. It really is Roy Galligan. I'd half thought everyone had taken leave of their senses."

"Maybe they have," she said. "But that doesn't mean they aren't right about Galligan."

"But why? Why would he get himself involved in something like this?"

"Because of what Dwayne and Guy were up to," she said. "Investigating what's been going on up at the King Coal and Grendel. Dwayne had been following whispers for a while. He brought Guy in on the story, and Guy talked to us. I think at first he was hoping it would make a better story, the scrappy environmental club versus a local captain of industry. Like that. But then it all got out of hand."

"Wait. What got out of hand? What in the hell are you talking about?"

Peggy said, "Anhydrous ammonia. At first, Dwayne thought it was meth dealers tapping the Knight Hawk's supplies, using it to make meth and sell it back to the miners, like what's happened in other parts of the country. But then they stumbled onto Galligan's involvement."

I said, "I suppose I don't have to ask whether you know Tony Pelzer."

She made a face and nodded. "Know him. Don't like him. And that's understating it a little, really. A friend of Guy's and a bit of a strong-arm. Promise me, Slim, you deal with him, watch your six."

"Been there, done that, won the hat," I said. "But Pelzer said Dwayne had a theory that Galligan was using meth to juice the King Coal's production numbers."

Peggy said, "I think maybe Dwayne ran that up the flagpole at one point. Truth was, none of us believed it. Anyway, it's a fantasy, Slim. There's nothing to it."

"Then what? If he's not using the ammonia to make meth, what's he doing with it?"

Anci broke her silence. She looked at Peggy and at me and said, "Water."

I said, "Half-pint . . ."

But Peggy nodded and kissed Anci's head again.

"No. She's right, Slim. She is exactly right. Galligan isn't stealing ammonia to make drugs. He's stealing ammonia to clean up dirty water."

Just then, the phone buzzed in my back pocket. I got up from the bed and went out into the hallway and answered. It was Pelzer.

"We might have a problem here, Hawkshaw," he said.

"Just the one?"

"Big one, maybe. I'm at Temple's place. Door's kicked in, and there's a busted window. I tried calling, but no one's answering."

"That doesn't sound so good."

"It sure doesn't. Doesn't look so good, either."

"Did you go inside? Look around a little?"

"Thought I'd wait on you for that," he said.

"Thanks a million," I said. "I'll be right there."

"I'm a statue," he said. "Oh, and Hawkshaw? It's okay to bring a piece this time."

I hung up the phone. Peggy was still on the bed, now hugging Anci to her. The teddy bear was finished.

She said, "What is it?"

"Beckett's wife has gone missing."

"Run away?"

"It looks like someone might have taken her," I said.

Peggy blanched. She said, "My God. Temple. They're killing everybody."

"That's what it looks like, anyway. But I'm hoping no one's been killed tonight." I turned to Anci and said, "How'd you know, by the way? About the water?"

"I guess I just thought it had to be that. If they're not using it for drugs, they might be using it to do what it's really for."

"Cleaning up acid drainage."

Anci nodded, "They teach us about it in school. We even did a class project."

"That's pretty good detective work, squirt."

"Thanks. Got an A, too."

"I've got to go."

Anci hopped down from the bed. "Then I'm coming along."

"Not this time," I said. "But I don't think you two can stay here, either. I'm assuming Galligan knows exactly where you live, Peggy, and you just can't stay."

She looked at me, her eyes bright and hard. A bit of her toughness came back. Maybe it was Anci's presence. Anyway, I considered it a good sign. If any of us was going to live through this foolishness, we were going to need all of us to pull weight.

She said, "Where, then?"

"The Vale," I said. "It's probably the safest place now."

I didn't want to leave them. I wanted to protect my daughter. And I wanted to stay and try to understand where things sat between Peggy and me, but there was no time for relationship healing right then. I kissed them both and put them in Peggy's car and watched them drive away, checking to make sure no cars slipped out of dark corners to follow them down the street. Then I got on my bike and hauled ass to the Estates, but these were country distances, and even hauling ass it took a half hour. By the time I roared down the hill toward the gates, it felt like someone had been tying Christmas bows in my guts.

Lilac was in the box again, and when he recognized me he smiled a little and waved his hand, but there was worry in his face you wouldn't miss twenty yards out in a hailstorm.

"Lot of bustle tonight, Slim," he said.

"I had a sense. What happened?"

"Truck came through here a while back. Yellow K20, I think it was. Came through like a bad man running from the devil. Wanted me to open the arm. I wouldn't, so they opened it for me. Big guy in an orange hat threatened to throw my ass in the water in case I called the cops."

"They still in there?"

"No. About ten minutes later, the truck flew out of here so fast it nearly went over the culvert. I'm guessing it wasn't a pizza delivery."

"Did you call the police?"

He sighed and shook his head, sadly, and looked at me and said, "Should do, but I'm having trouble bringing myself to do it. Slim, I'm a sixty-year-old black gate attendant at a mostly white subdivision. I work here for exactly as long as nothing goes wrong during one of my shifts, at which point I'm unemployed."

He was probably right about that and I was sorry about it and said so. I said I'd see what I could do to settle things down. I drove through and made my way toward the water. The streets were empty, and the dark woods loomed darker yet as night came on and the moon ducked behind the clouds. As I neared the lake, the sound of the licking water grew louder, and a breeze stirred off the cool ripples.

It was then I happened to look up, and there above the Estates all lit up and carelessly smearing its warning lights around in the wet air was the King Coal. Across the gap was a dark patch on the hill that I knew to be the Grendel coal mine, and one of the smeared lights from the King Coal seemed to reach from one mine to the other, like a thread of silver, like a straw, and for the first time it was as though I could see the direct line between them, and I knew. I knew like a flash why Roy Galligan needed so much anhydrous ammonia—so much that he needed to steal the Knight Hawk's supply—and why he would be driven to lie and cheat and even kill to cover up his need. But most of all I thought I might have finally solved the puzzle of what had become of Guy Beckett.

Pelzer was waiting on the street, in the spotlight of a streetlamp, like he meant to break in to song any time an audience happened by.

"Took you long enough."

"Sorry."

"Still nothing on the phone."

"You haven't been inside? I thought you said you were good at moving doors," I said.

"Yeah, but you know what I ain't good at? Getting shot to death by hired killers."

I looked at the house. The door stood open, but the house was dark and still, and if Lilac was right whatever happened had happened. It all had an abandoned-house look to it. I remembered what I had found at Luster's place and I shivered with it.

I swallowed a breath. I said, "You mind waiting here?"

"I ain't minded it yet. Don't plan on changing my mind about it, either."

"I bet you don't. It looks like the bad guys have come and gone, but someone has to watch the street, make sure no one comes back or sneaks up on me once I go inside."

"I'm your man." He sucked it around a moment. Finally, he said, "You think she's in there?"

"Maybe. Maybe not."

"Could be dead."

"Let's not get ahead of ourselves."

"Sure. I'll stay out here not getting ahead of myself."

I nodded and took the 9000S out of my pants and walked up to the house and went inside. I hugged the wall and shadow-hopped, but I needn't have bothered. I was right about being too late. The painting of Temple and the horse had been knocked off its hooks and rested at an angle against the wall. Someone had used a knife to slice the canvas. That just seemed mean. The marble-top coffee table was on its side and missing a leg; the fashionable broad-backed canvas chairs were overturned and stomped into lightweight matchsticks. Every photograph in the house had been taken from its frame. The kitchen wasn't an island of order, either. The dinner plates and teacups had been smashed into a bone china geometry lesson. The cabinets had been emptied, and the canned goods rolled around on the floor.

I searched the kitchen and went quietly through the house and into the living room. I searched the utility room, too, because you want to be thorough about this kind of thing. I went upstairs and found another shambles. The dressers in the bedroom had been emptied and the closets rifled. The fancy clothes were in piles on the floor. I searched the empty guest bedroom and the upstairs bath and found them in similar disarray. I opened the closets and looked inside, and in the last one I found Susan tied and up gagged on the floor.

"You sonofabitch," she said when I took the hankie out of her mouth.

"Me? I didn't do this."

"I know," she said. "I'm just angry."

"Where's Temple?"

"She's not in this closet, is she? I don't know."

I finished untying her. She looked frazzled but, all told, not too much the worse for the experience. There was a bruise under her right eye where someone had socked her, but nothing seemed to be broken, and she walked okay. We went downstairs. I tried to help her, but she shrugged my arm away and grunted a bad word at me. I figured she'd be fine.

"When?" I asked when Pelzer had come in from the street and joined us.

"Couple of hours ago," she said. "Maybe longer. It's easy to lose track of time when you're stuck in a dark closet. What time is it now?"

I told her.

She said, "It's longer. I must have been in there three hours or so. Some time around four, someone knocked on the door, and I went to open it, and that's the last thing I remember until I woke up in the dark."

"Did you get a look at anyone before your nap? Even for a second?"

"Your concern is touching," she said.

I said, "I'll be concerned later, when there's time. Right

now, you look healthy enough, but Temple might not be. So, I'll ask you again: did you get a look at anyone?"

She breathed in and shut her eyes and seemed to gather herself a little. She said, "I don't mean to be a baby."

"You're not. You've just had a shock, is all."

She nodded at me, and I figured that was the closest thing to gratitude she was capable of. "There was a big guy. In a camo shirt and orange hat. Great fashion sense. Redneck of the year. I didn't recognize him, though."

Pelzer said, "That might have been Sonny."

"Who?"

"Sonny Goines. One of Galligan's guys. His right-hand guy, in fact. He's always wearing an orange hat, like a trucker hat. Godawful thing."

Susan said, "That's what it was. I couldn't think of what to call it. With the high front. I think it said *I Hunt White Tail* on it."

Pelzer sniffed and nodded. "Sonny."

"Does that mean what I think it means?"

"Yeah. There used to be a drawing of a girl's naked behind on it, but the hat's old, and the girl kinda faded out. Now all that's left are the words."

I said, "You know an awful lot about this hat."

Pelzer frowned and threw up his hands. "I just noticed it, is all."

"Okay," I said. "Stop pouting. I think I saw it the other day, and you're right; it's an ugly hat. The question is, why take Temple? What's she got to do with it all?"

"Could be any number of things, you think about it for half a second. Instead of, say, insulting someone's powers of observation."

"Tony . . ."

"Like maybe they think she knows something," Pelzer said. "Maybe they think Beckett talked in his sleep. Or that he couldn't keep his mouth shut around his wife. A lot of guys can't, you know. Even guys who don't like their wives. Or maybe they think she knows where the picture of Jim Hart is." He looked at me. "You never brought it to me, by the way."

"Wasn't time," I said. "I'll see that you get it. Meantime, what are we going to do?"

Susan said, "Are you out of your mind? What do you mean, what are you doing to do? Call the police. Now."

"We do that, she's dead," Pelzer said. "She's probably dead anyway."

Susan glared at him. "Don't you dare say that again."

Pelzer said, "Hey, I'm not crazy about the idea, either, but that's where we are. They'll get what they can out of her. They'll ask her questions, maybe rough her up a bit, I don't know. And when they think they've got it all, they'll pop her. You go to the cops, they'll still be typing up your complaint when Galligan and his men are looking for a place to bury the body."

Susan blanched. She said, "I think I need to sit down."

We helped her to a chair. She buried her face in her hands.

"What do you want to do?" Pelzer asked me.

"I need to check something," I said. "I know we don't have a lot of time, but it has to be done. It's what I've been trying to do since I started this business, and doing it might help us in the end. As soon as I'm back, we're going to get Temple. Tonight."

I rode fast, and it only took a little more than twenty minutes to get there. The access road to the Grendel no longer existed, so I had to hike the dense timberland between the new mine and old. What remained of the colliery was a building skeleton here and there and a few pieces of junked equipment, abandoned where they fell and overgrown by grasses and vines. The shower house was still mostly standing, and the noise of the metal clothing hooks clanging and clanking together in the winter wind sent mortal chills through my blood. This was a slope mine, not a shaft, which means it had a walk-in entry, an adit twenty-five feet or so up a curved, stone-clotted slope. When I reached the top, I spied the ragged hole Guy Beckett had chopped in the concrete stopper. That's the way they did with some of these old mines. They'd abandon the works, and then, to keep out children or fools, they'd clot up the entries with concrete blocks or a steel hatch, whatever made sense for that mine. This one had concrete blocks, and Guy Beckett had used a pickax or a sledge to crack them open and bust his way inside. Despite everything, I'd kinda hoped to be wrong.

The air in the work area was stale and cold and tasted faintly of rusted metal, kind of like sucking on a dirty nail. You've ever had occasion to suck a dirty nail, I mean. And damn, it was dark in there. Dark as an exorcist's jokes but not as funny. The floors were bottoms—floors caked with deposited coal fine—and the batters had crumbled onto their arches and partially collapsed so that you could barely stand up, and the effect was something like being trapped inside a frozen black coffin. The first thing I did was step on part of an old crib can and damn near puncture my foot.

That was bad enough, sure, but then I ran into the bats. Literally ran into them, face-first, a colony hanging upside down in a dark corner like a bunch of overripe fruit. That pissed them off something awful, being woke up like that, and suddenly the cave front was filled with the slap of leathery wings and a piercing shriek that sent me diving for the floor, arms over my head, hoping to at least avoid a case of the rabies.

There are plenty of awful places to work and toil in the world, in many occupations, but man, that old slope mine had to be near the top of the list. Old enough to have remnant wooden beams and cradles and an alligator looked like it'd been built during the Civil War, the Grendel was as low as some scratchback mines I'd seen, and the only fire-prevention devices were in the form of cloth sacks and rock dust. The stopes were slick with slime and bat guano, and the backs winked eerily with some kind of rotting mushroom light that was somehow more disorienting than the dark. I guess it's no wonder Beckett ran into bad luck. You'd have to know mines pretty well not to, in a place like that.

I found him twenty minutes later. There was an open spot off the face where the shadows were so thick my spotlight couldn't flush all of them out. He was facedown in a deep pool, and there wasn't much left of him. His blue-veined features had been eaten away by liquid poison. Also known as acid mine drainage, the poison created when water comes into contact with sulfides in the rock. It's known by another name, on account of its color: yellow boy.

Farther down the tunnel, the sound of water was a restless drip, slowly filling the bowels of the mine. I made my way as far as I dared, farther than Beckett by maybe a hundred yards, until I found the jerry-rigged pipe system and saw the water pouring through it. Around the lip of the pipe, the ribs of the Grendel were broken, cracked through so deeply that in places the top had collapsed around them as though in surrender. It wouldn't be long before the earth shifted again and the water stored up inside the mine burst out and sluiced its way toward the wildlife preserve, with its trees and wildlife and water plants and good fishing. I got out of there before I froze to death.

I needed to make a call, but my cell phone was full of water. Or, as it were, the evidence. There was a bar up the road from the wildlife refuge. It wasn't a good place. It was a fighting place, a roadhouse that changed owners so often they could have used it as the basis for a new series of teenage slasher movies, Camp Crystal Lake with a liquor license. But it would have to do. I went inside and looked around for a pay phone. A guy tried to start a fight with me, but I wouldn't let him. After a while, he gave it up and stalked off to a table in the corner and had a pout about it. I found the phone at the back of the house, but someone had ripped it off the wall and it hung there from the busted plaster by a few cords. Something about that broke me inside. I flashed angry. I stomped back toward the front of the house. The guy who wanted to fight looked up at me. I kicked him right out of his chair and to the floor. I didn't want him to lose all hope in his fellow man. I leaned down and took his phone from his pocket and used it to make a call.

"I'm working," Jeep said. He was, too. I could barely hear him over the roar of the machines.

I said, "Might be time to consider a new line. Or at least a new boss."

"What's he done now?"

"Not much," I said. "You know, murder, kidnapping, an attempt to poison the world."

"I wouldn't put it past him."

"My place, soon as you can," I said, and hung up.

I gave the angry guy back his phone and thanked him. He seemed better, more centered after his kicking, and seemed not to hold any of it against me. Probably I'd made his night because now he had a story to tell, and that's the only reason anyone ever did anything anyway. We even shook hands and then I left the bar and went outside.

I crossed the noisy parking lot and climbed on the bike. The ignition switch on the Triumph is under your left leg, so you have to lean down to insert the key. I'd just done that when something slammed my head hard off the top of the tank, then grabbed me by the collar of my jacket and pulled me off the side of the bike. I was always getting kicked or hit or thrown off of my bike these days. Twenty years without falling off my bike, or putting her down, and now all of a sudden I couldn't manage to stay in my saddle. This time, though, I had on my helmet, and the pavement jumped up and hit me in the head but didn't do any lasting damage. I scrambled to my feet and pulled off the helmet and turned just as he materialized out of the shadows.

There was a pistol in his hand. He pointed it at my heart.

He said, "You goddamn cocksucker."

It was Jump Down.

FOURTEEN

He didn't need them—the gun was probably enough—
but he'd brought along two boys: big, meaty things with
scars on their awful faces and a frozen dislike in their eyes.
They were horrible and they didn't do anything to hide it.
You tried to imagine them having human mothers, but you
couldn't do it. Sharks, maybe. They put me in the backseat
of a green maxi-cab. The boys got in front. Jump climbed in
with me and we roared quickly away from the parking lot.
No one bothered to look up at us as we left. Probably they
had abductions there all the time.

I said, "This is kidnapping."

"Shut up."

"Well, it is."

Jump nodded. He turned his head slightly, as though to
look thoughtfully out the window. His eyes wobbled in his
head in that way of theirs, and then he suddenly swung with
his right arm and shoved me back against the seat.

He said, "It is. And I said shut up."

I shut up. The maxi cruised out of town and south a ways
on Spillway Road until we cut back west toward a gated
access into the wildlife preserve. The maxi lurched to a stop,
throwing us against the backs of the seats in front of us. The
big guy who was driving turned around and apologized to
Jump Down with a look, and the other guy got out and rus-
tled around in the bed for a moment and then there was the
sound of metal snapping. The door opened and the boy got

back in and we were underway again. I figured he'd used a pair of bolt-cutters to snip the chain off a barrier arm and take us into the woods.

You're about to die like that—and I was pretty sure that's where we were heading—your mind starts tearing off in all kinds of directions. I thought of Anci and Peggy and of what they'd think when they'd learned I came to harm. I silently asked Peggy to take care of Anci, and I asked Jeep Mabry to keep guarding over them and make it so they were safe. I found myself thinking of my old man and the bad he'd done and how maybe I'd tried to make up for a few of those things in my own way and through my own actions, but I didn't ask anything of him that didn't involve regrets and lost chances. When I was young, we'd come to this very preserve every fall to watch the migration of the Canada geese. One year, we found a goose with a badly broken wing, and instead of just leaving it there or killing it like I thought he would he'd wrapped it in his jacket and taken it to the rangers' station and then driven with the ranger to an animal rehabilitation preserve in Tennessee. Not much later, he'd gone away, and in that first year of loneliness I took my sisters back to see the geese on my own, but it wasn't the same and we never went again. I thought of Guy Beckett's body in the Grendel mine, and I wondered whether anyone would ever find him again. That was a lonely place of dying. I thought of how I wish I'd listened to my own good sense and refused to take Matthew Luster up on his devilish bargain, and how taking him up on it meant that Peggy and I would never get to make our life together, assuming we could have salvaged our relationship. I was thinking all that when the truck stopped at last and the engine died. The front doors opened and the big boys got out. One of them opened Jump Down's side, and allowed him to step out. The other pulled open my side and reached in and pulled me from my seat and to the ground like a sack of flour.

Jump came around the truck and over to me and squatted down. He rested his hand on his knee, and the big revolver filled his fist. I could feel the sweat trickling down my face. Jump said, "Shit just got real. You don't look so good, Slim."

"Don't feel so good, either."

"Yeah, and you shouldn't. Here I let you off the hook, and look what I get in return for my generosity. You've made a lot of trouble for me, cousin."

I said, "Not me, but I guess I understand why you think that way."

He nodded at that, more thoughtfully than I imagined him able. He scratched his head and spat into the dirt and said, "The cops are after me, man. They came to my place the other day and talked to my mother."

"You live with your mother?"

He shrugged. "Yeah. So what?"

"It's just kinda weird, don't you think? I mean, given your . . . occupation."

"I'm a coal miner, man. Nothing else. And the old lady was upset, and when she gets upset her phlebitis acts up. You think that's funny?"

I didn't realize I'd been smiling. "It's kind of funny," I said.

"It's not funny," he said, shaking his head. "You are wrong. It is a very painful and frustrating condition."

"Okay, I apologize. It just wasn't what I expected you to say."

"Top of that, the meds she needs to control it aren't exactly cheap, you know."

"I said I was sorry."

He wasn't listening. "So she gets mad and she's already in discomfort. She has to dip into her bingo money, and that makes her even madder, and she takes it all out on me. Guess who I'm blaming."

"Me?"

"Good guess."

"Or Galligan."

"There you go with that Galligan business again," he said. "We're talking about Roy Galligan here, right?"

"Less you know some Galligans I don't."

"How you figure?"

I shook my head and said, "Look, if you're going to shoot me, I'd just as soon as you get on it, save me the headache of trying to ram information into that bank vault between your ears."

"You're trying to piss me off," he said. "Get me to do you quickly. I get that. I'm not a zombie, man."

"You're close."

"There you go again," he said. He laughed quietly under his breath. The piles of meat shuffled nervously. One of them scraped a foot on the gravel path. He was like a horse scraping out the last ticks of my life with his hoof. "You should be careful, though. Guns have a way of just going off. At this range, the Commander here would rip a hole through your throat, and you'd bleed out in under a minute."

"Pretty thought."

"I told you the other day I'd hold my fire, and I did, but then someone told the cops that I'd sent some men to shoot you and your daughter, and now I'm on the hook for it. I'm living in one of the mobile labs, and I have to sleep in a gas mask, so if I wanted you dead, Slim, there'd be plenty of reason already to put a hole in your brain."

"So why not?"

"Why not is, I haven't built myself into something by going off half cocked. You deserve shooting, but I know who your old man was and I know who you're butt buddies with, and I'm not crazy about the idea of any more of my men going missing. Or me."

"Wait," I said. "Who went missing?"

"You're pissing me off, man. You know your boy Mabry pulled one of my men off the count in revenge for the other night."

"He didn't."

"Bullshit."

"He wouldn't," I said. "Tell the hard truth, I'm thinking he wouldn't need to."

"What? You think my guys can't look after themselves?"

I shrugged.

Jump Down said, "You think all that muscle's just for show, or what?"

I shrugged.

Jump Down said, "You think you could take them? You think you could take even one of them?"

"It's not my policy to piss off the guy holding the gun, but, yeah, I think I could. Without much trouble, either. Certainly I wouldn't need to turn Jeep Mabry loose on them. C'mon, look at those two. They're like something you won throwing baseballs at milk bottles. They're adorable."

He said, "So what you're saying is, you think you could

take, say, Lonnie there?" He waved vaguely in the direction of his boys. Both of them showed me mouthfuls of rotted teeth. I didn't know which teeth in which mouth belonged to Lonnie.

"Tell you what, let's make a deal," I said.

"I'm not sure you're in a deal-making position."

"Probably not, but here's one anyway: Let Lonnie and me go a round. He beats me, it's anything goes. I won't squawk. Put holes in me if you like. Whatever other wickedness you have in mind. But if I beat him, you give me twenty-four hours so I can go after Roy Galligan and put our troubles to rest. Yours and mine."

Jump Down thought about that some. He looked at his boys, but neither of them said anything or revealed how they might have felt about my idea. Probably they liked it fine. I didn't look like much. I was wet and cold and scared and had a bump on my head. My courage was as phony as a three-dollar bill. I'd laughed at an old woman and her phlebitis. Jump Down turned back to me and said, "Why on earth do you think I'd go along with something like this?"

"I don't know. Meanness maybe. Or boredom. And then there's always the off chance that I'm telling the truth. You can kill me, but tomorrow your problem is still the same."

"Galligan?"

"Galligan."

"Okay, maybe. But you got to put up more. Just not squawking isn't too much for me to win, and I plan to win anyway. I got the gun, after all."

"You'll win," one of the boys said. Lonnie, I guess. He studied me, and I studied him back. He was the larger of the two, which I found disappointing. Besides being smaller, the other guy moved with just the slightest limp, so I'd kinda hoped Lonnie was him. Lonnie was something else, though. He had arms like tree limbs and a head like a concrete block. His chest was as big around as a Hula-Hoop, and his hands looked like they could palm a Thanksgiving turkey. Fighting him wasn't my favorite idea.

I said, "What more can I put up?"

"Yourself, one," he said. "Mabry, two. In other words, after Lonnie there kicks your ass, you're both on my payroll for, say, a year. Except I ain't actually paying you, get it?"

"I get it," I said. "We'll be errand boys."

"Errand boys, or whatever else I need."

"Muscle?"

"Mabry, maybe. You, I ain't so sure. You're kinda wiry."

"Pot, kettle," I said. "Besides, Mabry won't ever agree to any such foolishness."

"He will if you tell him to. Everybody knows he'd strangle his mother for you. Anyway, it's either this or you don't walk away from here. So what do you say?"

There was just the one thing to say. I agreed. I figured that if I died, Jeep would murder the boy for killing me, and if I lived, Jeep would murder the boy for being such a lunkhead and hatching such a dim-witted scheme. Either way, he was in a world of hurt. That made things seem slightly cheerier.

Lonnie didn't do anything to help my mood, though. Jump Down and the other boy stepped back and Lonnie came over to me, cracking his knuckles and shaking a hitch out of his neck and making a noise in his throat like snot boiling. He went maybe six foot seven or so and was basically built like a Sherman tank. I figured him for a solid 325 at least. I'd seen plenty of big guys in my time, but that motherfucker was big enough to project a Charlton Heston

movie on. I stood off the ground and got into something re-
sembling a fight stance, and Jump Down barked something,
and Lonnie lunged in with a jab that hit me in the top of the
chest and sent me over backward.

That hurt like hell, but I'll tell you, I immediately felt better
about my chances. A single punch can tell a story, and Lonnie's
told me plenty. He'd done some bouncing work and probably
some other kind of hard physical labor—mine or farm work,
probably—but he'd gotten by mostly on body mass and bad
looks, and his fighting style seemed more haphazard than anything. His footwork was a series of stomps, and when he advanced on me he did it with his hands low and his head forward.

I clambered to my feet, and the boy came in again and
tossed off a painfully slow right hook. I cut inside the shadow
of his big body and kicked him in the gut. I rolled right and
went outside and hit him on the left ear so hard he went
down on a knee. He looked up and swiped at me with one of
his mitts, and I tried to get out of his way but he grabbed the
top of my leg and flung me across the road like a rag doll. He
laughed. He liked that one okay. I got up and we circled one
another. His buddy shouted some encouragement, and the
kid got cocky and lunged in again, swiping at my head. This
time I got lucky and he missed badly and overextended himself right into my jump front kick. That was a good hit, but
not my best, and it sent him spilling slightly sideways but not
down. He was stronger even than he looked, though, and he
came right back at me, lunging all his weight off his back
leg. He hit me a stunner in the left shoulder, and I felt the
arm go dead, but the boy's momentum was too strong and
he chased his own punch and lurched forward on his toes.
I moved slightly left and turned back into him. I stuck out

my foot and tripped him, then grabbed hold of his hair and bounced his face off the side of the maxi-cab so hard he left a shallow dent. He dropped to the ground and stayed there.

Jump Down looked at me and at his boy. He turned his head and spat again and looked at the gun in his hand and did some thinking. His eyes wobbled and shook like boiling eggs and finally I could see him make his decision. He shrugged. He said, "Okay. Like we agreed, twenty-four hours. Then we got to take care of this for good."

I stood there. Jump Down stared at me. He said, "Goddamn it, I said you got your twenty-four. What the fuck else do you want?"

I said, "I need a lift back to my bike."

I reached Indian Vale just as the first barks of thunder rattled overhead. That big front was pushing through, and this one was going to be a boomer. The sky darkened some more, and the stars ducked away and hid their bright heads. I got off the Triumph and walked up to the house just as a violent wind stirred and the weather cut loose. Rain slammed the house and rattled the windowpanes and a crack of lightning cut through the sky west of the valley.

Jeep Mabry and Pelzer were waiting for me under the overhang of my front porch.

"I'll say this for you, Slick," Jeep said, "you know how to make an entrance."

They'd already introduced themselves—I'm guessing with a grunt and a nod—but I did the pleasantries again anyway and watched them size each other up. I told them what had happened with Jump Down, and Pelzer laughed and shook his head. Jeep fumed.

He said, "Soon as we're done with this business here, that little bastard is dog food."

"I kinda thought you'd say that," I said. "But let's take one massacre at a time."

I walked past them and into the house and found Peggy and Anci calmly doing math homework at the kitchen table. There were some sodas and chips and other supper leavings strewn out, as was Peggy's Winchester Model 94 short rifle. She put her hand on it when I came in the room.

I said, "Easy there, deadeye."

She said, "Good lord, you gave me a fright. What the heck happened to you?"

"Ran into an old pal."

"And he kicked your ass?"

I said, "He had a momentary upper hand, but things evened out in the end."

Peggy said, "That's Tony Pelzer out there."

"Yes, it is."

"Well, he can't come in here. Apologies to whatshisname . . ."

"Jeep."

"Apologies to whatshisname, but I don't want him in here with us, and me and this rifle here told him so."

"They can wait on the porch," I said, and told her what there was of it to tell. She took it in and looked at me a long time. She ruffled Anci's hair and whispered something in her ear, and Anci hopped down off her chair and went quickly and quietly out of the room with a worried glance at me.

When we were alone, Peggy said, "You're going to leave that little one behind."

"Just for a while."

"That's not what I mean, Slim. What I mean is, you're going to go off and get yourself shot to hell and leave her behind for good and permanent. What kind of a father would do something like that? I didn't know better, I'd think you were enjoying this thing a little."

I don't mind telling you, that got me a little warm under the bandages, and I said so. Days of bad sleep, worse food, and hot-and-cold-running beatings had got to me some, I guess. I said, "And I think you're forgetting that our alternatives aren't too attractive, either. I let this thing go, I got to spend my midlife crisis looking over my shoulder for stray bullets. Anci, too."

"You could run."

"Run where? Another town? Another state? And what would that teach Anci?"

"It'd teach her that sometimes you get in over your head. That sometimes it's okay to cut your losses."

I said, "And someone taught you that, Peggy."

She stepped to me and hit me in the mouth. It was a pretty good shot, too, and I stepped backward twice and hit the wall. Thing like that can go one or two ways. Sometimes a punch makes you madder and sometimes it knocks your mad right out of the room, and Peggy's hit did the latter. We both looked at each other in that shocked way you get under such circumstances, and then we laughed a little.

Peggy said, "Goddamn it all. Look at me."

I touched my bloody mouth with my fingers.

"It's okay."

"I ain't apologizing, you asshole," she said, but she smiled sheepishly. "I'm just pissed I didn't knock your sorry ass out."

"Oh. Can I say that you've got a pretty good swing for a schoolteacher? Or will that just lead to more violence?"

"I grew up on a chicken farm with four brothers," she said, proud. She got her purse and dug until she found some scraps of pink tissue for me. "And I was the oldest. My mom made sure I knew how to fight."

"I knew all that," I said, "except the part about your mom. She sounds like a hell-raiser."

"You would have liked her," she told me, and smiled sadly at her memories. "She was as ornery as a Republican mule, and she could drink all the men in the county under the table."

"Sounds tough."

"She was. Maybe too much so. But something gets everybody, eventually. You sure you got to do this thing?"

"Pretty sure."

She picked the rifle off the table. She said, "You want some backup?"

"I want Galligan and his men in one piece at the end of this," I said. "You come along, there won't be enough left to fill an ashtray."

"Say that again. I don't know the last time I was so mad."

"Me, either. You mind keeping watch over Anci?"

"We'll be here when you get back."

"Thank you."

We kissed, and she touched my face and said, "I know I said I wasn't, but I am sorry about before. About hitting. I guess there's been some tension between us lately."

"Maybe a little."

"This is all my fault. Everything that's happening."

"It's nobody's fault. Or it's all our fault. Or something. It's the way we built our world, and I guess it was inevitable that it'd come to tears one day."

"Maybe," she said. She paused and looked into me deeply

for what seemed a long time, and then she said, "And Slim, my answer is yes."

"Your answer?"

"To what you've been asking me. You and me. Let's build that family together."

"You're sure?"

"Damn sure."

We kissed again and said our good-byes and a few other things, and after a moment I went out. Jeep and Pelzer were waiting. Pelzer was smoking a cigarette.

He said, "You're bleeding again."

"I know."

"You bleed more than a nun's vision. It makes a body nervous."

Nervous or no, we gathered up our things and moved out into the swirling night. Pelzer drove his beat-up van. Jeep and I shared my truck.

Jeep said, "Hell of a night for this."

Hell of a night for anything. The rain came down hard and pelted the windshield, and the wind shoved our vehicles around like scraps of tin. We'd settled on checking Galligan's De Soto residence first, but about halfway there Pelzer's van slid off the road into a ditch. He was banged up some, but when we stopped the truck and ran back through the washer to rescue him he seemed not much worse for wear.

"This is crazy," Pelzer said over the noise of the rain.

It was crazy, but it was the plan, such as it was. It took us a half hour to pull him out of the ditch and get back on the road, time we keenly felt. When we finally reached Galligan's place, we found the house dark and seemingly empty, something Jeep Mabry confirmed with a quick reconnoiter.

"Told you," Pelzer said.

I shrugged. "Time well spent, though. I'd hate to run all over the tricounties looking for them only to find out later that they were in the most obvious spot all along."

"Meanwhile, Temple Beckett is being put in a box."

"Pelzer," I said, "you open your mouth again for something like that, I'm going to let Mabry here turn you into a sock puppet."

Jeep grinned and folded his arms. Pelzer looked at him for a moment, assessing his chances, probably, then lapsed into a sullen quiet. His chances sucked, and he knew it.

Jeep looked at me. "Where to now, Slick?"

"Goines's place."

"You know where it is?"

I knew where it was. The place was a rental, and not even in Goines's name, but you look hard enough, you can always find someone to bribe. It'd taken a bit of doing—and a bit of cash— but eventually I'd come up with an address. The place was a stone-and-wood A-frame somewhere between Pomona and nowhere, in a lonesome spot at the dark edge of the national forest and without a neighbor anywhere in sight. A perfect hideout. We separated again and rolled out that way, our windshield wipers barely keeping up with the storm, and after a bit of knocking around in the dark and the wild rain we managed to find the place. Under the clouds, it looked a little like an Indian cave or some kind of black-magic church, and when the lightning flashed overhead it cast a fearful, peaked shadow on the grass.

Jeep said, "Okay, better. But are you sure they're inside?"

"Sure enough," I said. "It's a little late to be out for a stroll."

"They could be somewhere else entirely."

"I don't think so," I said. "Their cars are around back, hoping to avoid anyone noticing. Not that there's anyone out here to notice, but I guess they've elected to be extra cautious. You can't see the cars, but look there in the grass. Tire marks, and the grass is flattened down. Recently, too."

"Nice eye, buddy," Jeep said.

"If you two girls are done complimenting each other," Pelzer said, "maybe we should go see what there is to see."

I nodded. Jeep nodded. He looked at Pelzer. For a moment, I thought he might knock his head clean off. He must have decided we'd need Pelzer's gun, though, because instead of head-knocking he hopped down from his truck and raced off through the rain into the dark. Pelzer and I followed, quickly and quietly. We didn't really have much more of a plan than that. We ran through the yard, through the howling wind and sheets of rain, straight toward the house. We were tough men on a mission, and we had all kinds of guns. There would probably be murders. We were finally living up to our potential as Americans.

Jeep was fast, but surprisingly, Pelzer was faster. He got in front of us and hit the front porch at a leaping sprint. He caught air and slammed into the door with his shoulder. I guess he had a picture of it in his mind. This was a good door, though. An expensive door. The wood flexed less than a millimeter and spat him out like a wad of gum, and he landed on the concrete with a yelp.

Jeep looked down at him.

"You dumb little peckerwood." He shook his head. "I don't guess you thought of trying the knob first?"

Jeep tried the knob. The door clicked open, and Jeep pushed it once gently then reared back and kicked it hard with the bottom of his boot. A big guy with a tattooed face was there to greet us. The door greeted him first, smashed into his mush and drove him over and to the ground. He tried to get up, but Jeep stomped his knee and kicked him in the nuts, and the guy burped a word I'm pretty sure he made up on the spot.

I came in behind Jeep. Pelzer followed me, ducking low and to the left as soon as he was inside. I sort of hoped that they'd be hiding out in small numbers, but the room was full of assholes and firearms. The furniture had been scooted back against the walls and the den turned into a kind of situation room with a table in the center. The lights were on and some candles were lit in case the lights went out. There were bottles of booze everywhere and cigarettes and ashtrays. There were six guys present, too, besides tattoo-face: three rednecks, a mountain man with a big beard who looked like he ate weightlifters for breakfast, a fat boy with a leather jacket and one of those swollen faces looks like it's about to pop, and Goines, still wearing that silly orange hat. Seriously, he looked ridiculous.

Everything that happened next happened in a jumble. Redneck #1 slid a long-barrel .38 from the crack of his ass. But Jeep was ready. He whipped out his twelve gauge and emptied fire and steel into the room. Redneck #2 got hit and parts of him went down in a pool. The table pretty much disappeared. Everyone else jumped from under their hats and dove for cover.

A gun went off and there was a flash of heat and a spark and I hit the deck. It was like someone had hit me in the chest with a post-hole digger. When I got up, the dude with the beard was charging me. I didn't have time to get my footing, and he tackled me and down I went again, harder this time, but came up with the bastard's leg. I tried twisting him to the floor, but he was like a block of lead; he barely moved. He whacked me a good lick in the eye, and I dropped his leg and rolled over and away and came up two-footed and ready to fight. Just then, the storm picked up even more. The wind punched the house, and the wallboards rattled and moaned threateningly, and a window blew out. Rain and some freezing something came pushing in and the power flickered and died and darkness draped the room like a widow's frown.

I turned again and the Beard was there, like a nightmare. He punched me in the top of the chest, going for my neck maybe, and I fell over and rolled. I came up on the balls of my feet, leapt in. I snatched a small, decorative mirror off the wall and hit him with his own face, and the Beard went down and stayed there.

I looked up and wished I hadn't. The room was like an operating theater. Pelzer had Redneck #3 and Fatboy by the hair, one in each hand, and he was banging their heads off the coffee table so hard that both their faces were flattened like wet clay. He only stopped when I yelled at him, and the boys slid one way and other, sighing in relief as they slumped onto the smashed furniture.

"You're spoiling my fun, Hawkshaw," Pelzer said.

"Fun, hell. That was about to be murder." I looked around on the floor at the various bodies and parts of bodies. I didn't see anything orange. I said, "Where's Goines?"

"Here."

Back of the room was a kitchen and one of those kitchen cutouts. Goines must have slipped down behind the counter during all the excitement. There was a blur of Day-Glo as he stood and swung into the room and shot Pelzer in the head. Pelzer disappeared behind the sofa, and Goines turned the gun and shot twice at Jeep, who dove for cover. Then he turned his attention to me. I didn't have any cover available.

What I had was maybe half a second. A sawed-off shotgun rested on the pile of matchsticks that had been the coffee table, and I dove and reached for the pistol-grip gunstock but came up instead with a table leg. Good enough, I guess. I swung it hard at Goines's wrist and hit it, and he yelped like a calf and dropped his Dan Wesson .45 Bobtail. He tried to pull back and into a football kick, but it was a clumsy effort and I jabbed him between the eyes and swung the table leg at that silly orange hat, going for the home run.

The boy was quick, though. Quick as a greased cougar. He stepped under my swing and cracked me a good one in the ribs and then dropped to the floor and hooked my legs and brought me down with him. On my way, I reached out to arrest my fall and dropped the table leg, but the Bobtail was there beside me, and I grabbed it and fired off two wild ones. The air tore around us and Goines screamed and jumped backward off me and crab-walked toward the kitchen.

"Careful, slick," Jeep shouted behind me.

But I didn't listen. I launched myself into the kitchen, and Goines sprung suddenly back into view. He whipped something through the air, and the something hit me in the head, and I realized all at once that it was a toaster swinging by its cord. It was one of those old-timey ones, too, the metal ones that are built like bank safes, and I pitched over sideways, and there again was Goines.

"You goddamn troublemaking sonofabitch," he said. "I'm sending you to hell tonight."

I still had the Bobtail, but Goines grabbed my wrist and

twisted until I dropped the gun. He kicked it away. The kitchen was small, like you usually find in cheap rentals, and there wasn't much room to maneuver. Goines pressed himself away from me and spun right and hit me with an elbow-strike that sent me staggering against the stove. He moved in and jabbed again but missed, and I picked up a Teflon fry pan and struck him a good one across the chops with it. Blood looped from his nose and mouth and he bent down as though on reflex, and I hit him on the head again and again, like I was driving a rail spike, but the fucker refused to pass out or die. He avoided another hit and swung a right hook into my ear and grabbed me by the throat and sent me crashing into the wall. I hit the wainscot with such a thud that a clock dropped on my head and spat its little wooden bird across the linoleum.

I got to my knees and crawled into the living room and stood quickly. Before I could turn, though, Goines hit me in the back and drove me forward onto my face. He kicked me in the ribs until I rolled over, and he kicked me in the head and then reared back and made like to stomp me through the carpet and into the crawl space, and I rolled to my left and this time came up with the sawed-off and shot him in the foot.

Well, that was a sight. There was a roar and a blast of hellish smoke, and Sonny's foot just kinda vanished in a puff of suede and boot stuffing. His standing-leg buckled, and he sank down on his butt and grabbed his shoe. He looked up at me, and I looked down at him and suddenly found myself staring down the barrel of the gun, and man, let me tell you, all kinds of things run through your mind in a moment like that. I couldn't very well leave it lie, couldn't leave the little shit running around and unleashing hell on me and mine. My brain was going like a wheel, and it wasn't thinking about whether to add Goines to my Christmas card list. More like how much lye such a thing might require—Fatboy included—or where I might get a hacksaw that time of night.

But I didn't get to give any of that, or murder or self-defense or whatever it was, much more thought, because just then there was another shot, this one straight up into the ceiling and roaring loud. I looked up to find Roy Galligan, dressed fine in a suit as white as the season's first snow, coming down the stairs holding an antique Colt Kodiak double. His hair was the same pale blond, and upon his finger was a circle of carved anthracite. He was a fancy one, the kind of guy who made you want to use words like "upon." His belt buckle was mighty, and his alligator boots winked with silver buckles. The house seemed fairly to creak under his weight.

"That's enough, if you don't mind," he said, voice like a cave-in. He stopped to survey the room. "Holy God. It's an abattoir. How did it come to this?"

He didn't bother about my gun. He strode into the room, kicking pieces of this and that—furniture and employees—out of his way with equal disdain. He stepped to the kitchen and rested the Kodiak against a counter. He opened a cabinet and brought out a crystal decanter and a handful of glasses and set them on the bar.

"I saw you the other day up there to Coulterville. Buying chili. You're Slim, aren't you?"

"You Roy?"

We agreed we were who we were. Jeep came out and dusted himself off, and Pelzer stirred on the floor. He sat up and rubbed a swipe of blood around the side of his neck.

I said, "Thank God. I thought you were dead."

"I thought so, too." His hand went to the side of his head. He glared at Goines on the floor. "For a second anyway. Little shit shot my ear off."

"Better than your skull."

"Or my balls. Think they can sew it back on?" he asked.

"If you can find it," I said. "It might have gone under the couch."

He fished around until he found his ear under the sofa.

"Good eye. I bet they can sew it back on," he said.

"It's a world of medical miracles. Take this."

Pelzer put his ear in his shirt pocket and climbed to his feet. I handed him the sawed-off, and he stood there holding it and eyeing Galligan like something growing out of his nose.

Galligan looked back at him and smiled sweetly and said, "My opinion, boy, you look better without it. Evens out your head some."

I said, "You like gambling, don't you, man?"

"What else is there, boy?"

"A long, healthy life, one."

He regarded me with pity. "You're welcome to it. I'll take my money and my fun," he said. "I don't suppose I have to ask what this is about, do I?"

"Foremost, it's about Temple Beckett. Where is she?"

Galligan sighed. He drank his drink and looked at the loss with sorrow. I bet he always did that. He wanted his pie and to have it, too.

At last, he said, "Upstairs. First door on the left."

"Anyone else up there we ought to know about?"

"No," he said. He looked around the floor a little. "It looks like you got them all."

I nodded at Jeep, and he and Pelzer went upstairs. They took their guns. I had the 9000S to keep an eye on our host. You could only trust a man like Roy Galligan so far, which was to say not at all.

"It's also about Guy Beckett," I said when we were alone. I had to raise my voice, the storm was so loud, but the old man seemed not to have noticed it at all. "He's dead, you know."

"I wouldn't know about that," he said.

"I'm not guessing," I said. "I found him in the Grendel. Drowned in all the poison water you've been funneling into it."

"I confess, I'd wondered about that. He had to have gone somewhere, after all."

"He stumbled down there to pick up a water sample, maybe," I said. "Or to take pictures of your jerry-rigged pipe system. Whichever, he got lost in the dark somehow and couldn't find his way back out. Eventually, he panicked and got hung up on something and drowned. I found him in a room off the face."

Goines swore softly under his breath. His face was pasty white, but the boy was rawhide tough, I'll give him that. He toyed around with taking off his boot but gave it up when the job got too painful, and now he just sat there staring up at us with his crazy eyes.

Galligan looked at him, too, though maybe with less admiration. He said, "Foot full of lead, Sonny? Well, there are worse things. Sit tight, we'll get you fixed up." He turned to me again and said, "Did you bring him out? Beckett?"

I shook my head, and Galligan winked meanly at me and grinned like we were sharing diabolical doings.

He said, "Because you want money."

"Because I want to be left alone," I said. "Anyway, there wasn't time to bring him out. I'm not sure I could have done it by myself anyway."

Galligan nodded. He said, "Probably not. I had the sad fortune of moving some drowned bodies after the flood of '45, and they were as heavy as granite blocks, even the little ones."

"Let me ask you this: how much water would you say you've funneled from the King Coal into that old coal mine?"

If I'd hoped to surprise him with my brilliant detective work, I'd have gone home and cried into my pillow. His face didn't even change when he said, "Well, I don't know precisely. My calculations, the Grendel goes some four hundred acres or so."

"And it's full."

"And it's full. Well, it's more or less full, as such things go," Galligan said. "I'm not the first one to do this sort of thing, you know."

"You installed a false wet seal," I said, "from one mine to the other. Real seal directs acid mine drainage to a holding tank where you'd treat it with your supplies of anhydrous ammonia."

"Is that what I did?"

I ignored him. "But treatment's expensive and a pain in your ass anyway. You like doing things your own way and don't want anyone in the state capital or Washington calling the dance, so instead of treating the water you started funneling it to the Grendel."

"I'm awfully clever then."

I continued ignoring him. "I'm guessing you've been doing it for several years at least, funneling water and falsifying reports to the government. But then things hit a snag. The Grendel's slowly collapsing, as abandoned mines will, and the acid drainage pooled near some of its structural flaws and started leaking. If it all broke out of the mine—Martin County style—and ended up in the lake, everyone would know what you've been up to, and you'd be looking down the barrel. But to clean it up, you had to increase your supply of anhydrous ammonia, which you couldn't do on the books without attracting attention from the Feds. They'd want to know what you were using it for, so you decided to hit the Knight Hawk's tanks."

"What a wily character I am."

There were noises on the stairs. Jeep and Pelzer were coming down. Temple was in Jeep's arms, unconscious.

He said, "She's drugged out of her kettle, but she seems okay."

I looked at Galligan, "And man, are you lucky."

He smiled a little, but it wasn't a happy smile. He didn't like being under a thumb, and here he was under the biggest thumb of his life maybe, but he was smart enough to let it play out and live to fight another time.

He said, "You were telling my story back to me, I think."

"I was," I said. "You used up your own back supplies of ammonia, I guess, and then hit on the idea of tapping the Knight Hawk's tanks. Chances are, the local meth gangs would catch the blame, and anyway no one would ever think to accuse you of something like that. Only problem was, you didn't know that you'd been seen by Dwayne Mays and Luster's son-in-law, who were working on an unrelated news story. That is, you didn't know until things started getting hot and Beckett panicked and went to Luster for help. Luster must have figured out what you were doing, and he knew he had you. He came to you and told you what he knew and . . . what? . . . asked you for money? Coal mines?"

Galligan didn't say anything.

I shrugged and said, "Maybe both. Maybe magical fairy dust. Don't matter, really. Whatever it was, you weren't about to be outmaneuvered by him, so you killed him and you killed Mays. You would have killed Beckett, too, but he took care of that business all by himself. Then you learned about Beckett's environmental club and went after them, and Temple, too, fearing he'd told them too much. That's a lot of bodies to leave on the ground, man."

"I'm not saying anything," he said, then quickly held up a hand when I started to speak. "Let me finish. I'm not saying anything, except that we didn't do anything to Dwayne Mays."

Pelzer threw up his hands and said, "Oh, steaming bullshit."

Galligan looked at me. "Believe what you want. Believe that earless fool there. I'm just saying that no one in this room did anything to that reporter on my orders. That's a promise."

"Not sure I believe that," I said.

Galligan shrugged. "Like I said, believe what you want. I don't care. But what I will say is this: that sonofabitch Luster and I go way back. In a way, we were like brothers. Brothers who despised each other, but brothers nevertheless. We fought with each other during the fat times, and banded together against the unions during the lean. We did some things together that maybe you'd have a hard time believing, things that ought to have tied us together forever with blood. But when he came to me with his hand out and threats in his mouth, he broke our covenant. He broke the bond that our fathers took so seriously and the only thing that keeps this part of the world from drying up and blowing away."

"So you sent Sonny here to deal with him."

"If I did—and you understand that I'm not saying I did—it would have been a mercy, like putting an animal out of its misery. The man I knew was already dead, and all that was left was an old fool whose desperation threatened to bring down everything we'd both built up over the years."

I said, "Dwayne Mays threatened you, too."

"It's not the same," he said. "Any story about my mines would never have left his computer. Certainly it never would have been published. His boss and I are old friends. Besides, there are better ways to take care of nettlesome reporters. One thing, they think almost any amount of money is a fortune. Plus, Dwayne made noises about being a man of principle, and there's never anyone easier to bribe than that."

"That's a mighty cynical view of things, old man."

He said, "I'd say it's more realistic than cynical, but you have it any way you want."

"This doesn't leave us in a good place."

He said, "You've got the gun, boy. When you have the gun, you're supposed to use it, or use the threat of it to get what you want. A long time in this part of the world, I've managed to get what I want. Mostly, it's with money, but sometimes it's through threats and sometimes it's through other kinds of actions, some of them less wholesome than others. After a time, you can rely on reputation. People do what you want them to do because they're afraid of what you'll do otherwise, but that only lasts for so long. Sooner or later, all of this will be gone. Eventually the Grendel will let go of its hold on all that water, and my secret will be out, and I'll probably lose a few dollars here and there, either in court or by feathering the pockets of our noble civil servants. Maybe I'll get out of the business entirely, and a few more hundred or a thousand men will lose their jobs. But what's any of that mean in the grand scheme? You know I'll never be arrested, and you know I'll never see the inside of a cell. Son, this is the United fucking States of America. Land of the free market, home of the despoiler, where the only kings are citizen kings. When the hell is the last time you ever heard of a well-off white man going to jail for befouling the goddamn land? So I suggest you either use your gun or threaten to use it and tell me what you want."

I said, "It's a nice speech, but you didn't go through all this trouble for nothing. Truth is, you're scared."

For the first time, I'd touched a nerve. Sonny sucked a breath, and Fatboy stopped groaning, and Galligan drew himself up and turned as red as a radish.

He said, "You filthy little maggot. You dirty white nigger."

Jeep laughed. I brushed aside the insults and said, "How much is avoiding treatment saving you?"

"Depends," Galligan said when he'd collected himself. "Some months the flow out of that closed section is a bit heavier than usual. Treatment for our string is running more than a million a year."

"Used to, anyway." Goines.

"It's going to again," I said. "Here's what I want, me and my gun: Finish what you started. Clean it up. I don't care how you do it, or where you get your ammonia from, but clean the shit up."

"I'm not sure I can do that now, son," Galligan said softly. He breathed deeply and retook full control of himself. He smiled a little and shook his head, as though at the folly of his own weakness, and then he poured us a round of shots, even passing a double to Fatboy, who sat up long enough to moan about wanting a doctor.

Galligan said, "But hell, maybe you're right. It's not like we were saving a fortune on this deal anyway. That's the bitch of it all. All this woe, and all these unfortunate end-ings, and for what? A few bucks and the safety of a few fish?" He paused and drank and swished the liquid around in his mouth and finally swallowed and said, "I'll look into what you say. Doing what you say, I mean. I don't know that it's possible at this point, but I will give it a looking-at. I'll do it maybe because it was what I planned to do in the beginning anyway, but mostly I'll do it because I don't want my end in this world to be spent dealing with environmentalists and reporters and other kinds of fools."

"I take that personally," I said.

"Go right ahead. I meant it personally. Anything else?"

"Just take care of your wounded," I said. "And leave me and mine the hell alone."

"It's a deal, Slim," he said. He strode forward like a giant and gripped my hand.

"It needs to be," I said. "For your sake."

And the old boy showed me his teeth. "Oh?"

I gestured over my shoulder. "This is Jeep Mabry."

Galligan looked at Jeep. He betrayed no emotion, but his eyes lingered on the big man perhaps just a moment too long.

Jeep said, "It needs to be, for your sake."

Galligan nodded and said, "Any time, boy. Come for me, and we'll see. Maybe we'll go the devil together. I feel more ready these days than not. My time will be soon, and I'd like it to be memorable."

We went out. The rain was still coming down, but the worst of the tempest had passed and now rumbled away to our east. Flashes of moonlight licked the clouds. Temple snored.

I said, "We're alive. I can hardly believe it."

"Me, either, really," said Jeep. "Question is, do you believe him? Galligan?"

"About everything?"

"About Dwayne Mays."

I said, "I don't know why, but I kind of do."

"I kind of do, too."

"We're missing something," I said.

"Jump Down after all?"

"I don't know," I said.

Pelzer grunted under Temple's weight, "Maybe a little less talk, a little more doing?"

We climbed into our vehicles and got the hell out of there, leaving behind the wreckage for someone else to clean up.

FIFTEEN

I feel like I've been stepped on by an elephant," said Temple.

"You kinda were."

"I wonder what they gave me."

"All of it, apparently."

She laughed a little, but laughing hurt her head, and she stopped.

It was a few hours later, and we were back at Indian Vale. All of us. Jeep was there and Peggy and Anci and Pelzer. We'd taken Pelzer to a country doctor he knew, and the doc had sewed his ear back on and taped up his head and given him a shot to numb the pain some. Unbelievably, his wound was mostly cosmetic. The bullet had bounced off his skull and given him a shave, but that was more or less the extent of it. Pelzer joked that it made him uglier, but no one joked back because Pelzer was right. I'd called Susan and told her Temple was safe. She almost sounded relieved. No one wanted to call the cops.

The fear and excitement of the night started to wear off, and hunger moved in to take its place.

"I tell you, I could eat a car," Pelzer said.

"We could order up some takeout," Anci said.

"Probably too late. Everything worth eating is closed."

"We could run to that truck stop again," she said. "Get some of those scrambled eggs with orange cheese."

I said, "I think I can do a little better." I took out a big soup pot, filled the bottom with olive oil, then diced two big onions and a handful of fresh garlic cloves and threw it all in. I chopped up some chicken and threw that into the onion and garlic mix and hit it all with some fresh-cracked black pepper. Some stock and white wine and cannellini beans and spices, some rosemary and thyme and tarragon. Like that. Pretty soon the smells of my mother's pasta fagioli filled the house.

Anci looked into the pot and stirred it a little with the wooden spoon. She looked up at me and nodded. "Yeah, slightly better."

Jeep set the table. Anci sliced bread. Peggy tossed a salad. Pelzer shirked and went outside for a smoke, and Temple watched it all with a slightly dazed look. We were like a big, crazy family, maybe, but at least we were alive. After a while, Pelzer came back and pretended to help. I took down some bowls, and Anci ladled the steaming hot soup into them. Everybody found a place at the table, and we ate. Food never tasted so good.

"This is wonderful," Temple said.

"It is, Slim," said Peggy. She sounded calmer than she had in days. She touched my arm. "Thank you."

"Needs salt," Pelzer said, but everyone ignored him.

We didn't talk much during that first bowl. During the second, though, things started to loosen up a bit. Pelzer told the ladies the story of our assault on Galligan's house, and I have to admit, the way he told it was pretty good. He even did some of the fighting sounds. In the telling, it came off as more exciting and courageous than terrifying, and he clipped off the most violent parts for Anci's sake, which was a relief.

"You're heroes," Peggy said.

"I'll just be happy if Galligan keeps his word and leaves us alone." But I did feel kinda heroic, I'll admit it.

After we finished, and Jeep phoned Opal to tell the whole

story over again, I went and sat down next to Temple. "I'm sorry about Guy," I said.

She sighed. "At least he died doing something useful. Even if it was accidentally useful. Tomorrow morning, I'm going to see about doing something about this mess. It'll be a way to get to the old man. And I bet if we look under enough rocks, we're liable to find some bribe money floating around certain land and water management agencies."

"Probably," I said. "Anyway, I didn't really expect you to wait for Galligan to have a change of heart."

"He murdered my father."

"I know," I said. "Or he ordered it done, anyway. I'm sorry about that, too."

She just shrugged her shoulders.

Pelzer finished the dishes and drained the sink. Jeep sat at the table. Anci brought in her old computer and sat down with it, idly watching the video of my makeshift security feed. On the screen, Peggy was making her way through the house with armloads of Anci's things, shoes and books and clothes, like she'd told me that night at the hotel. Meanwhile, Temple gathered herself up and made ready to go back to her life or her revenge or whatever it would be. It was a little awkward, like saying good-bye after a long and bloody dinner party.

She said, "I can't thank you enough. I'll never be able to. You saved my life."

I said, "I just wish it'd all come out better."

"You know how it is."

I knew how it was. The best you could do was fight for the draw. Anything more was a pipe dream.

"You're okay to get where you're going?" I said. "I can call Susan. I'm sure she'd be glad to come get you."

"Susan's never glad to do anything," Temple said.

Pelzer said, "I'll give her a lift."

He looked at Temple. I thought she'd turn him down flat, but she nodded gratefully. You never knew with people. Pelzer turned again to me. We shook hands.

"You're sure you're okay?" I said. "Just a while ago, you were shot in the head."

"I'm a big guy," he said. "Sometimes you get shot in the head. A little thing that like hardly bothers me."

"That's a pretty sunny outlook."

"Sunny people live longer. I read that in a men's health magazine one time when I was getting my tires rotated."

"Thanks again for your help," I said.

"I like to finish a job, even if the client isn't around anymore."

"Anyway, I'm sorry about your ear."

His hand touched the spot and jumped away. "Well, it lends character, I guess."

"It does that."

"Just one more thing," he said. He leaned in and said in a theater whisper, "Jim Hart."

"You and that photograph. It's like a romance."

"You said you'd hand it over."

"I did," I said. "But now I'm thinking maybe I should keep it for a few more days."

He frowned. "That doesn't seem right to me. Going back on your promise like that."

"I'm not going back," I said. "I just think I should delay the handoff until I'm sure Galligan is going to keep his promise to leave me and my people alone. Plus, I'd like to run it over to the university, have someone in the photography school give it a looking-at. There's no telling what's on it."

Pelzer sucked that around some. He was a lunkhead, but I figured him to be pretty fair when it came down to it.

"Okay, just as long as I get it soon," he said. "Like you said before, maybe we can go get it checked out together."

"Maybe."

We shook hands again, and he and Temple turned to go.

The scene switched on Anci's computer. The motion detector had detected motion.

She looked up and said, "Hey."

I glanced at the screen. Someone was making his way through the house. Not Peggy. The time stamp said it was two days ago. The someone was searching the bookshelves and under the couch cushions. He must have found some change there, because he put something in his pants pocket. He went to the far end of the room and around the corner for a while and then came back, and as he approached the camera you could see that it was Tony Pelzer.

My head snapped up. I looked at Pelzer. I said, "Why, you devious little shit."

Some reason, he looked at Temple again. Temple shrugged at him.

"Okay," he said. "I guess that's it, then."

He reached into his jacket and pulled out a pistol and shot Jeep Mabry twice in the chest.

The computer hit the floor and smashed apart. Anci screamed. Peggy screamed. Hell, I think even I did. Jeep flew backward off his seat and crashed into the wall. There was blood everywhere and more flowing out of Jeep. Pelzer held the pistol on us.

He said to Temple, "Go find it. Now."

She hesitated, looked at me a moment, nothing in her face. Then she ran out of the room.

Peggy was holding Anci. Pelzer lunged, reaching for her. Peggy kicked out at him, but he was faster and stronger. He slapped her so hard across the face she let go of Anci and went whirling across the kitchen floor. I screamed again and jumped Pelzer, but I was off balance and my adrenaline was going too hard, and he was ready. He planted a kick in the center of my chest that knocked me backward, then lunged in and hit me with the grip of the pistol. I dropped to the floor in a pile.

"That's for before," he said. "For shooting me with that damn beanbag."

After a moment, Temple came back with the photo. "Got it," she said.

"Where was it?"

"What difference does it make?"

"I'd just like to know," he said

"Go to hell, Tony."

Pelzer nodded. "Let's go then."

Temple looked at Anci, "Take her."

"Why?"

"So he won't follow."

Peggy screamed. Pelzer shrugged. I climbed to my feet and made ready to charge, but he waved the gun in Anci's direction.

Temple said, "We need two hours. Maybe three. Then we're out of here. We won't be going back to the lake. You don't know where you're going, but if you follow us, if you try to find us, we'll kill her."

I said, "Either way, you're dead."

"That's up to you to try," she said. "That's your choice. But you can save her life by not following us."

Anci was crying, and I was tearing apart inside. I'd never experienced anything like that, even that night on the streets of Herrin. It felt like my guts were on fire, and I don't remember a time when I felt so helpless. Peggy stirred around on the floor. She crawled over to Jeep and tried to stop the blood pumping from his chest with her hands. It didn't look like it was doing much good.

Temple said, "When we're ready to go, I'll call you."

They dragged my daughter from the kitchen and through the house. I heard the front door open and then close, and I heard Pelzer yell a warning at Anci, who was fighting him. I looked at Peggy. Peggy looked at me, desperate. I ran out of the room and upstairs. I found the 9000S and ran back down and out the door. Pelzer and Temple were near her car, two hundred yards in front of the house. Pelzer saw me and fired off a couple rounds, but they missed badly. Then he climbed in the car and wheeled away so fast it was like he'd never been there. The gravel lot shredded and spat, and wet dirt spattered the air in thick clumps. I ran to the bike and climbed on and only then realized that he'd slashed the tires. Probably on his cigarette break before dinner. He'd done the trucks' tires, too, and Peggy's car.

I ran halfway down the long drive and nearly all the way to Shake-a-Rag Road before I gave out. I lurched into the grass and threw up my dinner. I was crying and searching the dark and I yelled her name but there wasn't anything to see and there wasn't anyone to yell back.

They were gone. The sonsofbitches had my daughter, and they were gone.

I went back to the house, fast as I was able. I had tears on my face and vomit in my shoes. The smell of cordite was stuck in my nose like a curse, and the memory of the gunshots rang in my head. I think I was in shock. I tilted over once and landed in the wet grass. It was like my body wanted to lie down and sleep away this terrible night, start over fresh in the morning. I fought it off and climbed to my feet and went inside. Peggy had staunched Jeep's wounds with some towels. She screamed again when I came in the room.

"Me," I said.

"Did you . . ."

I shook my head. She seemed in shock, too. She put a hand in her mouth and smeared blood on her face. She didn't realize.

"Oh, my God. Oh, my God. It's my fault."

"Listen to me," I said. I took her by the shoulders and shook her gently and held her eyes with mine. "There's no time for that. I'm going to get her back."

I tried to sound sure of it, but I didn't feel it. I felt like burning down the world. I looked at Jeep. Peggy's eyes followed mine.

She said, "He's alive. I can't believe it. He must be strong as a damn bear."

"More or less."

"Strong but fading. He won't last much longer, Slim. We've got to call an ambulance."

I shook my head. My thoughts were firing ahead of me like cannonballs.

"We do that, the police will be here. The police come, they'll get involved, and if they get involved, Anci will die."

"If we don't get him medical help right now, *he'll* die."

I thought about it for a half second longer. I grabbed my phone and dialed Dr. Cooper's number. He answered after about ten rings, sounding like he wasn't quite awake.

"There better be someone dying," he said.

Someone was dying. I explained the situation best I could and without going into too much detail, in case it came back on us later. I tried not to sound completely insane, but I have no idea whether I succeeded.

"This is twice you're asking me to leave the law out of suspicious doings," he said when I was done. "Not sure I can go along with it this time."

"Just for a few hours."

He paused a beat, uncertain. It was just a beat, but it felt like ten years.

I said, "My daughter's in danger."

He said, "I'm on my way. Put pressure on those wounds, and if you have a free hand, put on some damn coffee. I'm so tired, I'm liable to kill him myself."

I disconnected the call and put on my jacket and put the pistol in one of its pockets. I went out to Jeep's truck and got Betsy. Then I went back inside and kissed Peggy on the cheek and squeezed Jeep's hand.

"Jesus God, man," I said, "Don't die like this. Please."

His eyes opened a little, but he couldn't speak. His skin was ashen and he looked as close to the end as anyone I'd ever seen. I turned to go.

Peggy said, "What are you doing? You can't leave me here by myself."

"Doc Cooper lives just down the road. He'll be here soon. I've got to get Anci."

"They said . . ."

I shook my head. "They're liars. If I let them run, they might kill her. I can't leave it up to them."

"So you're going?"

"I'm going."

She started crying again.

"Alone?"

I said, "Not alone."

I drove into Marion on rims, then east of the town and out the other side until I found the spot. I left the ruined car in the lot and went inside the building. I convinced the woman at the front desk to let me in to see him. Visiting hours had ended long before, but a bit of persuasion and what cash I had on me turned the key, and I was allowed through the door and into the home. He had money, so it was one of the nicer places, more like a big hotel than a hospital. The lobby was fancy, with thick carpet and red curtains and a piano and a big-screen TV. I was led through the lobby and down a hallway past a library and into a private space, where four old men were gathered around a table holding playing cards and stacking plastic chips. Cheezie Bruzetti looked up at me, and it took him a moment but then he recognized me and smiled. The old man looked up at me, too, but he didn't smile.

He said, "What the hell do you want?"

I said, "Dad, I need your help."

SIXTEEN

Jonathan led me to the house. Luster had some real estate investments, apparently, and Temple knew about them. Two or three of them were in places that seemed too exposed to be useful to murderers and kidnappers. But one of them looked to fit the bill: a place inside the reserve, not far from the Estates, in a secluded spot that was just perfect for shadowy goings-on.

When I gave Jonathan the lowdown, he said, "She really did all that?"

"She did some of it anyway," I said.

"She . . . killed him?"

"No, but it looks like what she did led to his killing."

"It's the same thing," he said. "I'd like to say I'm surprised."

"But you're not."

"No, I'm not," he said, and he started to cry and the phone went dead between us.

The house was a big one at the northern edge of the national forest, off Eagle Creek Road and within shouting distance of Glen Jones Lake and the U.S. Fish and Wildlife area. Some reason, that seemed appropriate. The place was surrounded by thick walls of autumn olive and shivering common reed, and some big chinquapin trees bowed over what looked to be an old logging road. There was a deep ditch in the front yard, and a culvert, and the back was fenced in with high, sharp pickets.

The best approach seemed to be to sneak up to the house in the dark, and that's what I tried, but the going was rough. The undergrowth was thick and snatched at my clothes, and eventually my impatience forced me to take a clearer way where the moonlight didn't have to contend with the canopy. It was faster going, but I was exposed from almost every angle and at any moment expected gunfire.

There wasn't any of that. There was only the nighttime quiet and the wind. A big, black Navigator in the driveway was loaded for a long trip, and the front walk piled with boxes and palettes for the movers. She'd been planning to run for longer than a few hours. A sweeping view of the hill valley below was lined with honey mesquite, big bur oaks, and wax myrtles, and they shimmered now like metal leaf in the nervously chilly air. I stepped quickly to the house and around the back, toward the high wooden fence, and I was just getting ready to climb it when who should appear around the corner with a cigarette in his mouth and a hand on his zipper but Tony Pelzer. I pointed Betsy at his chest. He smiled.

"Well, here we are again," he said.

"Here we are. You mind finishing zipping up? There are some things about you I just don't need to know."

"Your loss." He zipped up. He said, "You actually followed us here. After all our threats. After we snatched your girl. After I popped your buddy. Jesus Christ with a chainsaw. You're unbelievable."

"You never should have taken my kid."

"Maybe not," he said. "Time will tell. I guess it's all academic now. You're here, after all."

"I'm here."

"Your buddy dead yet? I gotta tell you, I ain't never seen a guy bleed like that. He must've been a stuck pig in a former life. I'd have shot you and your woman, too, if Temple had let me. I saw the way you went after Goines earlier. I told her you'd never listen to reason. You're a runaway train."

"Feels that way sometimes," I said. "One thing."

"Oh, this should be good."

"The picture of Jim Hart you kept nattering on about. There's an account number on it?"

"Hidden in it, yeah. I should never have mentioned steganography to you, but what can I say? I don't always think too good on the spur of the moment."

"I guess I don't, either."

He said, "Temple changed the number after I told her what happened, of course. Goddamn, she was mad. I thought she'd pop me over it, but after a while she calmed down. Still, we couldn't let you keep it, even with the old number. Eventually someone might take a harder look at it, and proof of the existence of any account would tip them off to what we'd done."

"Okay," I said. I raised the gun a little more. "Thanks. Time to go nighty-night now."

"Betsy again? The little heartbreaker? Won't work," he said. He popped some buttons on his shirt and pulled it open to show me the quilted padding beneath. "I'm wearing a vest. No more beanbags, stupid."

I said, "No more beanbags," and pulled the trigger.

When the lead balls in the twelve-gauge triple-decker ammo hit him in the chest, Pelzer basically ripped in half. If it wasn't for his vest, he might have exploded like a balloon, so I guess it got him that at least. It was more noise than I wanted to make, but it was effective. He went into the dark in two directions and came to rest as a puddle and a closed coffin. I had to hurry now. I ran quickly to the fence, found a likely place, and threw Betsy over. Then I climbed up and dropped down on the other side.

She was in the backyard, pouring a drink from a glass pitcher of martinis and shivering slightly against the cool, but otherwise looking perfectly at home in the winter air.

"Well, *that* was loud," she said. She was almost cheerful. "But you never really defy expectations, do you? That was Pelzer bowing out, I take it?"

"That's one way of saying it."

"You did me a favor, then, believe it or not. Anyway, if it weren't this, it'd be something else. He was going to come to a bad end. It was inevitable."

"Character is fate."

She laughed. "For you, it's a death sentence. Can I finally talk you into having a drink with me? There might not be another chance."

"My daughter," I said, showing her the gun. "Then we can drink."

Temple hesitated a moment, then sipped her drink some more and shrugged and stood. I followed her across the yard and up the steps and into the dark house.

I said, "Anyone else in here?"

She shook her head.

"Susan?"

She said, "I let her go."

"You're awfully good at cutting ties."

"Maybe," she said. "But maybe that's why I'm so good at life."

We made our way through the back of the house, weaving between boxes. The place was a maze. Her things were everywhere in piles, luggage and clothes and what looked like bags of shoes. The furniture was draped with clean white cloths. A floor lamp stood in a corner like a ghost.

"I guess the plan is to leave town."

"And never come back."

"Someplace sunny, I suppose."

"And warm year round."

"Hell?"

Her answer was a snort.

Anci was on the second floor, in a bedroom and groggy. There was a bottle of pills on the bedside table and the smell of medicine was nearly overwhelming. I told Temple to wait in the doorway, and I walked over to the bed and sat down on it. I picked up Anci and held her and I felt her hug my neck.

Temple said, "She's fine. I know what you're thinking, but you've got it wrong. I would never hurt her, Slim. We always meant to let her go."

"I bet."

"As soon as we were gone."

"Cry fluphenazine tears."

"What?"

"I said you're so goddamn crazy it's leaking out of you. Now let's go."

She shrugged and turned and went out. I followed closely, carrying Anci downstairs. I wound my way through the dark living room and nearly fell over a piano bench, but I finally made the front door. I could feel Temple dropping behind me in the dark, hanging back. I fumbled getting the door open, struggling not to drop Anci. I turned the knob and went outside and stepped off the little covered porch. There was a blur and a whiff of cologne. He swung around into view at the same instant and hit me in the neck with the butt of his rifle, and I fell over sideways and dropped Anci in the grass. I tried to scramble to my feet and toward my daughter, but he hit me again and again until he finally tired of it and let me come to my knees. I guess he wanted me to see.

He must have been inside, maybe even saw me approach, and maybe that's why she stalled me, letting me have Anci while she waited for him to come out again. He was a big Average, balding, in slacks and a light blue sweater.

Guy Beckett, alive and well. The sight of him nearly made me swallow my tongue. That and the rifle he aimed at my chest.

"Well, I'll be fucked," I said, and Beckett looked at me like the scorpion stung the frog.

"Something like that. Surprised?"

"Pretty surprised," I admitted. "But not exactly shocked. Hell, I might not be much of a private eye, and I don't think I'll ever be an expert at solving murders, but you two aren't as clever as you think."

"Let's talk about it around back, okay? We get more privacy there."

I started to pick up Anci, but Guy kicked me in the ribs and I felt one of them flex out of place and crack. Beckett jabbed the rifle at me again, and Temple moved in and lifted Anci off the ground with a grunt. She was still completely under, and I found myself praying she'd stay that way, whatever happened. We went back around the house. Guy kept the gun on me, and Temple put Anci in a chair and sat again at her table and picked up her drink and took a sip and smiled as though nothing of any interest had happened, la-di-fucking-da.

Beckett said, "You were saying something about being fucked?"

Temple growled from her place, "Guy, there's no reason to talk to him now."

"What can it hurt?" he asked, but he was sheepish, like a dog called sternly back to heel.

"One thing," I said, ignoring the exchange, "I just got to know. Why did you kill Dwayne Mays? Couldn't talk him into going along with your scheme?"

"Never even tried. It would have been a waste of time. Dwayne was a lot of stuff, but he didn't have a dishonest bone in his body."

"I've heard."

"Yeah, well, he wasn't a saint, but you could never have told him that. He was a pro, though, and he would have gone ahead and published his story, and Galligan's secret would have been out and that would have been that."

"I can only imagine how happy you must have been when you realized who it was tapping the Knight Hawk's ammonia supplies. It can't be often that blackmail opportunities that perfect come along."

"Not too often, no. It was beautiful, like hitting the lottery."

"But then there was Dwayne to deal with. You couldn't bring him in on your deal, and you couldn't leave him running around collecting evidence against Galligan, so you took a trip to the Knight Hawk and talked him into going below and popped him there. During an active shift, too. That took guts."

Beckett shrugged. "I did it quickly and cleanly. I don't think he ever knew what hit him. Dwayne was my friend, after all. I wrote the old man's nickname on Dwayne's pad and put it in his mouth, and then I pulled my vanishing act. All of it was made to put Galligan under pressure without giving away the game. And we wanted the old man under as much pressure as possible."

Temple said, "Christ, Guy."

Again, Beckett said, "What can it hurt? It's all over now. Besides, this is the most fun I've had in days. I've been dead, you know?"

I said, "Speaking of that, I'm guessing you're the one who killed one of Jump Down's guys and tossed him into the Grendel coal mine."

"I needed a body. The dude had been talking to Dwayne, anyway, selling out his buds. He was trash. I told him I needed to do some follow-up, told him there was a few bucks in it for him. He was actually smiling when I popped him. Thought he was about to get paid. He got paid all right. I shot him right in his stupid smiling teeth. I burned down his flop and dragged him up to the Grendel and threw him in. I'll tell you, my back smarted something awful after that."

"Oh, I just hate it for you."

"Be like that if you want."

"And you don't think that's going to raise eyebrows when the cops figure it out? I mean, there are ways to tell that body isn't really you."

Beckett shrugged. "Maybe, but that was the point. The worst thing we could have done was honestly try to fool everyone. That just leads to a cell. Anyway, all you need to beat the cops is a little confusion. They'll piss around for a few weeks and then file the case away with all the other murders they're too incompetent to clear," Beckett said. "Not everything went how we planned. We hadn't planned on letting you in on the Galligan angle at all, but after Luster's murder, giving Galligan and Goines someone else to shoot at seemed like a pretty good idea."

"Thanks."

"Like I said, letting you in was dangerous, but it offered Galligan another target and tightened the screws on him some more. We'd never have let you go to the police with your suspicions. Temple would have killed you before that."

"Turned out I was useful anyway," I said. "After Galligan grabbed her."

"I couldn't believe our luck," he said, and he actually looked grateful. "It wasn't like I could go get her. I was supposed to be missing, after all. And your little rescue attempt was the final straw. Galligan had been paying us small amounts since Dwayne and I accidentally uncovered his little secret. I think he was hoping to get us to let our guard down, pop us then, but then Luster bullied his way into it and Galligan suddenly had his hands full."

"I had a theory that you tipped him off."

Beckett shook his head.

"Didn't have to. I'll give him this, the old guy was sharp. When he heard about the cold storage shed being tapped, he did the math and came up with the right answer. He went to Galligan and started making demands, and Galligan had Goines kill him, which solves one problem but creates another. Now he's on the hook for a homicide. Your little rescue attempt was the breaking point. As soon as you were out his door the old man was on the phone, agreeing to pay us off in full and settle the whole mess. That's when the whole thing really came together. It's one thing when they grudgingly agree to pay you. When they actually act *grateful* to give you their money, well, that's a thing of goddamn beauty."

"All this for some money," I said. "I hope it was worth it."

For once, Temple spoke up with more than complaints. "You're thinking too small, hayseed. Sure, there was money, but that was only for starters. We also wanted the lease for the mine. And we would have gotten it, too. The King Coal's on its last legs, but the land is still worth a fortune. It was hell watching my father sell out our legacy to that vain idiot Galligan, watching him diminish himself like that. He was a great man once, and seeing him grovel in front of Galligan and selling off our mines just to survive was like watching him die before his time. I know to you this was simple blackmail, Slim, but it was supposed to be justice. A restoration. If my father hadn't butted his nose in, he'd have lived to see that. He might even have appreciated it."

"Envy's a coal comes hissing hot from hell."

"What's that?"

"Nothing," I said. "Means anything to you, though, I know what it's like to have a larger-than-life father, too."

"God, shut up."

I turned back to Beckett. "So how much longer, do you figure?"

"Figure? Figure what?"

Behind me, Temple said, "Guy, do it."

Guy looked down the long barrel of the rifle, but didn't fire. I pushed a thumb over my shoulder at Temple.

I said, "Pretty clear she's the brains behind all of this. She's the one who knew Galligan well enough to know his vulnerabilities. She's the one who hated Mays, and I'm going to guess she's the one who convinced you that killing him was the way to go. Even getting her own father murdered didn't put an end to her plan."

"So?"

"So how much longer do you figure she'll keep you around?"

"Guy, for Christ's sake, just shoot him."

"Bodies are heavy lifting," I said. "In all kinds of ways. But pretty soon there won't be any more bodies. Just electronic fund transfers, and those don't weigh anything at all."

"Guy, goddamn it . . ."

I said, "And then who'll look after your kid?"

It was a desperate play, maybe, the last card in my sleeve, but I needed every second I could get, and it worked. Beckett sucked a breath and blanched, and Temple looked like she'd been kicked in the tits.

"Guy?"

"It's nothing," he said. "Don't listen."

"Oh, my God," she hissed, "Oh, my God, you lying piece of trash."

"I said it's nothing."

"It's not nothing. It's eight years old and living with his momma in Johnston City." I turned to Beckett. "What about him, man?"

"Goddamn you . . ."

"Mary-Kay Connor, man." I shook my head. "Love really is blind. Or stupid."

"*Guy!*" Behind me, I could feel her patience snap like lightning. She'd put up with his messes for a lifetime, and then all at once she'd had enough. But she struggled with her piece, and getting into a firing stance seemed to take three seconds. She'd let Beckett and the help do her killing for a reason. I don't know who she was aiming at, me or Beckett. Maybe both of us. I never found out.

I prayed it'd be then. I prayed they'd take her with the scoped M77, so it was a prayer to somewhere south of heaven, but it was answered and just then they tried. They tried, but the shot whispered out of the dark and went wide like a metal-jacketed bumblebee drunk on marijuana honey. The cylinder of martinis exploded in a silver shower, and the curved glass shards destroyed most of the left side of Temple's lovely face as she collapsed against the table and fired off three quick rounds with her lightweight Ruger.

The first and second shots went nowhere. But they must have been hollow-point rounds, because the third hit Beckett just below the elbow of his left arm and nearly severed it. There was a cloud of blood, and he dropped his rifle and hit his knees and made a sound I'll carry to my grave. Temple dropped her piece, too, and rushed to his aid, and I grabbed Anci and hugged her to my chest, and it was then that the back gate opened and the old men came through, out of the night.

These were the men I'd spoken about with Mary-Kay Connor. They were creatures of a different world and a different time, and they'd seen things and done things that most of us couldn't even begin to imagine. They'd lived through strikes and wildcats and attempted assassinations and beatings and murders, all of it over a few more dollars a month and the pride of whoever lost the fight. Even at nearly eighty years old, they were a terrifying sight. My father led the way, carrying the M77.

"You're late," I said. "Almost too late. I could have used your help a while back."

He shrugged and moved closer to stroke Anci's hair and without looking at me said, "We got turned around in the woods back there. We don't see so good in the dark these days." He looked at Temple and Beckett, who stared back at him in fear. He looked at them with a look that wasn't even disgust, because disgust was something you reserved for people who mattered. Beckett whimpered and Temple quaked like a frightened child. I almost brought myself to pity them. "These are the people who threatened my grand-daughter?"

"Yeah."

He nodded and leaned in and kissed Anci's head, but she didn't stir beyond the soft rise and fall of her breath.

He said, "Okay. Go on now. Get her out of here."

"I should be here. I'll drop her and come back."

He said, "Don't you dare."

I looked at him a long moment, and finally he looked at me, but nothing passed between us that might have told anything of our story.

I got out of there. I carried my daughter up the dark road. Cheezie was waiting in the car, and he smiled sadly at me when I opened the rear passenger door and the light came on. I put Anci in the back seat and buckled her in, then I closed the door and the light snapped off and at the same time there were two shots from up the road.

I got in behind the wheel and turned on the engine.

Cheezie said, "It's a hard old world for some folks."

I didn't say anything. I drove us away from that night-mare.

SEVENTEEN

I'd like to say it all worked out in the end, that the resolution of the case snapped back the pieces of an orderly life, but that wasn't the way things shook out. The only good thing was that Anci remembered almost nothing of her ordeal. Our therapist said that she'd probably have bad dreams, though, that at least some of the nightmare might one day worm its way through to her waking consciousness. I hoped he was wrong.

It was a slow and painful process, but Jeep Mabry eventually recovered from his wounds. Dr. Cooper said it was a kind of miracle. Jeep was literally too mean to die: that was the medical explanation. As soon as I had Anci stowed away, I spent as much time at his bedside as he'd allow, which wasn't much.

As for old man Galligan, I never found out whether he planned to keep his promise. Two weeks after Christmas, the camouflaged wet seal between the King Coal and Grendel mines gave way all by its lonesome, and the state EPA lumbered into action at last. With assistance from the local university, a team of investigators was dispatched into the old slope mine, and when they stumbled upon the bloated and acid-eaten remains in the Grendel coal mine, all holy hell broke loose at last.

Or so it seemed. Whatever else might be done to him, Galligan was right: he'd never see the inside of a prison cell. Guys like him never did. They probably wouldn't even take much of his precious money. In a similar case out in West Virginia, a mine owner was fined exactly one dollar for loosing untold AMD contamination into the Cheat River. Funny how bullshit's the same, wherever you go.

By March, the ugliness had moved into court, where the inevitable squabbling started over who was supposed to clean up old Roy's dirty ocean. They were still bickering about it when, just before the spring hatch, the Grendel's broken ribs gave way at last, and untold millions of gallons of contaminated mine water sluiced downhill into Crab Orchard and its three constituent lakes. Last I heard, the Parks Service was still counting the dead fish.

Not long after that, the Knight Hawk passed into receivership. With Temple gone, Jonathan inherited the works, but he wanted no part of it and put it up for sale. When no buyers stepped forward—not even Chinese ones—the banks eventually did. The entire workforce got put out on its ass, and they all lost their pensions. Me included. I guess nobody ever got around to setting it aside, Luster because he got murdered first and Temple because she never really intended to in the first place. It was rotten luck, all right, but I came out of it a lot better than a lot of them had. At least I was alive.

After I got word to Jump Down about Galligan, he dropped off my radar. I don't guess there was any question what career he'd moved on to, and I reckoned he'd do just fine for himself. These days, drug dealers were some of the only folk with any real kind of job security.

Me? Well, I had to find something to do to make ends meet. I looked around a bit, but it was hard going, and there were no other mine jobs to be had. It'd gotten so bad I was contemplating a Walmart greeter's job when Anci struck upon the idea of putting up the sign. A couple of weeks later she talked me into it. It said *Slim: Redneck Investigations*, which she thought was a hoot. I guess I kinda did, too, because every time I saw it I smiled.

"We've never run a business before," she said. "Might need some help."

"Maybe I'll call Susan. See what she's up to these days."

"Then start taking some cases," Anci said. "Small at first, maybe, and nothing too dangerous."

"Of course not. We'll only solve pleasant mysteries. Assuming anyone hires us at all."

"Right. Also, no more fights or guns."

"I figure you only get one like that anyway. Everything else will probably be pretty boring."

Anci said, "Probably."

I saw Sheriff Wince from time to time on the television, but didn't hear from him personally. One afternoon, though, Willard dropped by to deliver some welcome news: the DA had decided not to pursue charges against Jeep and me.

"Well, that's a relief," I said.

"Thought you'd like that," he said. He shook his head. "Damnedest thing. A lot of dead bodies around this business, and we still don't really know what it was all about."

"Some kind of meth war, probably."

"Yeah, I guess," he said. "But that don't really explain the disappearance of Luster's daughter. It's like the entire family just dried up and blew away. One of the networks is doing a special about it. You know, one of those programs about the unsolved cases."

"Who knows?" I said. "Maybe they'll get to the bottom of it."

He said, "That hurts."

I didn't see or hear from my old man again. He went back to his life, and I went back to mine, just like we'd been doing since I was a kid. That was neither a surprise nor especially disappointing.

Things with Peggy and I ran kinda rough for a while, like being around each other brought up too many bad memories. She stayed by Anci's side almost every day until she was convinced of her full recovery, but she and I didn't have much to do with each other, and then she was gone. I heard a rumor that she'd gone north to visit family, a sister of hers maybe, but I left it at that. For a while there, I thought that would be the end for us. After a couple of months, though, I found myself on the phone with her one night, and then the next and the next. She's a good woman, and unlike almost everyone else in this story, at least she was trying to do the right thing. We still haven't moved in together, though. Maybe one day.

Time passed, another year, and Anci turned thirteen at last, more beautiful than ever, and ever more the grownup I was proud to see her becoming. Peggy came by. And Jeep and Opal. Even old Lilac. We sang and ate cake and ice cream and gave presents. When they were gone, Anci and I found ourselves alone on the porch beneath the night sky.

I said, "Did you get everything you wanted for your birthday?"

"I guess so. Almost, anyway."

"Oh, what was missing?"

"Motorcycle."

"Come again?"

"Wanted one, didn't get one."

"Reason might be, this is the first I'm hearing of it. Besides, I'm not sure that's a very good idea."

"You got one."

"I'm a grown person, and when you're a grown person you get to have the things you want."

"That true?"

"No."

She thought about that for a moment, and then she said, "Hold on. I have an idea."

She disappeared into the house and came back a moment later holding a handful of white envelopes.

"One more present, then," she said.

"I'm almost afraid to ask."

"I got some letters."

"I see that."

"From mom."

"Okay."

She looked at me. "You knew?"

"Maybe."

"You old fox," she said. "And here I thought I was a snoop. Did you read them?"

I said, "Nope. They're not mine to read."

She looked at me until she was satisfied I was telling the truth. Then she nodded and said, "Truth is, I haven't, either. I opened some, but I never could read them. Guess maybe I'm scared."

"I guess maybe I'm a little scared, too."

"You? Of what?"

I said, "I don't know. The future, probably. How stuff

changes. Everything that can happen. It can be a little frightening sometimes."

"And after the gunfire and kidnappings and everything," she said. "Just look at us. Couple of chickens."

"Yeah."

She said, "Read them with me?"

"If you want me to."

"Well, that's what I want," she said. "Okay?"

"Okay."

"I love you, man," she said.

We looked at each other for a long moment, me and her, her and me. Partners in crime. The moon came out and touched my daughter's face, and a cool breeze whispered through the grasses, and it was a perfect autumn night at my father's house at Indian Vale, and damned if I wasn't crying.

ACKNOWLEDGMENTS

I couldn't have written *Down Don't Bother Me*, or for that matter created Slim, without my dad (who, never fear, is nothing like Slim's) and his cheerful service as technical adviser regarding all things coal mines and miners. Obviously, any details I might have gotten wrong are on me, not him. Thanks and bottomless love also to the rest of my family—Mom, Ian, Jiffy, Celia Rose—for standing by me when life knocked me down for a while. Deep bows to my wonderful agents, Anthony Mattero and Yfat Gendell, who guided this book from its earliest versions and without whom it probably would never have left my desk drawer. Fist bump to my editor, the magnificent Cal Morgan, whose support, enthusiasm, and insight I can never hope to repay. Finally, but mostly, to Laura, the other coast of me.

JASON MILLER is half of the Miller Brothers writing team, creators of the critically acclaimed graphic novel *Redball 6*. Born in southern Illinois, Jason currently lives in Nashville. Follow him on Twitter at @longwall26.